ELECTRIC CITY

ELECTRIC CITY

K.K.BECK

THE MYSTERIOUS PRESS

Published by Warner Books

A Time Warner Company

Mysterious Press books are published by Warner Books, Inc.,
1271 Avenue of the Americas, New York, NY 10020.

A Time Warner Company

The Mysterious Press name and logo are registered trademarks of Warner Books, Inc.

Printed in the United States of America

First printing: August 1994
10 9 8 7 6 5 4 3 2 1

Library of Congress Cataloging-in-Publication Data

Beck, K. K.
      Electric city/K. K. Beck.
      p. cm.
      ISBN 0-89296-536-3
      I. Private investigators—Washington (State)—Seattle—Fiction. 2. Women detectives—
Washington (State)—Seattle—Fiction. 3. Seattle (Wash.)—Fiction. I. Title.
PS3552.E248E44 1994
813′.54—dc20

                                                                                    94-9596
                                                                                    CIP

For Andrew, who led the way

Author's Note

While in this book
the Omak Stampede and World
Famous Suicide Race occurs in the spring,
in reality it is always held the second
weekend in August.

1.

When Jane da Silva opened the door one day around noon, two strangers stood there, staring at her with interest. The Greenpeace solicitors, who came around Seattle neighborhoods regularly, often looking like white Rastafarians, usually came singly. These two didn't look like Mormons or Jehovah's Witnesses either.

Whoever they were, Jane smiled nicely and prepared to come up with one of her canned rebuffs. A fanatical gleam in her eye and the phrase "I am very strong in my own faith" or "My political convictions are cast in cement" delivered with eager breathlessness ordinarily sent them packing. They usually seemed afraid that she would try and convert them to something, and scrambled off her porch. If they were selling something, a simple and sober "I just got laid off" killed any pitch.

The woman was young and pale. Her neat little face, with an upturned nose and big hazel eyes with orange bursts around the pupils, was dwarfed by a large squashy felt toque hat in bottle green, something a turn-of-the-century suffragette might have worn before she threw herself in front of a horse. She also wore a long wrinkled rayon print dress, the uneven hem of which grazed the tops of her logging boots.

That season, similar outfits had recently emerged from the streets of Seattle to make it onto runways in New York, but this woman wore the real thing.

Her smooth white arms were bare and lightly freckled in orange. Jane imagined the hat hid red hair. Her face looked intelligent and slightly nervous. She shifted a bag on her shoulder. The bag was made out of old Oriental carpeting, and Jane wondered what it contained. Clipboards with some cranky petition? Household products? Magazine subscription forms?

The man had a round face and body, and seemed somewhere in middle age, with salt-and-pepper hair parted neatly and held down by some old-fashioned hair preparation. Jane rather suspected the creamy, drugstore smell that hung around them came from whatever he plastered it down with, rather than any scent the woman was wearing. He had on a striped bow tie, a white shirt, gray slacks and a pair of red suspenders—a practical necessity for any man with such a large stomach. The whole impression was of a cheery toy shop proprietor from a children's picture book.

"Are you Jane da Silva?" said the woman in a fluty, dramatic voice.

"Yes," said Jane, trying to sound wary. Whoever they were, she doubted very much they were selling aluminum siding or anything predictable. Always drawn to eccentricity, Jane tried to resist the impulse to invite them right in and demand their life stories.

The two strangers exchanged nervous glances.

"We think maybe you can help us," said the woman.

"We think," said the man, "that we know who you are." He held up a blue file folder. "We have a file on you."

"Oh stop it, Clark," said the woman. "You sound too weird."

"Do you keep files on a lot of people?" said Jane.

2

Clark giggled. "Tons," he said.

The woman gave him an I-can't-take-you-anywhere look and said to Jane, "We work for a newspaper clipping service. Don't pay too much attention to Clark. He's very bright but he has a strange sense of humor. Sometimes he alarms people."

Clark just giggled again at this description of himself.

"Anyway," said the woman, shifting her weight from one boot to the other and jutting out her hip in a kind of nervous, fake-casual way, "I hope we're not bothering you, but Clark has a theory you're sort of a detective who handles strange stuff."

"Don't you want to see your file?" said Clark, looking smug and crafty.

"Why don't you come in?" said Jane. There was a chance, just a chance, that these two had something Jane needed.

She sat them down on Uncle Harold's old sofa, and eyed the blue folder in Clark's plump hands.

The young woman introduced herself. "I'm Monica Padgett," she said. "And this is Clark Rafferty." She arranged her wrinkled dress around her knees like an old lady. "I'm sorry we just burst in on you like this."

"Don't apologize," said Jane. She held out a hand to Clark, who gave her the folder.

Inside, were three documents. Two were newspaper clippings. The first clipping was a lengthy account of a murder trial in which Jane was mentioned once as a witness, and described as "the woman who had a business appointment with the victim, and who found the body." The second clipping mentioned her briefly in an interview with an apartment house owner, who'd found the body of another murder victim. Here, she was described as a horrified innocent bystander who happened to enter the apartment with him when he found the body.

"I don't like being in the paper," said Jane.

The third document was a Xeroxed copy of her uncle Harold's will. Jane didn't bother to read it. Its peculiar provisions were well known to her. It explained that she could live here in this house and receive funds administered by a crotchety board of trustees while she did the work of the Foundation for Righting Wrongs. Uncle Harold had been decidedly odd, but very rich too.

"Let me get this straight," said Jane. "You work for a clipping service. Presumably, you read newspapers all day. And you saw my name twice and started a file on me?"

"No," said Clark holding up a thick forefinger. "I started the file first. You see, I knew about your uncle Harold Mortensen. He made the papers occasionally, always at the edge of some case or other. I kept my eye out for him. Then, when I saw his obit, I went downtown and got a copy of his will. It's a public document. I figured you'd be carrying on his work, so I started to look for your name." He looked very pleased with himself.

"When Clark told me you ran some sort of freelance avenger thing, I thought he was nuts," said Monica, looking at Clark with apparently newfound respect.

Clark giggled again. He seemed to enjoy being thought a loon, so Jane decided to buy into it.

"Well even if he is nuts," said Jane in a bantering way she thought he'd like, "he's right on the money when it comes to Uncle Harold's foundation."

More self-satisfied chortling from Clark. "We got your address from the property description in the will," he said.

"I do continue my uncle's work," said Jane. "But I'm afraid I'm not allowed to talk about it. It's supposed to be kept very quiet." She was dying to know what kind of files Clark had on her uncle. His career as a pro bono, nonprofit busybody for people who couldn't afford good investigative help was very mysterious. All she knew was that the board felt her cases were messier than his, and acted as if this were due to some moral failing on her part.

Monica leaned forward. "So you do take on unsolved cases," she said. "We've talked to a private eye, but he wouldn't help us without a lot of money."

"I help people for free," said Jane. "People who need it. But in return, I ask for their absolute discretion about me and my activities." This pronouncement had the expected effect on Monica, whom Jane had pegged as the dramatic type.

Monica's big eyes opened wider in joy. "It sounds wonderful," she said. "Like something out of Chesterton or Robert Louis Stevenson." She exhaled lavishly.

Jane smiled. It was nice to have someone appreciate what she did and imbue it with some glamour, even if it was the faded glamour of another age. Anyone else who knew about her work tended to advise her to get herself a real job and stop acting silly.

"Tell me," she said, "about your problem. And would you like some coffee?"

"We only get a half hour for lunch," said Monica, looking nervous. "We were able to leave early, but we have to get back on time. Our boss keeps us on a short leash."

"Have you eaten?" said Jane.

"We were going to eat our sandwiches on the bus back," said Clark.

Monica looked faintly embarrassed by this revelation and indicated her large bag. It looked as if it needed vacuuming.

"For heaven's sake," said Jane. "Come into the kitchen and eat them here while I make coffee and we can talk while you're eating."

God, I hope they have something I can use with that

damn board, thought Jane. She was only as good as her last case, or the funds dried up.

Jane put on some water and sat down at the table. Her guests rustled with paper bags. Clark had peanut butter and jelly on white bread, a banana, and an Oreo. Monica's lunch was more grown-up—tunafish on whole wheat and an old yogurt container with something in it that looked like mung beans and smelled of cilantro.

Monica did the talking.

"Well," she said, "as we told you, we work at the Columbia Clipping Service. We read newspapers all day, and mark the items our clients want clipped and then the cutters clip them out."

Jane nodded.

"We're sort of close, in a strange way, even though we're all very different." She glanced over at Clark. "The readers are close, anyway. So when one of us vanished, we were naturally concerned."

"Who has vanished?" said Jane. The phrase had conjured up the image of a clerk with a green eyeshade, hunched over a newspaper down at the clipping service, all of a sudden dissolving into a puff of smoke, leaving behind an empty tall stool.

"It's Irene March," said Monica. "One of the readers. She's been gone a week, and we're worried about her."

"Eight days," said Clark, opening the Oreo and looking at the white filling before screwing it back together. "Didn't come in last Monday." He brushed some dark crumbs away from his mouth.

"And does that seem unlike her?" said Jane.

"Irene's worked at the clipping service for thirteen years," said Monica. "Outside of a little sick leave and her annual vacation, she's been there every day, like clockwork."

"In our business," explained Clark, "you never want to

get too far behind. The papers just pile up, and you've got to get through them."

The kettle whistled, and Jane poured the hot water through the coffee filter. Would the board go for this? Was it a hopeless case, an injustice that needed righting? Something that couldn't be taken care of any other way?

"What about the police?" she said. "What do they say?"

"Not much," said Monica. "I don't think they know where to look. But we're worried, because Irene seemed frightened about something."

"What makes you say that?" said Jane.

"I can't quite put my finger on it. Irene was hard to read. Not an emotional person. But she seemed kind of stressed. Something was up, I just know it. And then she got that personal phone call." Monica stirred up her bean concoction in an agitated manner.

"We're not allowed to have personal phone calls," explained Clark. "Our boss, Mrs. Webber, doesn't allow it." He was peeling his banana, and seemed to be scrutinizing it as carefully as if it were the first banana he'd ever encountered.

"Irene was all nervous about it," said Monica. "It was on a Friday, and then Monday she disappeared."

"It was probably someone who saw her on television," said Clark. "Someone who knew her from before or something."

"She was on television?" said Jane.

Monica put down her mung beans and dug around in her carpetbag. She produced a videotape cassette. "She was on *Jeopardy!* You know. The game show. It aired a few days before she disappeared. I've brought you a tape so you can see what she looks like."

Jane took the cassette, realizing that in accepting it she was somehow accepting the case. And why shouldn't she? If it didn't amount to anything, God would know she was trying and send something decent her way. Besides, she was pleased they'd found her and thought she could help. After years of skittering around from job to job, someone was finally consulting her like a real professional. It gave her a solid feeling of responsibility.

"I could use a still picture of her too," she said.

"I thought you might," said Monica. "I'm afraid this is all we have. She handed over a Polaroid snapshot. It featured a handful of people lined up against a wall as if they were waiting for a firing squad. Jane recognized Monica and Clark. In front of the group was a large cake, and an older woman was beaming down on it happily. "This was at a retirement party," explained Monica. "There's Irene." She pointed to a woman looking out of the corner of her eye at the cake and the retiree.

Irene seemed to be about fifty, with a square, solid body. Her mouth was thin and straight, her eyes slightly hooded beneath absolutely straight, thick brows. She had dark gray hair, parted on one side and held away from her smooth brow with a single bobby pin. Jane decided if she ever did find Irene she should try and get her a good haircut.

"I'll see what I can find out," said Jane. "But you know, you sound like pretty good investigators yourselves. You found me, after all. Maybe you can find her yourselves."

"We can't really get away," said Monica. "Mrs. Webber is a real slavedriver."

Clark leaned over to the photograph. "There's Mrs. Webber, at the end," he said. Jane had imagined the boss as a harsh schoolmistressy type with a fierce jaw, ready to whack her employees with a ruler if they took personal phone calls. Instead, she was dressed and groomed like someone who'd graduated from the Junior League to a prestigious charity board—well-coiffed honey blonde hair, silk blouse and pearls. She hadn't bothered to smile for the picture, and wore the resentful expression of someone who knew she was at a tacky party.

Jane poured coffee into three white china mugs. She really had no idea how to proceed, but she didn't want Clark and Monica to know that. "When she didn't come to work, did someone go over to her place and check it out?"

"I wanted to go that first day," said Monica. "But Mrs. Webber wouldn't let me. Later, the police said they went inside and she wasn't there."

"Mrs. Webber doesn't sound like a lot of fun," said Jane.

"We all hate her," said Monica in a tone of breathless urgency. "She's basically a controlling, demeaning Cruella De Vil sort of person who treats the employees like dirt, and other than being mean-spirited and gratuitously nasty, there's nothing wrong with her."

Clark nodded. "And she's not even that smart." He seemed puzzled that someone like that was supervising him. "I don't get it."

"I'm not surprised. Jerks run lots of things," said Jane, who felt that in many enterprises scum rose to the top, and that loyalty and the ability to pretend the world revolved around widgets counted for more than competence when it came to promotions.

"Anyway," continued Monica, "Clark did find Irene's next of kin."

"City records. Piece of cake," said Clark.

Monica continued. "We called them. Some cousins in the suburbs. They didn't seem too cut up. Irene had told me about them once. They'd had some family feud years ago."

"Someone should take a long look around," said Jane. "The explanation for her disappearance might be inside her house."

"The funny thing is," said Monica, "there was a spare housekey in Irene's drawer."

"We all have a drawer for our personal things," said Clark. Jane remembered a similar arrangement in kindergarten.

"She told me it was there if anything happened," continued Monica. "But Mrs. Webber cleared out the drawer and has all the stuff in her office. She won't let us have the key. I asked her about it and she said she would handle it, and give it to the police if they asked."

"Can you sneak in there and get it?" said Jane.

"I don't think so. She always locks her office behind her when she leaves. I'd be too nervous to try it anyway."

"Is she interviewing for Irene's replacement?" said Jane. An appealing plan was beginning to form.

Monica nodded, and looked nervously at her watch.

"Don't worry," said Jane. "I'll drive you back so you won't be late. Is the office downtown?"

Clark nodded. "On Third, between Marion and Madison." He looked at his own watch. "If you drive us we have about fifteen more minutes."

She asked them what they took in their coffee, and when she had fetched cream and sugar for Clark, she sat down, gazing for a second at the cassette box. "How did she do on *Jeopardy!*?" she said.

"She won twenty thousand dollars," said Clark.

"Yes," said Monica. "Irene had a lot of general knowledge. We all do. We have to, to do the kind of work we do." She smiled with a sort of shy pride, and Jane realized how young she was. Maybe not even twenty.

Jane wasn't quite sure why they were so anxious to find Irene March. Why weren't they able to let the police handle it? The answer was important. It could make the difference between a hopeless case that the board would accept and pay for, and something Jane would do just to see if she could help.

"I need to know exactly why you're so anxious to find Irene," she said. "I mean, obviously, you're concerned about a co-worker, which is perfectly understandable, but why can't you just let the police take care of this?"

Monica sighed and removed her big green hat and set it in her lap. She had pale red-gold hair, center-parted and caught up in a kind of Virginia Woolf knot. She brushed a few escaped strands from her pale face. "I guess we'd better tell you," she said. "Irene told us she left her money to us, her co-workers. The four readers, not the cutters," she added, as if that were self-evident. Evidently there was an intellectual hierarchy at the Columbia Clipping Service.

Monica looked over nervously at Clark. "That's one reason I thought she was frightened. She told us we were her heirs. Why else would she tell us that?" Monica didn't wait for an answer and leaned forward. "I was shocked that she would leave her money to us. To be really honest, it seemed kind of pathetic. We were all she had in the world, I guess. I don't think we were even that nice to her. She could be irritating."

"She kissed up to Mrs. Webber," said Clark with a dark look. "But it was nice of her to leave us her money."

"That's why we feel we owe it to her to find out what happened to her," said Monica. "She didn't have anyone else. If she cared about us enough to leave us her money, it means we were the most important people in her life. So we should care enough to find out what happened to her."

"And," said Clark, "we want to know. We like to know things."

Jane looked back and forth at both of them. "I'd like to help you," she said. "And Irene too, if she needs help. I don't know what I can do, but I will try to help."

Jane divided twenty thousand dollars by four newspaper

readers. Would any of them be willing to kill for five thousand dollars? One thing was certain. If they didn't find out what happened to Irene, and Irene never showed up, they'd have to wait for years to collect—until their benefactress was declared legally dead.

2.

Clark sat in the back seat and Monica sat next to Jane. On the short run from Capitol Hill to downtown, Jane got Monica to write down her home phone number. And she asked her how Mrs. Webber filled a job opening.

"She just runs a little ad in the paper, telling you where to show up and how to apply in person," said Monica. "The ad is pretty enticing. It's always a mob scene. It should run in tonight's *Times.*"

Jane nodded. "And that collection of stuff from Irene's drawer, where is it exactly? Is it in plain view?"

Clark piped up from the back seat. "It's on the shelf above the radiator next to a jade plant. In a big cardboard box that used to have typing paper in it. The label on the box is orange and black, and the box is kind of smashed."

"Clark has a photographic memory," said Monica.

"And what's in the box exactly?" said Jane, partly to see just how good Clark was.

"A bottle of Jergen's hand lotion, a key ring with a couple of keys, a small package of Kleenex, a business-sized yellow envelope, and I think maybe a bus transfer or something," he said with a flourish.

"So can you describe the layout?" said Jane. "Do the job applicants all arrive at once?"

"That's right," answered Monica. "They hang around the waiting room and Mrs. Webber has one of the cutters usher them in, one by one."

Jane pulled into the bus stop in front of their building, and they got out of the car, thanking her. Jane sat there for a while, engine idling, watching them walk into the narrow Art Deco building. Clark had a cartoonish rolling, purposeful gait; Monica took ladylike little steps in her combat boots, her Salvation Army dress swirling around her slim hips.

It wasn't until Jane heard the rubbery wheeze of hydraulic brakes behind her and caught sight of the front of the bus in her rear-view mirror that she realized what she'd done. She'd been waiting there at the curb to make sure they made it to the doorway, as if they were children. She pulled out of the bus stop with an apologetic wave at the bus driver.

There was something fragile and brave about Clark and Monica. Having spent a significant part of her own life underemployed, Jane felt a kinship with them. Now, with a couple of cases behind her and lots of Uncle Harold's money to give her the respectability and freedom she'd always craved, Jane looked forward to giving them any help she could give them. She also felt a kind of energetic sense of purpose that she hadn't had for some time, redecorating and massive wardrobe rehabilitation courtesy of Uncle Harold notwithstanding.

As soon as she got home, she went up to her bedroom (formerly murky and yellowish, now newly papered in gray and white stripes) where the VCR was, curled up on the bed and played the *Jeopardy!* tape.

Irene strode out to the opening music with the announcer's voice saying: "A clipping service worker from Seattle, Washington!" Jane was relieved to see that Irene's hair looked a little better. It had been styled into a wave around her face, and that awful bobby pin was gone. Irene stood behind her podium, smiling a little nervously. They'd put some coral lipstick and blusher on her.

Since coming back from Europe a year ago, Jane had managed to catch up on a lot of the American culture she'd missed. *Jeopardy!* was an old-fashioned game show all razzle-dazzled up with electronic visuals. The contestants had to exhibit a lot of general knowledge in order to win. The gimmick was that the contestants had to phrase answers to clues in the form of a question. The polished host, Alex Trebek, pronounced all the foreign words and phrases properly, something Jane appreciated, and the whole thing rattled along at a fast clip. She'd seen it a few times and found herself shouting answers (in the form of questions) at the screen.

Irene March had a tough time during the first round. She could be seen jabbing ineffectually at the buzzer, trying to be the first one to log in with an answer. A lawyer from Santa Monica raced through a lot of baseball questions and started working on national parks, but when he said "What is Yosemite?" instead of "What is Yellowstone?" Irene got in and seized control of the board.

The third contestant, a good-natured housewife from Portland, Oregon, named Margot Dodge, managed a few forays. She knew who wrote *Black Beauty* and recognized the state motto of Virginia. But when Irene ran through a category devoted to Greek mythology, Margot seemed to visibly crumple and Irene started to look confident.

After a commercial, Alex Trebek interviewed the contestants. The lawyer, still in the lead, looked smug and seemed to expect to win. He talked about his law practice until the host cut him off. Even though she knew the outcome, Jane still found herself hoping he'd lose.

The housewife from Portland managed to sound like the whole thing was just a lark. She said her hobby was gardening and that she loved to travel.

Irene looked up at Trebek meekly. She seemed shorter than Jane had imagined. He said that reading newspapers all day was probably excellent training for *Jeopardy!* She beamed at him like a woman in love, and she said she sure hoped so.

When play resumed, Irene looked fully in charge. She seemed to develop kind of a rhythm with the buzzer. She knew that the Potomac and the Susquehanna fed into Chesapeake Bay and that Grover Cleveland was the only American president to serve nonconsecutive terms.

Jane found herself yelling answers at Irene, as if to coach her, but she did all right all by herself. The lawyer got himself in trouble by buzzing in when he didn't know the answers, which cost him points, and by wagering a lot on the Audio Daily Double, then failing to recognize "Baby Elephant Walk." Margot from Portland mostly smiled and looked uncomfortable, then began a lot of stabbing at the buzzer in an extravagant way, and examining it quizzically, as if it might be defective.

When they rolled into the end of the game, Irene had a hefty lead. She waltzed right over her opponents, and bet over half of her winnings on Final Jeopardy. The category was Oscars. She was the only one who realized both Liza Minnelli and her father, Vincent, had won Oscars.

By the end of the show, as Irene graciously received the congratulations of her opponents, Jane was wrung out, and relieved Irene had won. It was absurd, really. She'd known the outcome. But hadn't Jane agonized during repeated viewings of *Casablanca,* wondering whether or not Ingrid

Bergman would get on that plane with Victor Laszlo? How many evenings at the opera had she prayed that the firing squad in *Tosca* was shooting with blanks?

Jane watched another game. As the winner, Irene was now the defending champion. She neatly dispatched a nervous graduate student and a blustery pharmacist and got her total up to twenty thousand dollars, mostly by making a huge bet in Final Jeopardy, and knowing that Wagner had married the daughter of Liszt. Jane was a little surprised at the size of Irene's bet. It was a risky thing to do.

In the brief chat with Alex Trebek between rounds, she came across as relaxed and happy, a nice smile lighting up her face. He asked her what she'd be doing with her winnings, and she said she'd take some of her co-workers out to dinner, then looked straight into the camera and said, "But not my boss," and laughed. Alex Trebek smiled and the studio audience tittered. Jane wondered if the despised Mrs. Webber had been watching.

In the third game, Irene's challengers included a fortyish clergyman with a sweet face named Roy, and a lean, tall young man with dark hair, thick and tousled on top, shaved down to the skin on the sides. David bounced onto the stage on the balls of his feet, and wore a weird early-sixties green sport coat that was probably older than he was.

David flashed a big white smile and was clearly prepared to trounce everyone, which is exactly what he did, starting with "What was a Studebaker?" on through "What was the Treaty of Versailles?" including "What is a Singapore sling?" and on to "Who was Nathaniel Hawthorne?"

Roy and Irene got in a few licks, but David usually barreled right back. His technique seemed to be to answer everything and assume he'd be right ninety percent of the time, and it was working.

As Alex Trebek chatted with the contestants after the

first commercial, Jane learned that the irrepressible David was a graduate student in physics who played the saxophone and tended bar. The clergyman smiled graciously and said in a pleasant low voice that he'd been a longtime fan but he felt he was out of his league. Alex told him kindly that anything could happen in Double Jeopardy.

In his chat with defending champion Irene, he asked her about her hobbies and she said tersely that she liked to read and crochet. Irene losing was quite different from Irene winning. Her body had taken on a defensive posture, with her shoulders hunched. Her neck looked shorter, as if she were a turtle trying to pull her head back into her shell. Why couldn't she be gracious, like Roy next to her? Jane felt let down.

In the next round, Irene, selecting from a category called "Saints and Sinners," hit the Audio Daily Double, which meant she had to wager some of what she'd won on her ability to answer. She wagered it all. This time it wasn't her usual risky betting; it was her only chance to get back in contention.

The camera ruthlessly closed in on her as she screwed up her face in concentration. She was supposed to come up with the saint's name in the title. After a long brassy intro that sounded completely unlike the rest of the song, Jane recognized it. "What is 'My Funny Valentine'!" she found herself screaming, but Irene just stood there, nodding her head a little as if to indicate she knew the tune but just couldn't place it, until Alex Trebek said, "I'm sorry," in mournful tones.

And then, Irene seemed to fall apart, bending her head forward so a piece of hair hung over her face and looking so utterly defeated that Jane felt like bursting into sympathetic tears. But at the same time, Jane was furious with

Irene for being so vulnerable, for taking a game too seriously.

Irene brought her face up again, and gave a weak smile. Jane stopped the tape and studied Irene, stock-still for a moment beneath a blur of video snow. The coral-lipsticked smile was perfectly symmetrical. But the eyes didn't go with the lips. The eyes were dark and angry and hurt. The result was more than unsettling. Jane felt that by stopping the tape she had glimpsed an unattractive corner of Irene March's soul. Irene March was a bad loser.

3.

Shortly after rewinding the tape and preparing herself a grazy late lunch of cheese, bread, some olives and leftover salad, Jane heard a familiar thunk on the front porch. The *Seattle Times* had arrived.

She ate reading the help-wanted ads, an experience not without a certain gut-numbing terror for one with her own spotty job history. There but for the grace of Uncle Harold go I, she thought to herself as she skimmed through jobs she knew she'd never be able to get and the ones she thought she could but would hate. Eventually, she found it. If she had been looking for a real job she probably would have applied. There was something so sweet about the ad.

It didn't say what the job was exactly. It just said that job seekers with the ability to read quickly, with good general knowledge and a good memory should come by the Columbia Clipping Service between nine and noon tomorrow if they were interested in a position with a monthly salary and a health plan. "Ideal for a quiet individual who loves to read," the ad said, which sounded rather peaceful and nice.

Even though Jane knew about the supervisor from hell, and realized that the job entailed reading day-old newspapers from dreary towns, the ad managed to evoke a charming picture. Quiet individuals who loved to read sat in cozy nooks or at old oak library tables with the light from mullioned windows slanting into the room through cheery pots of geraniums, the silence broken only by the sound of turning pages.

There were times, during Jane's last real job, singing old Gershwin and Kern and Porter standards in smoky little European clubs, when such a genteel, anonymous atmosphere would have seemed immensely appealing. Jane had grown tired of artfully tossing her head back, narrowing her eyes or jutting out a hip to give the act some pizazz. (She had never been under any illusion that her voice alone had been enough to carry it off.)

Jane always provided an imaginary wardrobe for herself in any daydream. Now she could see herself in comfortable shoes, Katharine Hepburn slacks and a tweedy old cardigan, reading serenely in the world conjured up by the ad. Of course, in real life, after a few weeks of reading newspapers she would probably go berserk from underutilized adrenaline. But still, she thought she could come up with enough gentle enthusiasm to engage Mrs. Webber's interest for twenty minutes or so.

Later that afternoon, she was able to get in touch with Bob Manalatu where he worked out, a hard-core gym swirling with testosterone and probably veterinary-strength steroids. The large Samoan had helped her out in her very first case. His ability to project an amiable ruthlessness, not to mention his awesome size, was very comforting. She told Bob she wanted to hire him for an hour or so.

"Someone giving you trouble?" he said with a kindly, protective air. "Do I have to hit anybody?"

"No. It's not a muscle thing at all. All you have to do is show up in an office and act weird enough in the waiting area to give me some time in the boss's office alone.

21

"To be honest, Bob, I want to take something while she's distracted." Jane sketched out the scenario. Both of them would be posing as job applicants, and there should be plenty of other people in the waiting area.

"Maybe we can just bust in there after hours," said Bob. "What kind of security they got?"

"Oh, let's just try it this way," said Jane, who could easily imagine one of Bob's huge feet kicking through a door, and one of his giant hands yanking out an alarm system. "Anyway, aren't you busy after hours with the band and all?" Bob played bass in a Hawaiian band.

"Just Thursday through Saturday. Yeah, I guess I could do what you wanted. I can think of a couple of ways to shake things up there." He gave a throaty chuckle.

"I only need a minute."

"Got any particular stunts you'd like me to pull?"

"Surprise me," said Jane.

The next day, Jane arrived promptly at nine at the shabby old office building that someone had forgotten either to wreck and replace with a black glass office tower, or restore and then charge fat rents to trendy tenants.

On the seventh floor she found an oak door with a frosted glass window on which the words "Columbia Clipping Service. Please Enter" were painted in black letters.

The waiting area had some nice old oak trim, and a worn old red carpet on the floor. The tables and chairs were vaguely Danish modern with Naugahyde upholstery. A dusty plastic philodendron, listing slightly, sat in the corner.

Jane got one of the last chairs. Applicants, many of them reading paperback books, lined the room. They were all steadfastly ignoring each other. In chatty Seattle, where a shared elevator ride was a good enough reason to start a conversation, their lack of eye contact could be attributed to the fact they were preselected for quietness, that they were all competing for a job, and perhaps to the fact that they had been infected with the humiliation and self-loathing that affects almost all but the most brazen job seekers.

The applicants were mostly women, and Jane felt well disposed toward all of them. After all, they had answered an ad for "a quiet individual who likes to read," which set them apart in a world where everyone was encouraged to be noisy and oozing self-esteem all the time. A lot of the other ads Jane had read were looking for "energetic, highly motivated self-starters."

After about fifteen minutes, the chairs had filled up and people were beginning to line the walls, some leaning against them reading. Soon Bob Manalatu arrived in all his glory.

At about six foot eight, and God only knew, somewhere approaching three hundred pounds of Pacific Islander bulk, Bob stood out from the crowd. He managed not to smile at Jane when he came in, and surveyed the room with his bright, dark eyes. His beautiful satiny face remained impassive.

Bob wore a massive aloha shirt revealing his barrel-sized, pillowy arms. Mirrored sunglasses hung on a cord around his thick neck. He wore a Walkman with the headphones stretched to the max (a tinny buzz of escaping sound came from the area around his head), black trousers and black tasseled loafers. At his side was a large Nordstrom shopping bag. It looked like it might contain an enormous lunch. The quiet individuals who liked to read seemed to be trying not to stare.

Bob sidled up to a neurasthenic-looking man with a beret and a fat paperback. "How you doing, bro," he said. "What's the book?"

The man looked up wanly. "*Basic Chess Endings* by Reuben Fine," he said.

"I played a little of that in the slammer," said Bob affably. "What a stupid game."

"It all depends on your perspective, I suppose," said the man in the beret, plunging back into the book with a frown.

Bob laughed heartily. "Total waste of time."

"So is pointless conversation," said the man in the beret snappishly.

"No need to get bent out of shape, friend," said Bob, resting one huge brown hand on the man's shoulder. "We're all in this together. We're all looking for work. Do we take a number or what?"

The man in the beret didn't answer, and just then a cowed-looking young woman in stretch pants and a big sweatshirt handed around clipboards with pencils and job application forms. Everyone dutifully filled them out, and they were collected.

Jane rather enjoyed making up a completely phony life. She decided she should look like an intelligent dilettante with little work experience. She gave herself a BA in English from the University of Washington, when actually she'd dropped out of college during her junior year abroad, her major still undeclared. She listed her last occupation as housewife. She decided she'd be an impoverished widow, which was what she had been until Uncle Harold's will was probated.

She said that before her marriage she'd worked as a clerk at Frederick and Nelson's, a nice old-fashioned department store that had gone bankrupt and was therefore conveniently out of business in case anyone checked.

A door to the inner office opened and everybody's head swiveled over toward it. The young woman in stretch pants summoned one of the applicants, who spent about twenty minutes in the office, then left in a kind of nervous flurry, while a second applicant was ushered in. It really was a humiliating way to interview for a job, thought Jane. Couldn't they set up appointments so these people weren't all furtively eyeing each other?

Jane was called in third, and had by now worked up a vigorous resentment at the way Mrs. Webber was treating all these out-of-work people. As she left the room she caught a quick glimpse of Bob reaching into his Nordstrom bag.

Mrs. Webber's office had the same low-overhead look as the waiting area. She sat behind a desk littered with papers. There were some steel file cabinets and a few African violets that on closer inspection were revealed to be fake and in need of dusting, just like the philodendron.

Mrs. Webber, however, looked much more soigné than her surroundings. She was a little too perfectly groomed, with ivory makeup that gave her a rather ceramic look. Jane recognized her from the picture she'd seen. She wore a very nice dark blue blouse in heavy silk that Jane wouldn't have minded owning, and a double strand of pearls that looked real.

Jane glanced over to the side of the room. There, on a shelf above the radiator next to a jade plant, was the slightly squashed box Clark had described, down to the orange and black label. It looked forgotten, and there was something pathetic about Irene's few possessions sitting there.

Without looking up from Jane's application, Mrs. Webber fired off a few of the details. A very low salary, some skimpy benefits, hours from eight to five with a half hour for lunch, a week's vacation after a year. She looked up at Jane, as if expecting her to leave. "How does that sound?"

Jane thought it sounded wretched, but she smiled shyly and said it sounded all right.

"You know how a clipping service works?" demanded Mrs. Webber. "You'd be given a bunch of papers to read— the same ones over and over again so you get familiar with the area. We read papers from all around Washington State here. Our clients are national, but we're just part of a network of offices. It's cheaper to send the clippings around the country than the whole newspaper."

Mrs. Webber sat back and scrutinized Jane. Jane heard a faint plonky sound coming from the waiting area. It was a familiar sound but she couldn't place it. Mrs. Webber didn't seem to notice.

"So you haven't worked for a while, huh?" she said, gesturing to the application.

"No. While my husband was alive, I stayed home," Jane said. She was envisioning her false self as a vaguely agoraphobic woman looking out the window uneasily into a rainy garden, waiting for her husband to come home from work. "He died recently," she added.

Mrs. Webber didn't offer any condolences. "We need someone who can read fast and who's smart enough to know what our clients are looking for. You get a list of them, with a number, and you code the clippings for the cutters. You have to be fast, and efficient. If you aren't, it comes out of your hide, because we pay you a commission on each clipping."

"You mean in addition to the salary?" said Jane.

Mrs. Webber smiled sadistically. "The salary is, strictly speaking, an advance on the commissions. If your counts get below a certain total, we take it out of next month's check. Of course, you get a bonus if you do better."

The way she said this last, in a tone that seemed designed not to get anyone's hopes up, convinced Jane that the thing was structured so no one ever got a bonus.

Jane said meekly, "I do love to read."

Mrs. Webber looked puzzled for a moment, as the plonking grew more audible. It sounded as if an instrument were being tuned.

"That's good," said Mrs. Webber begrudgingly, "but remember, you're not here to read for yourself. We aren't paying you to amuse yourself, so you have to make sure you don't let yourself read items that our clients can't use. Some people are compulsive readers and they can't break that habit. They don't make it in this business."

Jane nodded. The low pay, the threadbare benefits, the unattractive surroundings, all of this was depressing, but what Mrs. Webber had just said depressed her the most. It seemed heartless to lure in quiet individuals who loved to read and then tell them not to.

Jane accidentally allowed a flicker of hostility to cross her features. Mrs. Webber seemed to notice it immediately, and leaned forward with a triumphant gleam in her small, glittering eyes. "I cannot emphasize this part strongly enough," she said. "You aren't here for your own pleasure." Her voice lingered just a second too long on the word "pleasure." She had pronounced it with contempt.

This woman, thought Jane, was suspicious of people who liked to read. To Mrs. Webber, reading for its own sake was a puzzling form of weakness that had to be stamped out. No doubt she had nothing but scorn for the people she supervised, smart but not particularly aggressive people, who toiled here for about fifty cents an hour more than the minimum wage.

"How did you like selling at Frederick's?" asked Mrs. Webber now, surveying Jane with the air of a carnivorous feline who had already seized its prey, but was toying with it for the fun of it.

"I liked it," said Jane, feeling more like herself, because she actually had worked in retail. "I liked helping people and finding out what they needed and encouraging them to go ahead and get something they really wanted and making it fun for them."

"You liked selling?" said Mrs. Webber.

"Well, yes," said Jane.

"I don't think you'd be right for us," said Mrs. Webber. "You have to be assertive to sell. And you had some time at home, doing whatever you wanted. Watching soap operas or whatever." She curled her lip. "Here, everyone takes their break at the same time. You want me to tell you when to take your break?" Mrs. Webber snorted, as if she knew the answer.

"Well, if that works out better . . ." began Jane feebly. She felt the interview slipping away from her. It was ridiculous, because she didn't want the job anyway. But it irked her that Mrs. Webber had seen through her and ferreted out the truth: Jane wouldn't take at all kindly to Mrs. Webber blowing a whistle and telling everyone when to take five.

The brief silence was filled with some chords of Hawaiian music. The instrument was clearly a ukulele. "What *is* that?" said Mrs. Webber sharply.

"I think it's 'Aloha Oe,' " said Jane.

Mrs. Webber frowned and started to rise, then seemed to think better of it and sat back down. "There is a general knowledge test," she said. "For finalists. But I don't think you're suited to the work."

"Well, I guess there isn't much more to say," said Jane. She thought for a moment of launching into some tirade against Mrs. Webber to give Bob some more time. Suddenly, they heard a booming voice singing "Michael Row the Boat Ashore" and more ukulele, followed by a sharp, peevish voice shouting, "Just stop it!" This was followed by a mighty roar and a few girlish gasps and screams.

"Jesus Christ," said Mrs. Webber, clambering out from behind her desk. Jane stepped back to let her get out of her office, then whisked over to the squashed box and pocketed the keys. A second later, she was out in the waiting area where Bob was shaking the philodendron with one hand, and waving the other, curled into a huge fist with a ukulele coming out of it, in the face of the man with the chess book.

"You know what's the matter with you guys who wear berets?" Bob was shouting. "Nobody can tell you guys shit." He looked over Mrs. Webber's shoulder at Jane, who gave a tiny nod.

"Okay, I'm leaving," said Bob, releasing the philodendron, which snapped back into place. He stashed the tiny ukulele in the Nordstrom bag, gave Mrs. Webber a beautiful smile, and made his way to the door rather buoyantly.

The man in the beret looked shaken. "I just asked him not to play that thing," he said to everyone in the room. He flapped his chess book. "I was trying to concentrate." A few reassuring murmurs came up from around the room.

Jane caught up with Bob outside the building and handed him four twenties. "Nice work," she said.

He folded the bills in half and put them in his shirt pocket. "I spotted the guy right away as someone who'd snap real easy."

" 'Michael Row the Boat Ashore' would push me over the edge too," said Jane, who never felt any nostalgia for the hootenanny era. "Aren't you a little young to remember that one?" Jane couldn't imagine Bob having been part of the folk movement in any case.

"They used to play that at vacation bible camp all the time," said Bob. "Take care. You let me know if you need anything else." As Jane watched him roll off down the street, she reflected on the fact that Bob never asked her any questions about what she was doing, or told her how to do things properly. He just took any assignment in stride. It was a professional quality she appreciated, especially as she wasn't always sure just what she was doing herself.

4.

That evening, Jane drove Monica over to Irene March's house. It seemed like a good idea to take Monica with her. She'd know more about Irene's life, and would be able to shed more light on what they found there.

Monica was dressed like a cat burglar in tight black jeans and black cotton turtleneck, her red hair twisted into a serviceable knot, giving her pale face with its wide eyes an undeniably chic but slightly scary look.

Jane had a sinking feeling she'd come on a fool's errand, dragged into some ridiculous little drama cooked up by the employees of the Columbia Clipping Service in their overheated little office because their intrigues against their unpleasant boss had begun to pall. She supposed that years of reading newspapers and enduring mental abuse from Mrs. Webber had taken their toll on the fragile sanity of the people who worked there. Monica was clearly high-strung and melodramatic. Clark appeared to be an idiot savant. And here was Jane herself, hiring Bob and his ukulele, stealing from an office, sneaking around someone's house at night, buying into the whole thing.

Irene lived on a steep little street called Argyle off of Phinney Ridge, near the zoo. Jane parked on the flat street half a block up next to a big brick Lutheran church, because she felt funny about poking through the house, and it seemed more discreet not to park right in front. There were some blue and black stickers with an eyeball logo on the windows of surrounding houses, a sign that there was a neighborhood block watch designed to foil residential burglaries. The last thing Jane wanted was to have neighbors with pitchforks or the police asking her what she and Monica were doing there, although she supposed it was better to be letting themselves in with a key than kicking in a basement window.

They walked the half block down the steep hill with special concrete treads on the sidewalk. Phinney Ridge was a neighborhood clinging to the side of a bluff, overlooking the flat neighborhood of Ballard, marked out below them with rows of street lights that were just beginning to come on. Beyond lay Puget Sound and the Olympic Mountains, far away and dark blue against a peachy dusk sky beyond.

Irene March had lived in a small bungalow, half obscured by ugly old ornamental cedars. Inside, the living room was crammed with grim furniture—oily-looking upholstered pieces in ugly florals. Bookshelves lined the walls. The place smelled of old cigarette smoke.

Monica locked the door behind them, punching a button in the center of the knob. Jane felt like whispering, but forced herself to speak in normal conversational tones.

"Let's just take a general look around," she said. "There certainly aren't any signs of a struggle or anything."

Monica crossed her arms and scanned the room. "We should also look for some clue as to what Irene was up to. In retrospect, I realize she was acting mysterious. I thought she was just eccentric, but she had, I don't know, a secret life."

"What makes you say that?" said Jane, examining a collection of four cigarette butts in a heavy glass ashtray. They all seemed to be the same brand.

Monica screwed up her face in concentration. "There were those bus trips, for one thing. Once in a while, she'd go away on the weekend to strange places all by herself. Little towns around the state. On break someone would say, 'How was your weekend,' and she'd say, 'I took the bus to Cosmopolis' or something, and when you asked her why she'd kind of roll her eyes and smile enigmatically." Monica began to stroll around the room, taking in her surroundings.

"Maybe she wandered off somewhere on a Greyhound bus," said Jane. "Did you get the impression she knew people in those towns?" Jane loved the name Cosmopolis.

"Not really," said Monica. "Of course she knew the towns themselves, in a way."

"She did?"

"Sure. They were towns she knew about because she read the papers from there. You get so you sort of know the places. I can tell you how much a house costs in Pullman and what's playing at the movies, and who gives good parties in Ritzville and like that."

Monica frowned and picked up and examined a dusty old needlepoint pillow, a wreath of roses on a wine-colored background. Jane wondered if the girl was mentally dividing up the estate.

Monica dropped the pillow hastily. Apparently Clark, or one of the other two readers, could have it.

They went into the dining room, taking in the dark old table and matching glass-fronted cabinet. There was a lot of flowery-looking china with worn gilt rims.

Beyond was the kitchen—neat and orderly, although there was what appeared to be a breakfast plate and coffee cup in the sink. The appliances were old, the linoleum worn. Monica fingered some curtains with a pattern of olive green pepper mills and garlic bunches.

In the dark hall, the floorboards creaked. "Did she own this place, do you know?" Jane asked.

"She lived here with her mother for years, and then got the place when her mother died, all paid for and everything," said Monica. "I guess this is the house she grew up in."

There were two bedrooms off the hall. One, Jane guessed, had been the mother's, and later Irene had moved into it. A big suite of matching furniture—dresser, bed, bureau—furniture a department store might have sold in the forties—was crowded into the room. At the window was a cracked manila window shade pulled down all the way with white net curtains hanging limply at the sides.

Jane checked the bedside table. There was a copy of a trashy-looking novel. The cover depicted a swarthy pirate in a tight clinch with a 36D wench in satin and lace.

Jane picked up the book. There was a bookmark in it. "If she went away, she didn't plan to stay overnight," said Jane, "unless she's like me and reads a couple of books simultaneously. But I usually take them all on a trip."

Monica suddenly had the bright idea of checking in the bathroom. There was a toothbrush there. The two women looked at each other. "I suppose she could have had an extra one in her suitcase or something," said Monica, "but it doesn't seem as if she planned to leave overnight."

"You know what's missing?" said Jane. "Her purse. What did it look like?"

"You're right!" Monica looked impressed, but Jane was wondering why she hadn't thought of it sooner. "You couldn't miss it. A great big navy blue vinyl thing, with sides made of braided strips. Always the same one."

There was one more bedroom, smaller than the first. It

looked as if it had been Irene's bedroom when her mother was alive, and had been halfheartedly converted into an office when Irene moved into the master bedroom.

There was a maple Colonial-style bedroom set from the fifties, but the bed was covered with papers, and there were filing cabinets and untidy piles of newspaper clippings dotted around. There wasn't any sign of a purse.

"Guess she brought her work home with her," said Jane.

"Some of the readers do that," said Monica rather apologetically. "It gets to be kind of an addiction. Clark collects UFO sightings. I sometimes snag reviews of books I want to get from the library later. Mrs. Webber tries to stop it, but we have a deal with the cutters. We put a secret mark on the thing we want, and we do it for each other too. Margaret likes anything about ancient instruments and Norm is interested in restored airplanes and trains and ships."

Monica yanked open a file drawer, which gave a rusty squeak. "You'd think her personal records would be in here too, wouldn't you?"

She pulled out a few old files. They all seemed to contain crochet patterns for lacy vests and afghans. "She used to crochet on the bus to work," explained Monica. "Weird sort of tunics and awful stuff in bright acrylics."

Another file drawer yielded recipes. Pumpkin soup. Lentil loaf. A cabbage casserole. "Real taste treats," said Jane, who liked foods with cholesterol in them, and who felt emboldened to be snippy about Irene's taste, seeing as Monica had slammed the crochet projects.

In a third drawer were canceled checks in shoe boxes. They were all written on the main office of the Washington Mutual Savings Bank, downtown, near where Irene had worked. Jane picked up the last month's worth. There were just a handful of checks—mostly for utilities and a Ballard supermarket, with several to cash for thirty-five or fifty dollars.

"I think Irene used cash a lot," said Monica. "After she won, but before the show aired, she took us all out to dinner at the Hunt Club in the Sorrento Hotel."

Jane approved of her choice.

"The tab must have been hundreds of dollars," said Monica, "and she took a big old bankroll out of her purse and peeled off some bills. I remember thinking at the time that she looked like someone in an old gangster movie or something."

It was the first thing Jane had heard about Irene that she found appealing. Picking up a big tab for her underpaid co-workers and paying cash in an expansive way for a great meal spoke of a certain joie de vivre she found lacking everywhere else around her. It wasn't right, perhaps, that money should make such a difference, but Jane knew it could.

"Poor Irene," said Monica, her face crumpling up a little, as if she might burst into tears. Jane stepped protectively toward her, in case she did. "She was just on the brink of feeling happy, I think. That *Jeopardy!* thing made a big difference in her life."

"Maybe it made her realize she was smart," said Jane.

"Oh, she always knew that. But she'd always seemed sort of bitter that even though she was, she hadn't been a big success or anything. I was always afraid I might end up like her, to tell you the truth," said Monica.

Jane put a hand on Monica's shoulder. "Don't be ridiculous. You have a sense of style, some dash. I can tell. That can take you pretty far."

Monica gave her a sweet little smile that seemed to say she appreciated the thought but wasn't quite ready to believe it.

"In the movies," said Jane, casting her eye toward a small

metal wastebasket with yellow irises painted on it, "the trash is always a little gold mine." She reached inside and pulled out a newspaper.

Monica touched her arm. "Quiet," she whispered. "Do you hear that?" Someone was rattling the front door in the living room. This was followed by a series of thumps, as if someone were kicking at the door, and then there was the sound of splintering wood.

"Let's go," said Jane. She figured they had time to get into the kitchen and out the back door if they hustled. She didn't know who the intruder was, but the splintering sound indicated a certain ruthlessness.

Monica, however, seemed frozen, and Jane had to jog her arm a little, and finally grab her by the elbow. When Jane got her moving, Monica staggered sideways and knocked over the metal wastebasket with a telltale clang. Despite her racy cat burglar ensemble, Monica was a klutz when it came to surreptitious entries.

Jane thought briefly about the window in this room, but it had an unused, painted-shut look to it. They had made it to the back door in the kitchen, and Jane was scrabbling at the locks and a chain when a big man came in and shouted at them.

"Who are you?" he demanded belligerently. He was about twenty-five years old and maybe six foot three, with a big gut, a dirty tractor cap, lanky blond hair coming out from beneath it, and a florid face with a scowl. He wore a black windbreaker, a white T-shirt with the legend "Marv's Tavern," and black Levi's that had faded to a steel gray color.

In one hand was a crowbar. The other hand was balled up in a fist. He looked like the kind of guy who'd force you off the road and stomp you if you cut him off in traffic.

Jane kept working on the door. "We could ask you the same thing," she said, actually smiling at him as if there were nothing surprising about a big goon with a crowbar smashing into the place. "But we won't," she added hastily. "We were just leaving."

To make him think before attacking them, Jane added, "They've got one of those block watch things around here."

"Big deal," said the man. "Who the hell are you broads?"

"Just some friends of the lady who lives here," said Jane, now conscious that Monica was clinging to her upper arm like a limpet.

Jane shook her loose. Fear was the wrong kind of body language to convey in a situation like this. Jane believed thuggy specimens such as the one before them attacked when they smelled fear.

She backed out of the place while trying to keep Monica from clambering all over her. They ran down a flight of squeaky steps and barreled out of the backyard, which went out onto North 55th Street. Jane's heart began to race, now that they were out of immediate danger and she was allowed to fall apart. Monica was looking as if she were going to faint.

"Hey, relax," Jane said to her. "He's not coming after us." By the time they got up the street and to the car, Jane's heart had stopped pounding and she felt an agreeable sort of giddiness she associated with getting away with something. She also noticed she still had the newspaper in her hand, the one she'd fished out of the wastebasket. She tossed it in the back seat, then put the car in gear and drove down Phinney, looking for a pay phone. "We'd better call the cops," she said.

Monica put a hand on her elbow. "We can't tell them who we are," she said.

"Why not?" The brakes squealed as Jane made a hard right into the parking lot of a convenience store. "Got a quarter? Oh, never mind." She opened the ashtray, which she had begun to keep full of quarters for Seattle's greedy parking meters.

"But we really weren't supposed to be there," said Monica.

Jane set the brake. "Okay, I won't give a name." She bounced out of the car, discovered she could call 911 without a quarter, and said breathlessly, "I was just driving by a house at 125 Argyle right below Phinney, and I saw a man kick open the front door. It looks like he was breaking in." She hung up the phone.

"Now where are we going?" said Monica nervously, as Jane peeled back out of the parking lot.

"We're going to cruise by the house," said Jane. "There's a pen inside the glove compartment, and some old deposit slips or something to write on. I want you to get the license number of anything parked outside. Okay?"

There was a car in the narrow driveway of 125 Argyle. It was a sagging old red Pontiac with some big rust patches and one black door.

"I got it," said Monica, who seemed to be hyperventilating. "And I think there was someone sitting in the passenger seat."

The sound of a police siren came nearer. Jane wondered if they'd done the right thing, calling the police.

After all, maybe the thug with the crowbar knew something about Irene. He hadn't acted entirely like a burglar. Why did he want to know who they were, for instance? If the cops whisked him away, Jane's only lead would be gone.

5.

In the past, when Jane had needed Calvin Mason's help, she had been broke. Now, thanks to Uncle Harold's money, she was rich. For now, anyway.

Being rich, a state for which Jane had always thought she had been mentally and emotionally prepared, had proved to be slightly different than she had imagined. During the many years she had lived on the edge, Jane had always assumed that having money reduced many problems to stunning simplicity. Got a little problem? Write a little check.

In large part, this proved to be the case, and just as heady and liberating as she had imagined. But sometimes it was hard to break old habits. Jane had to admit that she rather liked the idea of getting Calvin to help her the old way— with the faint hope of future payment, the camaraderie of the lost cause and the occasional well-timed smile. Now she'd just have to take out her checkbook. It was too easy, and she couldn't congratulate herself on her charm when he did the legal or investigative chores she needed.

Not that she wasn't happy to pay Calvin some real money. God knows, he deserved it. But she was afraid things would change, and understood for the first time what the word "cold" was doing in the phrase "cold cash."

Calvin was in his mid-thirties, maybe a year or two younger than Jane. He was a tall, rumpled guy with thick dark hair and horn-rimmed glasses, and he ran a shabby but sincere solo law practice, supplementing his income with some investigative work for more successful firms around town. He also managed the Compton Apartments, an old brick building in the Fremont neighborhood. His office was there, in the living room of his apartment.

Jane sat in that room now, on the worn but comfortable sofa, taking in the familiar surroundings—the old green file cabinets, the big battered desk with its dog-eared Rolodex and stacks of papers, the blinds at the window, their slats marking the room with bars of shadow and bars of light that swirled with the faintest dust motes.

"I think I found another hopeless case," she told him.

"That's good news," said Calvin. "The way you've been blitzing through Uncle Harold's money you're about due for another one."

Jane smiled with relief. Good. Calvin wasn't above giving her a bad time. Their relationship hadn't changed abruptly.

"Well I was beginning to panic, to tell you the truth. At first, after that last go-round when I got all that fabulous money, I just kind of wallowed in it. It seemed as if I needed everything. And then I had some work done on the house. I wanted to invest more, but interest rates are so low."

Calvin clicked his tongue. "You didn't do too much to the house, I hope. It belongs to the foundation. You screw up and don't come up with another case the board likes, they'll throw you right out."

"I know, but I have to live somewhere. The kitchen was really bad." She didn't mention she'd done all the other rooms too, and was planning on installing a new arbor for wisteria in the back and punching out a bay window in the dining room. Or that she'd taken off for the south of France in the middle of the work. First the plaster dust got to her. Then her relationship with the contractor took on the feeling of a bad marriage—periods of whiny dependence alternating with gruff hostility. "What's the point of having money if you can't have pleasant surroundings?"

"Yeah, I know. It's some kind of female nesting thing. Me, I'd rather have a reliable car."

"I've got a very nice vintage Jaguar back in England," said Jane. "It's been in storage for years, waiting for me to be able to provide it with a stable home."

"Sounds very chic and a potential pain," said Calvin. "You having a British mechanic shipped over with it?"

"It has some sentimental value," said Jane, who feared she was coming across like a princess. Calvin had admired her pluck when she was broke, and she rather relished his admiration and wanted it to continue. "Bernardo gave it to me. That and my white Chanel suit are all that's left of the old days with him."

At the mention of her late husband's name, Calvin's face took on a sympathetic cast and he looked as if he were sorry for having joked about the car. She gave him a reassuring smile. "Anyway," she said. "Until then I'm leasing a Ford Taurus. It's nice and reliable. Actually, it's a car thing that brings me here. Can you run a license plate number for me?"

"Uh huh, if it's a Washington State plate. It'll cost you a hundred bucks."

"Great." She handed him a piece of paper. "You want to hear about my new case?"

"Dying to."

"It's a missing persons thing. I might need your help. Do you have some sources who can see if credit cards have been used, that kind of thing?"

"Not really. I can tell you if they've been arrested or

something. Your best bet is to get some publicity. Who's missing?"

"A middle-aged lady from Phinney Ridge who lived alone and worked at a clipping service. The quiet type."

"I can't see them remaking page one for that," said Calvin. "You need money or sex." A gingery cat came into the room, glared at Jane and plunked itself down on Calvin's desk in a flurry of hair.

"She won a bunch of money on *Jeopardy!*" said Jane. "Maybe I can use that."

"She probably met a guy," said Calvin. "Some young stud after her money. She's probably having a good time, doesn't want to be found." Jane watched him pet the cat with his square hands.

"You know, Calvin," she said, "I'm kind of surprised you own a cat. It seems out of character, somehow."

"That's very perceptive, Jane," he said, "because I hate cats. They're sneaky bastards who aren't grateful for their free three squares a day. This one belonged to an old girl-friend, and she took off and I got stuck with it. It's kind of like a client you can't stand, but there's no one else to look after them, you know?"

Jane knew. Calvin had a whole roster of deadbeat legal clients who spent their lives getting into low-level scrapes from which he extricated them on a pro bono basis. "What's the cat's name?" asked Jane.

"Name?" said Calvin. "I don't know. I just call it the cat." He looked down at it, seemed startled to find himself pet-ting it, and stopped. "I can give you the name of a reporter on the *Times*," he said. "I want some remuneration if she goes for the story. Like maybe lunch."

"Deal," said Jane, who figured she could have called up the papers on her own without his help, but who looked for-ward to lunch with him.

*   *   *

The next evening at six, Jane found herself presiding over a small gathering at her house. The four readers from the Columbia Clipping Service sat waiting for the reporter. Jane had been curious about Margaret and Norm, the two readers she hadn't met.

Margaret was a pretty, plump women around sixty with a soft round face, a halo of fine wavy hair, and remarkably intelligent gray eyes. Norm was tall, thin, silent and nervous-looking. She imagined him to be around thirty-five. It was clear they had been brought up to speed on Jane's efforts in whispered conferences at break time under the beady eye of Mrs. Webber, and they both seemed pleased to meet Jane, although Norm's face broke out in bright red patches when they shook hands.

The reporter arrived, a dark-haired woman named Carla, who wore big earrings and bright red lipstick. "And how do you all feel about her disappearing," she said, in the tone of a group therapy leader, after brief introductions.

Monica told Carla how amazed they all were. "It's really strange. She led a very ordinary life. Same routine every day. The exact same bus to work, everything. We're really worried about her."

Clark's attention seemed to wane. Jane observed him examining the old engraving of Saint George and the Dragon that hung over the mantel, recording the image, no doubt, in his photographic memory.

"No family, huh? Just you guys. Do you all miss her very much?" said Carla in a sentimental sort of way, obviously looking for an angle. There was a brief strained silence, during which Jane was reminded of Calvin Mason's relationship with his cat.

The kind-faced Margaret filled the silence with a quote. "We're all very concerned about Irene," she said. "We need to know what happened to her for our own peace of mind, and as friends and colleagues."

"And this *Jeopardy!* deal, how much did she win exactly?" said Carla, scribbling away.

Clark turned away from Saint George. "Twenty thousand four hundred and two dollars," he said.

Carla nodded approvingly and wrote that down, then checked her watch. "I'll tell people to call the Seattle Police Department if they know anything," she said.

"Ha!" said Monica. "The detective on the case just has an answering machine."

Carla ignored this. "And I need a picture," she said.

"We just have a fuzzy Polaroid," said Jane. "But I'm sure we can get you something better." After all, they had a key.

"Okay," said Carla. "I'll hold on to the story until you can get a better picture. I guess I could try and get a driver's license picture or something." She sounded as if she thought the latter option would be too labor-intensive.

"She didn't drive," said Clark.

Carla shrugged. "Hey, without a picture, I'm not sure we want to run it. Let me know if you find one."

Jane walked the reporter to the door. "This could be an interesting little story," Carla said. Her voice dropped to a conspiratorial whisper. "All those clipping people are sort of sweet." She wrinkled up her nose as if she were talking about puppies.

"They're quiet individuals who love to read," said Jane in a dignified tone meant to make Carla feel tacky for being condescending.

When she got back into the living room, Norm had broken his silence. "*She* won't like our having used the name of the clipping service," he said, obviously referring to the feared and loathed Mrs. Webber. "I just know it. We didn't check with her. She'll get us for this." He gnawed on a cuticle.

Jane considered offering them all drinks, but also wondered churlishly if they'd hunker down for the night and expect dinner if she did. Her better nature took over, and she smiled. "Would anyone like a drink? There's some Scotch and gin and everything and sherry and some white wine. And there's Coke in the fridge."

When Jane's guests had all settled in with their drinks, and some cheese and fruit, and with festive, pleasant expressions on their faces, Monica said, "I meant to ask. What was that newspaper you found in the wastepaper basket in Irene's room? You had it in your hand when we ran out of there, I know, because it kind of flapped against my face on the stairs."

"My God," said Jane, "I never took a look at that. It must still be in the car." She was a little embarrassed by this lapse, excused herself and went out to the garage.

There it lay, in the back seat of the car, where she had flung it. It was a page of want ads, with some of them circled. Jane's first reaction was that Irene was looking for another job. After meeting the odious Mrs. Webber, Jane could hardly blame her. But the page seemed to be apartment rentals.

Back in the living room, she showed them what she had found, and handed it to Norm, who was sitting closest to her. "I guess she was planning to move," said Jane.

"Why rent when she already owned that house?" mused Margaret. "Irene was reasonably practical."

Norm swallowed, and Jane watched his Adam's apple slide up his long neck and back down. "I see a pattern here," he said. "Did you notice? All the ads she's circled are for security buildings. You know, with intercoms and special locks and like that." He looked up at the rest of them. "I think Irene was afraid," he said.

"Check the date," said Jane.

"It was the fourteenth," said Norm. "That's the last Friday she came to work."

6.

The next morning Irene's house seemed less sinister and more depressing. Jane circled the block and ascertained that there were no cars parked in either the front of the house on Argyle, or in the back on North 55th. In the yard next door, a young mother was pulling spring weeds from a bed of tulips and talking to a child of around three who was playing in a sandbox.

Jane tried the front door and found that it was locked. Whatever the guy with the crowbar had done to the door to get in, he'd managed to lock it back up again, or maybe the police had done that after she'd called them the other night. She took out the key, which still worked, and went inside.

She heard herself let out a little cry. The place had been ransacked with a vengeance. There were books pulled from the shelves all over the close, tobacco-scented living room, and a small table was overturned. Jane stood stock-still and listened. The house was silent, and there hadn't been any cars parked in front. Just to be on the safe side, she left the front door wide open as she went inside. That way she could get out fast, or, worst-case scenario, the woman weeding her tulip bed could hear her scream. Jane glanced around the room. In the corner was a television set, dusty and untouched. Wouldn't a thief go for that?

The dining room and kitchen had been searched too. At the sight of dishes on the floor, broken plates and teacups, and some plates still intact lying on the carpet, Jane found herself getting a horrible queasy feeling. The pattern, some old-fashioned pansies and California poppies, looked old and out-of-stock. Jane couldn't help but think it was criminal to wreck a set, then realized what a minor matter a few incomplete plate settings was. A person was missing.

She had a sense that this wasn't vandalism. After all, the dishes weren't all broken, and some were still in the cupboard. Just enough of them had been pulled out of the cupboard to search behind them, by someone without Jane's sensibilities about keeping a set of china intact. Someone like the thug with the crowbar.

The kitchen was a similar mess. Even the refrigerator had been searched. Jane looked down at the floor and saw an onion and a pile of dishcloths sitting next to a nest of mixing bowls and a box of Spic and Span on its side, the green powder spilling out onto the red-brick-patterned linoleum.

The bathroom sink was full of bottles of Tylenol and cough syrup. There was a mound of towels outside the linen cupboard in the hall. The bedroom had been pretty thoroughly gone over too, with clothing piled onto the bed. Overturned on the floor was a gray metal box—which looked as if it had been dragged from under the bed. On the bureau, a jewel box lay on its side, spilling out brooches and rings.

The center of the search, however, had clearly been in the second bedroom. The floor was a flurry of yellowed newspaper clippings and opened file folders. Jane just backed out of the room. Two things were clear. First of all, this wasn't a burglary, this was a search. The television and the jewelry were still there. Second, whatever they'd been looking for, it didn't look as if they'd found it. The search was too extensive.

Jane decided she should call the police, but first of all she decided she'd look for what she'd come to find.

She got lucky right away. That overturned metal box on the floor in the first bedroom looked like one of those fireproof boxes people used to keep insurance policies and other papers. Its position suggested it had been kept under the bed and Irene's idea was to be able to grab it and run out in case of fire.

Jane tipped it up and underneath was a nest of papers. Jane sat on her heels and went through them. There was a homeowner's insurance policy, a high school diploma from Lincoln High School, which would suggest Irene had indeed grown up in this house, the counterfoil of a Social Security card. And there was a small stack of photos including a few awkward group shots, and a baby picture that looked from the eyebrows as if it might have been Irene at about six months or so. She was sitting up in little dress with big square white baby shoes, looking inquisitively at the camera. It was sometimes easy to forget that nearly everyone had once been someone's darling baby.

There were some other shots too. A thirtyish Irene with a large, gray-haired woman, presumably her mother. Vacation snapshots. Jane finally found a studio portrait that looked maybe ten years out of date. The hair hadn't gone completely gray yet, there were just a few streaks, but it was enough like the woman on the *Jeopardy!* tape. Irene looked relaxed and pleasant. It was a nice picture, which pleased Jane. She was protective enough of Irene by now to want to make sure the newspaper had a nice picture of her.

Jane thought she should stay and look around some more. But she was overwhelmed by the task of sorting through the huge mess, and she didn't really know what she was looking for.

Anyway, she already knew several things.

First, Jane believed from the absence of her purse, or signs of a struggle, that Irene had probably left the house in some routine, voluntary way. But the bedside book, the breakfast dishes in the sink and the toothbrush made her think that Irene had not planned to be gone long. Second, she agreed with Norm. Those circled newspaper ads meant Irene was frightened. Third, there was someone else interested in Irene right now. And that someone, according to the state of this house, didn't have Irene's best interests at heart.

Later that day, in a small Italian restaurant on Queen Anne Avenue, Jane dipped bread into olive oil and herbs. Across the table from her, Calvin Mason did the same. They were surrounded by a lot of gently animated white-haired ladies lunching at pretty tables with green cloths and pink napkins before a matinee at the theater around the corner. The world, as represented by the matinee ladies, seemed a kind, intelligent, orderly and predictable place.

"O Solo Mio" on tape floated in from the kitchen, and an Asian waitress came with Jane's hearty lunch of angel hair pasta with sardines and roasted garlic. Calvin was having the special—singing scallops—which he dug enthusiastically out of the pink fluted shells.

"So did you call the cops about the place being tossed?" said Calvin. Jane thought he was trying to sound stern. "You should, you know. I know you like to mess around yourself so you can drag some case back to the board . . ."

Now he was starting to lecture her. There were times Jane wished Calvin didn't know what she did for a living. "Of course I did," she said firmly. "Well, actually, I had Monica at the clipping service do it." Monica had left another message on the answering machine in Missing Persons.

Calvin had touched on a sore point. If Jane really cared about right overcoming wrong in the pure way her uncle had, she'd want the police to find Irene. With their superior resources and skill, they could probably do a pretty good job if they ever hacked through all the cases they must have, judging by their apparent lack of activity.

But Jane also cared about Uncle Harold's lovely money— money that enabled her to lead a quiet, dignified life after years of marginal living. And the only way she could get her hands on that money was to take on some hopeless case, and solve the problem herself, to the board's satisfaction. Which meant rooting for the police not to do their job properly.

Surely Uncle Harold had realized, when he set up the trust, that her motivation would be different than his had been. He had even alluded to it, not unkindly, in a posthumous letter to her, mentioning her love of luxury. After all, he was rich and hadn't needed the money. Jane was sure if she had plenty of her own money she'd be free to behave just as decently too. "What do you think the police will do?" said Jane.

Calvin shrugged. "Not a lot. She could be anywhere. Without screaming relatives, it might take a dead body to get their attention. Or maybe if Carla runs that newspaper story it will produce some leads."

Jane suddenly had an unpleasant realization. She didn't want the police to get those leads. She wanted them herself.

"So what did you find out about that license plate?" she said. Calvin reached into his pocket and handed her a piece of paper with a name and an address in Renton. "Guy's name is Craig Swanson," he said. "Does that mean anything?"

Jane shook her head. "No. I had the idea he might be some kind of hired thug."

"Why didn't you say so?" said Calvin. "I can see if he's got any outstanding warrants."

"How much?" said Jane.

"For you, since you're buying me this nice lunch, nothing."

"Deal," said Jane. "While you're at it, could you find out whether the cops arrested him the night I called in? What really confuses me is that I know I heard sirens maybe twenty minutes or so after I was there, so how could the guy have searched the place so thoroughly?"

Calvin shrugged. "Maybe he came back later."

The warm, fragrant pasta dish and the nice Italian wine were making her sleepy. She woke herself up with a cappuccino, because she still had a few things to do later that afternoon.

Jane had planned to drop off Irene's picture with Carla at the newspaper office after lunch. Now, instead of dropping by Editorial, she went to the Retail Advertising department with the picture, and wrote a check for $3,276 to buy a quarter-page ad to run in both Seattle dailies, the afternoon *Times* and the morning *Post-Intelligencer*. She wrote her address on the back of the photograph and asked that it be returned as soon as the ad was produced.

The ad, a rough layout of which she sketched on a piece of paper, featured Irene's picture, and underneath it the words "Have you seen this woman? Concerned friends of Irene March want to talk to anyone who saw her after May 14th, when she was last seen leaving her office in downtown Seattle." Jane added her own number and said anyone with information could call collect. She decided to forget about a reward. She'd get too many false leads, and the board wouldn't like it.

She hadn't told Calvin about her plan. She was a little ashamed that she was hogging this case for her own selfish reasons. She was also afraid he'd tell her it was foolhardy to put her own phone number there, and link herself to Irene's disappearance. But Jane wanted to shake things loose fast, and this seemed like a good way. Something that would get things moving, even if it were a little dangerous, was better than doing nothing. Jane also took satisfaction in the fact that the ad might put whoever else was interested in Irene, whoever might have done her harm, on notice. Someone cared what had happened to Irene March.

7.

The day after her ad ran, Jane spent all morning on the phone. Thank God, she thought, she had call waiting. The first call was from a woman named Donna MacLaine from a town called Pateros. "I hope I'm not calling too early," she said. "I go on shift in twenty minutes, and we get real busy, so I thought I'd better call you now."

"Pateros," said Jane, as if the name were familiar. She was wondering where it was. She didn't want to start out insulting her informant by her ignorance of the place. Washington was a big state and people in Seattle were notoriously vague about anything outside the city limits.

"East of the mountains," said Donna. "In Okanogan County. I'm calling 'cause I think I've seen that lady in the newspaper."

"And when was that?" said Jane.

"I can tell exactly," said Donna. "Because it was the weekend of the Omak Stampede. That makes it almost a year ago. She was in here for lunch. With a strange guy."

"And you remember her after all that time?" said Jane.

"I know it sounds funny, but I do. Things were real tense at their table."

Donna spoke to someone in the background. "Just a sec,

honey," she said. She turned her attention back to Jane. "I knew there was some story behind it all. If you didn't watch the people and see what they're doing and thinking, waiting tables would get pretty boring. I like to know where people are coming from. If I don't, it drives me nuts, to be honest. There was some weird story there, I'll tell you that."

Donna was a woman after her own heart. Jane sometimes felt like an adult Harriet the Spy herself, wondering about strangers, eavesdropping in waiting rooms, and even making up histories for intriguing people on buses or airplanes.

"Listen, I gotta go," said Donna with reluctance. "Maybe I can call you back later. What happened to her? She's missing, huh?"

"Yes," said Jane, who had made a quick decision. "Can I come and talk to you more about this, Donna? It might be important."

Donna sounded thrilled, and she sounded like an excellent witness. Maybe she could cast some light on Irene's weekend excursions. Jane took Donna MacLaine's phone number and best times to call, and hung up with a nice heady sense of anticipation.

She'd have to get a map and find out where in God's name Pateros was. Somewhere East of the Mountains.

East of the Mountains was the generic term for most of the state, the area that began east of Seattle's King County at the peak of the Cascade Mountains. On the west side, everything was green and wet. Parts of it were even rain forest.

But beyond the mountains that kept the wet clouds from moving inland, the land was dry. In some places it was desert. Jane had a vague and jumbled impression of sagebrush, cowboys and pine trees. Plains Indians in teepees. A couple of pretty old college towns.

Through it all, moved the Columbia River, captured here

and there by big concrete dams. The river irrigated the apple orchards along its banks, and salmon swam against its current to spawn. It was a huge river working its way west to the ocean and to Portland, Oregon, where, wide and swollen, it flowed out to the Pacific.

Overwhelmed by geography, she was about to go out to the car where she thought she had a map of the state, when the phone rang again. Someone wanted to tell Jane they'd seen Irene on *Jeopardy!*

As soon as she got rid of them, the phone rang again. This time, it was a man who sounded as if he were in his fifties. He had a slow, patient sort of voice. "I'm reluctant to get involved in this," he began.

Jane rushed in to reassure him. "I'm so glad you called," she said. "There are people worried about Irene."

"I worried about her too," said the man. "She was doing something dangerous and, I'm afraid, sinful."

"She was?" said Jane. She believed in sin, all right, but she thought mere mortals should be pretty careful about categorizing others as sinful. She wondered if the caller was some kind of fanatic. Maybe he'd never even seen Irene, but his mind had just gone off on some tangent when he read the newspaper.

"Do you know where she is?" said Jane.

"No," he said. "But if she had any loved ones, I thought maybe I should tell them what I know. It's hard to decide what's right. Are you her family?"

"No," said Jane. "I'm helping her friends. Have you seen her?"

"Just once. Some months ago." He said it impatiently. The facts about Irene seemed unimportant to him. It was clear he was primarily interested in doing the right thing.

He sighed. "I wouldn't want to hurt anyone. If she's passed away, it might be better to let it all lie, let the Lord take care of it. But if she's missing, I might be able to shed some light on why."

"Please," said Jane, trying not to sound exasperated. "What you've told me makes me fearful for her safety. What was she involved with?"

He didn't answer.

"Can we meet and discuss this?" she said. Jane felt that in person she could be much more persuasive. The caller had given her a couple of clues as to what motivated him. "Maybe if you have time to pray on it, then we can talk."

"All right," he said, sounding slightly relieved that he was dealing with either a believer or someone who had respect for his belief. "I'm over in Westport. You can come by Dave's Charters and ask for me."

"I can be there later today," she said. She tried to remember how far away Westport was. It was on the West Coast, three hours or so west of Seattle, which isn't on the Pacific at all, but inland on Puget Sound.

"What's your name?" she said.

"I'm Dave," he said. "What's yours?"

"My name is Jane da Silva," she said. "And I'm very glad you called. I will try and make it today. But what if I get there too late? How late are you open?"

"I live above the place," he said. Then he added, "I hope I'm not making a mistake here, but I know I've got nothing to hide."

What did *that* mean? Jane felt uneasy. At least she'd tell Calvin Mason she was going to see this guy. She decided she'd better bump him up to the top of the list, before Donna in Pateros. He sounded less reliable, but his voice had an urgency about it.

The phone rang again and another caller told Jane that Irene had been on *Jeopardy!*

Jane thanked her and got off the phone. She bustled

around and collected a few things for the drive out to West-port—an extra sweater and a Gore-Tex parka. It could be cold on the coast. She packed a few overnight things too, in case she was too tired to drive back tonight.

She began to leave a message on Calvin's machine, and had recorded "Gone to Westport to interview Dave of Dave's Charters," when Calvin came on the line.

"I found out what happened to Craig Swanson, the guy you called the cops on over at Irene March's house," he said. "They didn't arrest him or anything. He said he was a relative. Concerned about her well-being."

"Yeah, right," said Jane.

"Apparently he was legit. He had an old lady with him, waiting for him in the car. They said they were cousins or something."

"That does fit," said Jane. "I heard she had some cousins. She was estranged from them, and after meeting Cousin Craig with his crowbar, I can understand why."

Jane decided to check on the next of kin when she got back to town. While she was thanking Calvin and saying goodbye, a click on the line told her she had another call coming in.

"Collect call from Amanda Jenkins. Will you accept the charges?"

"Yes," said Jane, wondering if her brain could take one more lead right now.

A child's voice came on the line. "Hi. You know that lady in the paper? The one that's missing? Is there a reward or anything? I saw her. So did my mom. Well actually, my mom more than me. Is this the right number?"

"Yes," said Jane. "Tell me about it."

Just then there was a commotion in the background and the sound of an angry adult female voice. At first, Jane couldn't make out what it was saying, but as the voice came closer she heard a sharp "Just what do you think you're doing? Hang up that phone now!"

The child hung up the phone.

Jane stood there for a moment, wondering if the child really had seen Irene, or whether she'd seen her on *Jeopardy!* like the other callers. Maybe she was just playing with the phone. She could follow it up, she supposed.

She wrote down the name Amanda Jenkins on the pad next to the telephone, and headed to the garage.

By two in the afternoon, she should be talking to Dave in Westport about the sins that had tarnished the life of Irene March. Actually, the way Dave had talked, it almost sounded as if he thought her sins could have been the death of her.

8.

By two in the afternoon, Jane was on board a forty-five-foot charter boat, being tossed around Grays Harbor off of Westport. She was bracing herself, holding on to a rail and gazing at a migrating gray whale that loomed up momentarily between the white-capped waves and exhaled through its blow holes. Its warm breath created a roundish cloud of mist in the cold air with an audible whooshing sound.

She had driven south along the Interstate 5 corridor where most of the state's population is clustered, down to Olympia, the state capital.

With the capitol dome looming above stands of trees, she had headed west, away from the stucco postmodern malls and the familiar logos of franchises, hoisted high along the interstate to catch the eye of the driver looking for the known entity.

Away from I-5, the landscape took over. The road climbed uphill, past green meadows with cows and horses, through forests of fir, hemlock and alder, past rock walls with waterfalls running over their surfaces, past signs pointing to old towns too shy to flank the road.

Finally, she reached the coast and Aberdeen, a mill town with an old-fashioned gritty, industrial look. Big sturdy steel bridges, booms of peeled logs floating in the harbor, solid old buildings from the turn of the century in dark brick.

South from Aberdeen, it was only a short run to Westport. The town seemed strangely elongated, running along a long strip of road lined with gappily placed motels and businesses. The road led to a small grid of streets near the marina. Facing the marina and looking out at a fleet of bobbing vessels was a street that featured a big old Cape Cod–style Coast Guard station with white shingles and green trim, and a row of charter businesses and gift shops selling dried sea stars and bits of coral, abalone jewelry, books about sea life, fresh bait and plush seals.

Dave's Charters was busy with a handful of tourists with cameras and binoculars around their necks, putting rain gear on young children.

She introduced herself to Dave, who was dressed in a windbreaker and a baseball cap, a pleasant-enough-looking man with a lean, lined face and crisp dark hair turning gray.

"We're about to go out whale watching," he explained. "I'll be back in a couple of hours. We can talk then."

"Is there room for me?" said Jane, who couldn't imagine what else she could do to amuse herself here for two hours and who thought it might be good to start bonding with Dave as soon as possible.

"All right," said Dave a little warily. Jane made arrangements with the woman at the counter, presumably Dave's wife, a fresh-faced lady with short brown hair. Jane had already noticed that she had a nice way with the children, instilling them with a certain amount of festive anticipation about their outing.

On board, one of the fathers of the children spent a lot of time talking to Dave, which allowed Jane to listen and take the skipper's measure. He didn't seem like a raging nut case.

He talked about how court decisions giving more of the salmon to the Indians back in the seventies had changed the charter business. "We've had to get creative. Now we go out after lingcod and tuna, and we go whale watching in the spring. And, when the tourists aren't around I do a little crab fishing. Things work out if you just have a little faith."

The radio crackled, and the skipper of another boat came on and told Dave where some gray whales were to be found. He turned the boat and raced off, bouncing over some tremendous waves and the wake of a vessel laden with logs for Japan.

Soon he was regaling the children with details of the whales' feeding habits, their migratory patterns, which took them from feeding grounds in the Arctic to calving grounds in lagoons in Mexico, and the hundred pounds or so of parasites the poor things had to lug around—barnacles embedded into their hides and orange lice an inch long that lived between the barnacles and in folds of skin.

The children screwed up their faces in delighted horror, and Jane felt that nature had been unnecessarily cruel saddling the whales with an ugly encrustation of parasites. She was consumed by an urge to take a wire brush to the animals and clean them up.

By the time they saw the whales, ponderous creatures emerging now and again and blowing their vaporous clouds, it had begun to rain. Jane was freezing cold, having foolishly allowed herself to get wet when waves had crashed over the railing instead of huddling under shelter, and her hands were red and numb.

She wished she could see the whales in those Mexican lagoons where the waters would be calm, the air nice and hot, and where there were lots of appealing baby whales, the only ones, apparently, free of all those hideous parasites. After an afternoon of whale watching there she could have margaritas and go dancing with attractive dark men to wonderful salsa bands.

Her teeth began to chatter, bringing her back to reality. She'd seen the whales, now she wanted to go back to land. Not only was she cold, she wished she'd taken some Dramamine.

She sat quietly on a bench, turning green, she was sure, willing herself not to throw up and wishing the boat would turn around. Dave seemed cheerful and happy, standing up nice and straight at the wheel, answering questions and making small talk. Jane decided a life running these vessels had to be sheer hell. An eight-hour salmon charter would kill her.

Finally, they did make it back to land, and Jane, feeling like a drowned rat, managed to lure Dave, disgustingly perky, off to a restaurant where she ordered a large pot of tea for herself and hoped she could keep it down.

Dave ordered a cup of coffee. "I prayed about it, like you suggested," he said. "And I feel much better about it. I realize I wanted to tell someone about it, but I didn't know who. I didn't want to call the police. I believe you are a person of goodwill, and maybe you can help this poor woman somehow."

Jane tried to look deserving of his confidence, and like a person of goodwill—serious, with a grave expression in her eyes, a slight furrowing of the brow; yet pleasant, with a small half smile.

Actually, despite her queasiness, she felt like rising in her chair, leaning across the table, grabbing Dave by the throat and demanding that he get to the point.

As if in answer to prayer, he did. "She showed up here in town and tried to blackmail me," he said.

"What?" It occurred to Jane she may have come on a fool's errand. What did she expect, running an ad like that.

The world was crawling with nuts. But then he said something that made her realize he wasn't a nut at all.

"She came to the office in the middle of the day. Wouldn't tell me her name. Said we had to talk. There was a funny expression in her eye. Kind of smug like. I couldn't imagine what she wanted. Then she reaches into her purse and brings out a couple of newspaper clippings stapled together."

He sipped his coffee.

"Yes?" said Jane trying not to sound too surprised. "Then what?"

"I looked at the clippings. One was from a newspaper in the Tri-Cities." The Tri-Cities were three towns in eastern Washington, Pasco, Kennewick and Richland, clustered together. "The other was from our little paper here in Westport.

"The one from the Tri-Cities talked about some vice roundup. They were arresting these fellows who were patronizing prostitutes, and putting their names in the paper. Not a bad idea, really, except it might hurt the wives of these guys. They'd picked up a guy who gave my name."

"You mean someone with the same name as you." Jane considered the possibility that they'd picked up Dave himself, but she wanted to sound as if she was sure he'd never do anything like that.

"No, someone who gave them *my* name. I happen to know who it was too. I have a nephew who's been nothing but trouble to my sister over the years. He didn't have any ID when they picked him up, and he gave them my name and address here in Westport. It just popped into his head, I guess. I'll give him the benefit of the doubt. I'd hate to think he was being out-and-out malicious."

Jane sensed that's just what Dave did think, but he was trying to be charitable. "I knew all about the whole deal," he continued, "because they went ahead and let him out but there was a fine or something, and they came after me. It was a real mess, but fortunately, they finally straightened it out. My nephew is a lot younger, so they knew I wasn't the guy."

"And the other clipping?" said Jane.

"It was a notice that I'd been made a deacon of my church. Somehow, she put two and two together and figured I'd be ashamed here in Westport to have people know what I was up to over there in the Tri-Cities. It seemed so strange she would have come across both those things and put them together like that. My last name is sort of unusual, I'll grant you that."

"She worked for a clipping service," said Jane. "She sat around reading newspapers all day. Just what is your name, Dave?" said Jane. She was still getting used to the fact that in America, except for a few legal dealings, you could go through life on a first-name basis.

"Twentyacres," he said, making it sound like two words. "They translated it from German a long time ago. It had something to do with the family farm, I guess."

"And she tried to blackmail you," said Jane. "How awful."

"It was dangerous, what she did," he said. "She was just lucky I was a Christian. I told her so."

Jane remembered thinking Irene was a risk-taker when she had watched her betting on *Jeopardy!* "You were right," said Jane. "If she tried the same thing with someone else they might not have been so forgiving."

"And she might have found someone who actually had something to hide," he said. "She had her facts wrong as far as I was concerned."

"How much money did she want?" said Jane.

"A thousand dollars," he said. "She wanted a thousand dollars. Of course it's all relative, but it doesn't seem like a whole lot, does it? I could have come up with it easily enough. But I guess she might have come back for more later."

"I would have tried to get it all at once; minimize the contact and the risk," said Jane, who instantly regretted it. She didn't want to sound like a potential criminal herself.

"Maybe," he said. "But in a way, I don't know if she cared that much about the money. When I told her she had it all wrong and she could tell the world whatever she wanted and I wasn't giving her a dime, she looked disappointed. But not because of the money." He squinted a little, as if trying to remember, exactly. "She looked upset with herself for having it wrong. It was like she wanted to impress me with how smart she was to know something about me. I really do believe she hated being wrong more than she hated not collecting the thousand dollars."

"Pride more than greed, then," said Jane. Pride was supposed to be the deadliest sin. But the sin of pride was more than just the arrogance Dave was describing. Wasn't it supposed to be playing God yourself? Which is what a blackmailer did, in a way, by deciding whose behavior deserved punishment.

"It's horrible, what she tried to do to you," Jane said, feeling apologetic that she had anything to do with Irene, and trying to make it clear she didn't condone her behavior. "But in a way, it's sad too."

"The absence of God is always a sad thing," said Dave Twentyacres. "She had to be far from Him to take such pleasure in the sins of others."

Jane leaned forward over the table. "If you had wanted to find out who she was, could you have done it?"

He thought for a minute. "I don't think so," he said. "She didn't give me her name. She wasn't driving a car."

In a quirky way, it made sense to arrive on public transportation. Jane had a bizarre vision of Irene, crisscrossing the state by Greyhound bus, maybe transferring at odd points to elude anyone following her. Did she find it tedious? Or somehow exciting? Maybe she liked to see the places she read about at the Columbia Clipping Service. And how many other blackmail victims had she managed to discover there, reading quietly at her oak table?

"To tell you the truth," said Dave, "I never thought about finding out who she was. I just prayed for her. I figured she needed it."

9.

Jane decided not to go back to Seattle. Her clothes were wet, she still felt a little rocky after her ocean ordeal, and the prospect of hitting rush-hour traffic on I-5 didn't appeal to her. At first, she'd felt resigned to the trek back but then she reminded herself she wasn't broke anymore and she may as well be comfortable. A few inquiries at the local tourist office and she'd found herself booked into a resort a few miles up the coast where she could get a hot bath, a good meal and a good night's sleep for a nice fat amount of money.

The place was on a bluff overlooking a wide stretch of ocean. Jane's modern, anonymous sort of room with European-looking birch furniture and muted blues and peaches featured a fireplace and a panoramic view of crashing waves, framed by a fringe of dark rain forest. The crashing waves looked just fine on the other side of the glass, Jane decided, stretched out in front of the fire (real logs with sputtering pitch, no irritating gas jet arrangement, she noted with pleasure). She sipped a brandy from the mini-bar in the terrycloth robe thoughtfully provided by the management.

Now that she'd learned more about Irene, she realized that going back to Seattle would have seemed anticlimactic and frustrating. Jane felt a delicious sense of momentum.

Tomorrow, she'd head straight for Pateros, east of the mountains, and talk to Donna.

Tonight, there were a few phone calls to make. First she called Calvin Mason. She asked his answering machine if he'd go down and interview Craig Swanson, Irene's crowbar-wielding relative.

"I'm sort of curious to see if he ransacked the place," she explained. "Why would he smash those pretty dishes with poppies and pansies? See if you think the guy might have wanted to kill a relative for her *Jeopardy!* winnings. Maybe they think they're next of kin and stand to inherit. I'd appreciate a general impression. Is your usual hourly rate okay?" Then she added: "And Calvin, can you get the number and maybe the address of someone who called me collect? It should be in a computer somewhere, shouldn't it? I accepted the charges. It was a little girl named Amanda Jenkins."

After she hung up, Jane decided against getting dressed and eating in the restaurant. She suddenly had a vivid picture of a room full of couples who'd come to the ocean for a romantic weekend. Perhaps they'd come out of an erotic fog for a few moments to notice her dining alone and feel sorry for her. This was a disturbing thought. She had traveled alone for years and it seldom bothered her. In fact, there were times when she watched couples and felt sorry for them and relished her own freedom. And then there were other times, like now. She sighed and called room service.

While she was waiting for a bowl of clam chowder and a Caesar salad, Jane forced herself to remember the name of one of Irene's opponents on *Jeopardy!* She recalled her first name—Margot. And the last name, she knew, was the name of a car her grandfather once owned. It took a while but she finally remembered it. Margot Dodge. From Portland, Oregon.

Jane had been wondering why a blackmailer who had managed to stay anonymous would blow her cover on a nationally syndicated television show, and she wanted to find out more about Irene's state of mind when the show was being taped. Margot Dodge had seemed accessible and open, and it wasn't too late to call her.

After calling Directory Assistance in the 503 area code, Jane got three possible Dodges and got lucky with number two. She was a little nervous making the call. Doing this kind of work, there was always the possibility she'd sound crazy.

"Hello, this is Jane da Silva. I'm calling from Washington State, and I'm looking into the disappearance of Irene March. She was a *Jeopardy!* contestant when you were."

Margot hesitated and then sounded uncertain. "Yes?" she said.

"I'm a private investigator," said Jane, thinking to herself how corny it sounded, but realizing it was true, even if she didn't get paid by the hour and her client was dead Uncle Harold.

Fortunately, Margot sounded fascinated. "Really? Disappeared! Irene?" She had a nice throaty voice.

"So you remember her?"

"Of course I do, she shellacked me." Margot sounded like a good sport about it. "I'm all recovered now, but it was reasonably humiliating. I never quite got the hang of the buzzer."

"It must be nerve-racking," said Jane sympathetically. The room service cart clanked to a stop outside her door. She managed to continue the conversation while she opened the door. A shy-looking teenage waiter pushed the cart inside. His uniform was a little big for him and the sleeves were too short, revealing thin white wrists.

"Not really nerve-racking," said Margot thoughtfully.

"Just frustrating when you know the answer—or the question, actually—but can't spit it out right away. You have to tell yourself it's just a game."

"I suppose so," said Jane. "The whole idea is to have fun, right?" She signed for the meal, included a generous tip and shooed away the waiter, who wanted to peel the plastic wrap off her soup and unfold her napkin.

"I guess so," said Margot, sounding as if she were trying to convince herself. "Some people take it pretty seriously. Like Irene. And you say she's disappeared? Involuntarily?" The phrase was telling. Here was a woman who read detective novels, thought Jane with satisfaction.

"We don't know," said Jane. "But we have reason to believe she was frightened before her disappearance. I don't know if you got to know her at all—"

Margot jumped right in. "We got to know each other pretty well," she said. "It's sort of like being on jury duty. You have a lot of downtime where you all sit around and talk about your lives."

"What was Irene like?" said Jane. As she peeled off the plastic wrap from the soup, a cloud of steam rose into the room.

"Kind of defensive. Some people are pretty nervous and I assumed that's what it was, nerves. But she wasn't too friendly or forthcoming. The other people were admitting they were nervous and showing each other family pictures and stuff. She was just watching."

Jane dipped her spoon into the soup and tasted it. Nice and creamy.

Margot continued. "To tell you the truth, I felt sort of sorry for her, so I made a point of being friendly and trying to calm her down. Then it turned out they drew our names as competitors. I was a bit sorry I'd been so nice to her, because it made it harder to compete against her."

"Oh well," said Jane, "at least you did the kind thing."

"I suppose so," said Margot. "Except to be very honest I think I thought I could beat her or I wouldn't have been so kind. She didn't look as competitive as she turned out to be."

A lot of people might have underestimated Irene, thought Jane, who now asked: "Did she seem to have any trepidation about appearing on the show?"

Margot thought for a beat. "Well, come to think of it, she did something kind of paranoid. I thought so at the time. We were all in this sort of waiting area and a guy comes and touches up your makeup, and these very nice women go over all the rules and stuff. And Irene wanted to use another name. She even lied about her name, but they made you show them your Social Security card. So you won't rip off the IRS, I guess. They told her she had to use her real name and she sat there for a second, looking like she was thinking real hard, then she said okay."

"I see," said Jane, who had managed a few more spoonfuls.

"Do you think it's important?" said Margot breathlessly.

"It certainly could be," said Jane, who wasn't about to tell anyone who helped her that her contribution was worthless. In this case, though, she thought Margot's information was actually very interesting.

Jane thanked her profusely, hung up, and finished her soup. So Irene had been afraid of revealing her identity, but the temptation of appearing on *Jeopardy!* was too much for her.

To blackmail someone in the first place took a lot of nerve. But to follow it up by appearing on a show watched by millions, carried nerviness even further. Maybe she thought because she hadn't asked for much money she would be safe.

But when had Irene received that mysterious phone call at work? Right after the show aired. After she was taped telling Alex Trebek she worked for a clipping service in Seattle. You wouldn't have to be a genius to look in the Yellow Pages, find the Columbia Clipping Service, call and ask for Irene.

When was she was looking for a security building? After the phone call. And when had her house been ransacked? After she disappeared. If Irene had made blackmail a habit, maybe one of her victims wanted to find out if she'd left any evidence of their secret. Jane thought she knew what they'd have to look for. Clippings. She sighed. But where were they? Mixed in with the lentil loaf recipes?

10.

The next morning, while waking in the massive bed, Jane suddenly remembered that she'd dreamed of Bernardo. She felt a sudden ache. She willed herself to remember, and felt that she had somehow betrayed him by letting the dream slip away to a point just out of reach where it hovered and shimmered. She knew, though, that she had seen him so vividly—his dark eyes and that beautiful line of violet pigment right beneath them—and had inhaled the scent of his skin and felt the shape of his mouth. This pleased her because sometimes she found herself forgetting how he looked and felt, and that too seemed like a betrayal of sorts.

She willed herself to remember the dream but was left with just a vague, unsettling void, and the strange sensation that she had cheated herself of the opportunity to leap across the distance.

She dressed and called her own phone at home to listen to her messages. First of all, there was a pleasant-sounding voice that identified itself as a Seattle police detective working on the disappearance of Irene March. "I saw your ad in the paper yesterday, and I'd like to talk to you about any possible response you got," it said.

But she was supposed to be working on a case no one else

could solve, so why help anyone else solve it? Maybe it was tacky, but she told herself that if he really cared, he'd call back.

There was a second message, from Calvin Mason. "I'll be glad to take care of that matter for you," he said. "And I won't turn my back on him."

A third message was from a woman with a gentle voice who identified herself as Peggy from Coulee City. Jane decided she needed a map of Washington State to sort out all the players. "I think the lady in the *Times* stayed with us here in Coulee City," she said. "We operate the Sage Motel, right here near the junction of 17 and 2. I hope the lady's all right." She left a phone number.

Jane packed her few things and headed out. In the car she consulted her state map and found Coulee City. If she went east on I-90, then headed north toward Pateros, she could turn off to Coulee City and it wasn't too far out of her way. She'd drop by there.

Maybe she was overdoing it to make a point of interviewing these people in person, but she felt strongly that she could get a lot more out of people face-to-face. And there was something more. She wanted to see what Irene had seen, go where she'd been. And besides, she thought a little bitterly, why shouldn't she do a completely thorough job? It wasn't like she had anything else to do.

In a matter of hours she had reached the pass at the summit of the Cascades. She drove through patches of cloud, gray mist that seemed to hang between the branches of the glistening wet tree trunks, past rock-faced walls, mountaintops overhead, deep gorges below.

In the spring, the forests of the Northwest are deep green with flashes of the bright acid green of new growth on the tips of the hemlock branches; the young leaves of the alders, dogwoods, sycamores and vine maples; and sword ferns and horsetails at the side of the road.

But once over the summit, the landscape changes right away. The mountains stop the clouds and water, and a rain shadow desert begins.

There's a narrow band where the two landscapes mingle briefly, and a few spiky-needled pines share space with firs and hemlocks. On the eastern slops of the Cascades, the pine takes over, its heavy dark branches stretched out over grass-covered ground, spare after the lushness of the forest floor on the western side of the mountains.

At the base of these foothills, eastern Washington begins. Suddenly, the sky takes over and spreads itself out over arid rangeland, covered with golden grasses and gray-green sage.

East of Ellensburg, a college and cattle town of fine old brick buildings, Jane crossed the Columbia River, wide, blue and slow-moving, tamed by dams into something that resembled a lake.

She forgot entirely about Irene as she drove alongside the Columbia through a landscape of castellated rock. Ancient volcanos had formed these layered mesas that loomed above the road, and ancient floods had cut out the flat valleys beneath them.

She turned north, off the interstate, and found a Spanish-language radio station—something that didn't exist west of the mountains. It played Mexican songs and ran ads for car dealerships ("Ask for César Guzmán, who speaks Spanish") and restaurants in Yakima County and the Tri-Cities down near the Oregon border.

North into Grant County, she lost the Spanish station, settled for some glitzy country, and headed deeper into the Scablands, a landscape composed of three planes: the flat tops of the mesas; the towering perpendicular walls, their surfaces segmented into columns, gouged out into caves and streaked with lichen; and finally, piled in perfect hills of forty-five-degree angles, at the base of the walls in the valley floor, neat piles of dark gravel, like buttresses connecting the eye to more flatness. The dry valleys were covered with sage and bunchgrass, and clumps of wildflowers, blue lupines and some flowers Jane didn't know, bright yellow, creamy yellow and white.

She got out of the car once, filled it with gas, smelled the sage, heard a buzz of insects, felt the dry, clean heat and went into a mini-mart to buy something to eat and a Coke. Inside, there was a blast of air conditioning.

The place had everything you'd find in an urban convenience store, and a lot more. Opposite the counter was a wall full of fishing lures with fanciful names. Overhead were rows of movies on tape and at the counter a pile of bargain audio cassettes. There was a rack of used paperbacks—romances and Westerns and a few thrillers. There was a bulletin board that advertised hay, Weight Watchers, kittens, puppies, guns and a co-dependency workshop.

Behind a window that led to a kitchen, there was a hefty young girl chatting with a tanned man in jeans, cowboy boots and a T-shirt that said "Chicago Bulls." Jane checked out the menu posted overhead: burgers, Jo-Jos, fries—curly and reg., biscuits and gravy, burritos and pie.

Jane opted for some premade sandwiches in a refrigerator case and a can of Coke. As she paid, she realized she had expected the young girl at the register to speak in some kind of country-western twang. Maybe it was the landscape, maybe it was some kind of ingrained snobbery from west of the mountains. Instead, the girl spoke just like anyone from Seattle, the kind of standard American English that meant no one could ever guess where you were from.

Outside, Jane caught a glimpse of a young couple kissing. The girl was leaning against the building, her back flat against it, one knee bent, her face upturned. The boy had one hand on her hair and the other bracing himself against the building. She just caught a glimpse of them and thought how sweet they looked.

Then she thought of this morning's elusive dream, and realized that these kids were just babies when Bernardo died—and wondered when someone would be kissing her next. As she pulled the car back out into traffic she told herself to stop thinking about it. She was convinced that lust would show on her face and make her look desperate, when all she wanted to look was desirable. Damn, she thought to herself. She could go without a man for a pretty reasonable length of time, but then it would come over her suddenly. Jane told herself to concentrate on Irene and stop feeling like a ripe fruit ready to be plucked. Or worse yet, like an overripe, unplucked, and falling-forgotten-to-the-ground fruit. She cranked up the radio—a hard-edged honky-tonk ballad about whiskey and deceit and love gone wrong.

11.

When Calvin got to the house, a woman came to the door. She was short and around sixty or so, thick around the waist and heavy around the shoulders. Her gray hair was in a poodlelike perm, and there was a wary, and slightly belligerent look on her face. From within, the TV blared. He had the feeling no one was watching the show. It was just one of those houses where the TV provides continuous audible wallpaper.

The woman coughed once—the rough congested hack of the heavy smoker—and said, "Yeah?"

He wasn't quite sure where to begin, but he thought he was probably talking to Craig's mother—the one who'd been waiting in the car when he broke into Irene's house with a crowbar. Maybe she'd been too wheezy to go up the porch stairs into the house.

"Mrs. Swanson?" he began. He wasn't sure what tack he'd take. He was certain, however, that he wouldn't mention the word "attorney" around this woman. She was clearly of the class that thought of lawyers not as employees who expedited matters, but as demons whose mission it was to confuse, intimidate, harass and to suck up money.

"That was a couple of husbands ago," she said. "My

name's Thibadeau. So if that big Swede's in any kind of trouble, it's not my problem." She began to close the door.

"Are you Craig Swanson's mother?" said Calvin. He should have started right in about Irene, he supposed.

The door froze about six inches away from the frame. She wasn't closing it but she wasn't opening it back up, either. "Did he write you a check?" she said.

"No," said Calvin, "nothing like that. What I really came about is Irene March. Are you related to her?"

"That's right," said Mrs. Thibadeau. "Our mothers were first cousins." The door opened a little more.

"You did know she was missing, didn't you?" said Calvin.

"Someone from where she worked called. They told us about it. Later, the police called us and asked us if we knew where she was, and they asked our permission to get her dental records. They still haven't found her, huh?"

"I'm afraid not. My name is Calvin Mason, and I'm helping the people she worked with look for her. Could I ask you a few questions?"

"I guess so," she said, in the embarrassed and therefore slightly hostile tone of someone who didn't know quite how to act in a given situation.

They went into the living room, a little room full of knickknacks and bric-a-brac. Mrs. Thibadeau kept her eye on Calvin as he maneuvered past a whatnot shelf bristling with Hummel figurines, porcelain birds, cut glass, and a massive oval plate, suitable for a Thanksgiving turkey, with a double portrait of the screen versions of Scarlett O'Hara and Rhett Butler in one of the couple's happier moments.

Mrs. Thibadeau gestured toward a chair opposite her and Calvin sat down.

"Irene's co-workers are worried about her," he began. "They say it isn't like her to just take off like that."

"I wouldn't know, to tell you the truth," said Mrs.

Thibadeau with a superior little sniff. "I haven't even talked to her for years. Her mother at least used to send Christmas cards, but not a word from Irene after her mother died. We've never been close, so I don't know why everyone keeps asking us about her. We'd be the last people to know what she's up to."

So why was her kid busting into the place with a crowbar if they didn't care about her, wondered Calvin. "Seeing as you weren't close, I can't imagine then that you've made any attempt to find her," he said.

Mrs. Thibadeau gave him a sly, sidelong look, pursed her mouth up into a little rosebud shape, and remained silent.

"You see my associate ran into someone at her house recently, and I thought it might be your son," he said. "She said he was carrying a crowbar."

"We are her next of kin. We checked on Irene, sure," said Mrs. Thibadeau. There was a little silence. Calvin just smiled. He knew that a little silence sometimes precipitated further confidences. "And the things, too," added Mrs. Thibadeau. She reached over to the coffee table and shook a Kool out of the package, then lit it.

"The things?"

She leaned back against the sofa, stretched one plump arm along the top of it, and brought the cigarette to her lips, tossing back her head to exhale a deep plume of smoke. There was something a little too brash about all this expansive body language.

"All my grandmother's things," she said sharply, as if he should be up to speed. "Irene and her mother were supposed to divide them up with us when my grandmother died back in 1959, but Uncle Stan was the executor and he just stalled around until he died. The lawyers involved was all crooks too."

Calvin nodded sympathetically, as if this were a given.

81

"The upshot was we never did get nothing but that old clock that was broken, and a couple of cartons of junk—ashtrays stolen from restaurants like."

"I can see why you didn't get along," said Calvin, his brow furrowed in fake sympathy.

"They treated my mother badly. To tell you the truth, the whole deal stank," said Mrs. Thibadeau with spirit. Then she smiled a grim little smile. "Well," she said, "what goes around comes around."

"I suppose you mean that if anything has happened to Irene, you, as her nearest relative, will inherit," said Calvin, trying not to sound as if he thought Mrs. Thibadeau was a human vulture.

"That's right," she said. "We're her next of kin, Craig and me." It hadn't seemed to occur to her that Irene might have left a will, in which case it was hardly likely Irene would leave her estate to them.

Mrs. Thibadeau leaned over confidentially. "There was a lovely set of dishes," she rasped. "They just sat there all those years in that house. It broke my mother's heart, she was so sentimentally attached to them, and I don't think Irene and her mother gave a damn."

Calvin had heard it all before. In the squabbling over effects, the challengers invariably based their claim on their more profound and sensitive feelings for the objects in question. It was usually women who carried on about old dishes. Men were more likely to try and steal cash, although Calvin had presided over one fierce dispute between brothers-in-law over a vintage Thunderbird. Calvin himself had already thought about asking for it as a fee, so he kind of understood.

"It must have been hard for you," he said now, sympathetically. "Did they have flowers on them? Poppies or something?"

Mrs. Thibadeau narrowed her eyes. "That's right," she said. "What do you know about them dishes?" She didn't seem to like his even talking about the sacred relics. "They were supposed to go to my mother and then to me," she said.

"I understand someone tore through there and they smashed some of those dishes," he said. "I thought it was a shame."

Mrs. Thibadeau rose from the sofa in a fury. Her whole body seemed to be shaking. "God, no!" she said in what almost sounded like a battle cry.

"Not all of them," he said hastily, afraid the woman would have a heart attack. She was getting quite red in the face. "Maybe it was just some teacups or something."

Just then, a loutish young man, presumably Craig, rushed into the room. He was wearing a pair of faded black Levi's with an inch or so of jockey shorts showing above the waist. He wasn't wearing a shirt or shoes, and looked as if he'd just woken up. "What is it, Mom?" he said. "What the fuck's going on," he said, his hands in fists at his sides.

"Language," snapped Mom, a touch of gentility Calvin guessed was trotted out for company. "This guy here is a friend of Irene or something. Craig, did you break those plates? I've told you about those dishes—"

"I never touched those goddamn dishes," he said, waving a hand dismissively. Apparently, sentimental attachment to the china didn't extend to the third generation. Calvin could well imagine him offing the Hummel figurines and the Rhett and Scarlett platter at a garage sale before his own mother's body was cold.

"He says he knows one of those women you saw at Irene's house," she said.

"Oh yeah?" said Craig. He pointed a finger at Calvin. "We're her relatives. You're not. We're like entitled to check

83

it out. After all, if she doesn't show up again, it's our house, right, Mom?"

"And the things too," said Mrs. Thibadeau.

"Unless of course, there's a will," said Calvin.

"Craig and I were checking on that," said Mrs. Thibadeau with a little smirk. "We didn't find one in her filing cabinet."

"So you're saying you went there one time, looked for the will and didn't trash the place?" said Calvin.

"Why would we do that?" demanded Mrs. Thibadeau. "It's our stuff anyway, isn't it? If she's dead of course," she added as an afterthought.

There didn't seem much sense in pointing out they'd jumped the gun, or in prolonging the conversation. Calvin said goodbye. Once he reached the front yard, Craig, in the doorway, pointed at him and said hoarsely, his arm outstretched belligerently, "Stay the hell out of there. No one goes in the place without our permission." He was bouncing around a little, like a barking dog safe on its porch.

Boy, if this Irene's alive those two are gonna be some real disappointed folks, thought Calvin. He wondered for a moment if they'd killed her for the dishes. The old girl was clearly a fanatic on the subject. The son knew all about it too. Probably had been hearing about it for years, which made it seem unlikely he'd broken them. But who had?

If the unpleasant relatives had eased Irene out of this world, though, in hopes of inheriting her house, her *Jeopardy!* winnings and her effects, they'd been fools to hide her body. It would just make it that much harder to collect.

12.

It was about six by the time Jane got to Coulee City. At this latitude and at this time of year there was still an hour and a half until sunset and the sky was a pale blue streaked with skimpy, feathery clouds. It was easy to find the Sage Motel on the highway, past a campground and a sign that pointed left and said "City Center." It was a single-story building stretched out in front of a big gravel parking lot with a couple of garden trolls in the low shrubbery in front of the office, a swimming pool behind a cyclone fence, and a miniature golf course with neatly painted plywood tunnels, ramps and windmills.

Peggy was in the office, giving instructions to a young boy, and looking like she was about to leave. "We've got one room. The bass fisherman in number twelve got disgusted and quit," she was saying. "I could have rented that out five times over, what with the rodeo and all." She was a big, comfortable-looking woman with freckles and crisp auburn hair.

She turned to Jane with an expression both hopeful and friendly. Jane assumed she was hoping she could rent her number twelve, and felt vaguely sorry she couldn't oblige her.

"I'm Jane da Silva," she said. "From Seattle, and I'm sorry I don't need a room. You called me about Irene March."

Peggy, who had nice hazel eyes, nodded. "Yes," she said. "Gosh, I didn't expect you to come all the way over here."

"I have to go to Pateros anyway," Jane said. "I hope you don't mind my dropping by. Could we talk just a little bit?"

"The thing is," said Peggy, "I was just heading over to the bull-a-rama. My nephew Scott is riding."

"Oh," said Jane, wondering how long a bull-a-rama took. And what it was, exactly. "Maybe afterward?"

She decided she must look a little pathetic, because Peggy gave her a sort of motherly smile and said, "If you want, you can come with me. To be honest, there's not much else to do in town."

So, fifteen minutes later, after handing three dollars to a man in jeans and a polo shirt and a baseball cap that said "Lions Club" on it, she found herself sitting on wooden bleachers in the bosom of Peggy's family, watching a series of trim, serious-looking young men in chaps and spurs and cowboy hats do their best to hang on to huge, furious bulls, who were foaming at the mouth, thrashing and pawing and twirling in circles.

Peggy's family consisted of two couples who immediately paired off by sex, the women talking softly, the men joking good-naturedly, and all of them keeping an eye on several small children in tiny cowboy boots and jeans; a teenage girl with a pretty, sulky face who seemed to be scanning the stands looking for her friends, and an elderly patriarch who paid the most attention to the bull riding, and seemed to take issue with the judges most of the time.

They all took Jane in stride, greeting her politely when Peggy introduced her, perhaps assuming she was a guest from the motel.

The bull-a-rama, it transpired, was the kickoff event to

the Coulee City Rodeo, which had performances the next two days. Tonight there was only one event—bull riding, embellished with some homey civic touches like the head of the rodeo committee thanking the reigning rodeo queen, a wholesome-looking girl completely at home on her pretty palomino horse and who wore a rhinestone tiara over her cowgirl hat. "Just a terrific little gal," he said, "a great gal who's done so much for the Coulee City Rodeo."

A couple of local kids sang some bittersweet country songs, and the rodeo clowns filled all the downtime engaging in endless banter with the slick announcer, providing the kind of hopelessly corny humor Jane had assumed died with vaudeville. A rodeo fan from Seattle was thanked for contributing the money to string the arena with electric lights.

Peggy leaned over to Jane. "It's just a cute little country rodeo," she said half apologetically, half in an apparent desire to let Jane know she knew the whole thing seemed small-time. "Not real glitzy like the Ellensburg rodeo or anything."

"I love it," said Jane, who had found herself rather thrilled with the whole thing. Especially, though she wouldn't want to admit it, all those lithe young guys looking fabulous in chaps and fancy shirts. There was something of the Latin male show-off thing about it that appealed to her—the riders had the same unsmiling expression as flamenco dancers—and she assumed the whole thing was descended somehow from bullfighting and had its roots in Spain, just as the country-western tunes she'd been listening to lately sometimes had a sweet south-of-the-border melodic line that revealed a Latin root.

She was glad they had seats near the chutes where she could see the riders looking brave and casual, stretching out their hamstrings and quads like runners and rubbing their gloved hands on rosined ropes. She could hear the bulls slamming against the gates, and when they were trying to toss their riders, feel the dust they kicked up and see the foam that flew out of their mouths.

Peggy's nephew ("Scott's a Coulee City cowboy, so I know you want him to do great today, and, he says he's got some fine hay for sale by the way . . ." said the announcer.) flew off his bull before the allotted time. ("No score for Scott Mayhew, but I know you'll want to pay off this young cowboy with your applause.") Scott managed to scramble to his feet, and pick up his hat. The bull went after him, but was diverted momentarily by one of the clowns, allowing Scott to dash for the fence and flip himself over before the two mounted pickup men came and herded the huge animal back through the gates and into the pens.

By the time it was all over, Jane was almost sorry she couldn't come back tomorrow and see the bareback riding, the saddle bronc riding, the steer wrestling and roping and the ladies' barrel racing. The big parade was starting at ten.

Peggy and Jane sat on the bleachers as everyone streamed past them. "My, I am sorry," Peggy said, "to drag you over here, but I wanted to see Scott ride. I realize you're worried about Irene."

"She wasn't a friend or a relative," said Jane reassuringly. "I'm sort of a private investigator, looking into her disappearance." She had to learn not to say "sort of." The truth was, Jane felt like a fraud saying she was a private investigator, and she was afraid people would think she was delusional. Peggy, however, just nodded politely and said, "I see."

"I'm helping her co-workers find Irene. They're awfully worried about her."

Peggy shook her head. "So many horrible things happen these days. You watch *America's Most Wanted* or something, and it makes you wonder just how bad things are. You think this lady was murdered or something?"

"We don't know," said Jane. "It wasn't like her to take off without telling anyone or calling in sick. Tell me about Irene."

"Well she was out here last August. I'm sure it was the lady in the paper. Except I think her hair was grayer."

"It was," said Jane. "A lot grayer. It was kind of an old picture. Was she alone?"

"Yes. That's sort of unusual, really. She just checked in for the one night." Peggy smiled shyly. "To tell you the truth, a lot of the time I find out something about my guests, especially someone traveling alone. They like to chat. She kept to herself all right."

"So you never figured out why she was in town?"

"No. She seemed sort of keyed up. Was she in some kind of trouble?" said Peggy.

"I think so," said Jane. "This doesn't seem like the kind of place to find trouble, though."

"It's just like any other town. We've got plenty of troubles. But here, everyone knows about them," said Peggy. "She had a visitor, you know," she said.

"A visitor?"

"That's right. A good-looking blonde lady. She came to see her in her room and they walked over to the mini-mart and had coffee. About an hour later, the lady from Seattle checked out. You say her name was Irene?"

"That's right," said Jane.

"Well she checked in as Doreen Martin," said Peggy. "I looked it up after I called you. Isn't that strange?"

"Maybe she came here just to meet the blonde lady."

"Well that's what I thought," said Peggy in a mild, circumspect way, as if it was somehow pushy to venture an opinion.

"And the blonde lady, she wasn't from Coulee City?"

"No. I didn't recognize her. She was very glamorous. Wearing Western clothes—real fancy boots and jeans that fit perfectly—but kind of a Las Vegas cowgirl, you know?"

Jane thought she got the idea.

"How old was she do you think?"

"I don't know. Maybe in her thirties. I didn't see her up close."

"And what was she driving?"

"A thing like a Jeep. Brand new. I don't remember the color."

"You noticed a lot," said Jane, in an effort to encourage Peggy.

Peggy blushed. Jane felt she'd blundered. Peggy thought she was calling her nosy. In a town like this, she supposed, everyone had to develop a certain distance so they wouldn't all drive each other mad knowing each other's business.

Jane leaned forward. "Really, that's a very good thing that you're so observant. This could be very useful. Do you think you could recognize the blonde woman again?"

"I doubt it. I think I could recognize her boots, though. They had little yellow lightning bolts on them. Coming out of clouds. Very unusual and flashy. Not the kind of thing you see around here much."

A few more questions didn't elicit much more information. Jane was sure Irene had been up to no good here. And the glamorous blonde sounded like a more likely black-mail victim than the born-again skipper in Westport.

"Thank you so much," said Jane. "You may have been a big help to us. And I liked the rodeo a lot. This is a nice town." She had enjoyed the rodeo and the atmosphere in the stands—the teasing and joking, the familiarity all these people had with each other.

"It is. A nice place to raise kids, I guess. I don't have any of my own, but I have nephews and nieces here. They have a good time; everyone's looking out after them."

Just then Jane saw two young girls picking their way through the bleachers. They had identical pierced noses and ears, identical flat, short, unfluffy hairstyles, and urban ensembles—one wore a nappy old sweater and a retro plaid skirt over black tights, the other distressed jeans and a seventies polyester blouse. Peggy nodded at them and said, "Hello, girls," in a stiff way, as if she were holding something back. Like her approval.

The lives of the two girls flashed before Jane. They were best friends who'd pierced each other's noses in an act of solidarity and to their parents' horror; best friends who plotted and schemed to leave town as soon as they graduated from high school, and who were pining away here in Coulee City sustained by each other and the conviction that somewhere more exciting, Spokane, Portland or Seattle, there was a place for them.

Jane had always respected small-town life with its sense of belonging, its special sort of tolerance that came from having few secrets, its good-natured, self-deprecating humor.

But for some people, like Jane, and maybe those two girls with pierced noses, it would never work. A few minutes ago, Jane had envied people like Peggy and her family. Now she looked up at those two girls. Their heads were bent together. Behind them in the dusky light were the rodeo horses and bulls, now off-duty and grazing peacefully in a field behind the chutes. Jane found herself feeling some of the excitement the girls must be feeling as they planned their escape.

13.

The first thing that Patrolman Lombardi had said as he looked down at the crumpled heap some twenty-five or so feet down from the trail was: "Why did it have to be all the way down there." With a sigh, he set off with an awkward, sideways gait, trampling on bracken and horsetails, and taking small steps to avoid skidding in his shiny black shoes on the dry, slippery grass.

At the top of the hill stood his partner and the two twelve-year-old boys who had called 911 and had waited patiently until the King County Police showed up. Unlike Patrolman Lombardi, the boys were anxious to head back down the hill one more time, but he made them stay up on the trail while he went down. They were leaning on their bicycle handles and watching with fascination.

At the bottom, Lombardi took a quick look at the crumpled form, which lay facedown at the bottom of the slope. Her head was higher than her feet, and she was kind of wedged there at the bottom amongst some big chunks of granite rocks. She had matted, gray hair, a cardigan sweater and skirt. Gravity had pulled the blood down the hill to her feet, and her legs were swollen and the color of old wine. He knew that underneath, where her body touched the ground, insects had already begun their work.

"Forget the aid car," he yelled up to his partner and began to clamber back up the hill. "Do we have any yellow tape?"

"No," said his partner. "We never have any yellow tape. I'll get on the radio and see if anyone has some."

"Better get a plastic bag big enough for that backpack too," said Patrolman Lombardi as he reached the crumbling edge of the path. "And call the sergeant. Looks like an old lady fell down there and broke her neck."

His partner, younger and less jaded, said, "God I hope she died right away. I hope she didn't lie there for a week or so waiting for help."

A little later, the knot of men on top of the hill had grown to include another couple of King County patrolmen who had come by with yellow tape to secure the scene, and the sergeant, whose first words had been: "Why does she have to be all the way down there?"

When he got down the hill, he took it upon himself to unzip the day pack, which lay a few feet from the body, opening the sides to examine the contents. Inside was a banana that had turned jet black, a grocery deli department sandwich wrapped tightly in plastic wrap that looked remarkably well preserved (a little orange sticker said it was roast beef and havarti) and a glass bottle of apple juice. "You guys had lunch yet?" said the sergeant without cracking a smile. Patrolman Lombardi snorted a little in appreciation.

There was no wallet. The sergeant went over to the body, squatted down on his heels, and reached into the pockets of her cardigan. The second pocket yielded a bright red plastic card that said "Quest Card" in white letters, with below it the motto "It has all the answers!" A smaller line of type indicated that the Quest Card was actually a Seattle Public Library card, presumably a name without the same marketing appeal.

He flipped over the card. There, above the bar code, was a

carefully written card holder's signature. "Irene March," he said. He trudged back up the grass, past some beer bottles and a Doritos bag, and huffed and puffed a little when he got to the top.

A Dodge Aspen station wagon arrived a little later, with a medical examiner at the wheel. He got out of the car, stood with his hands on his hips, looked down the slope and said to no one in particular, "Why does she have to be down there?" Then he took his bag out of the car, sighed and started off down the hill himself.

A few hours later, the body had been removed from the bottom of the hill and was waiting in a chilled room at Harborview Hospital for an autopsy. Patrolman Lombardi had filed an apparently accidental death report back at the Third Precinct in Maple Valley. The backpack was in a large plastic bag waiting to be sent to the evidence locker downtown. And Patrolman Lombardi's sergeant, having found Irene March listed in the computer as a missing person with the Seattle Police Department, had made a phone call to the number listed in the report, a co-worker named Monica Padgett. She hadn't been home, but she had a machine, so he left a message, saying he wanted to talk to her about Irene March. Maybe she knew who the next of kin were.

14.

Dusk fell as Jane drove up highway 17 to Pateros. The road took her up and across flat farmland—acres and acres of wheat, underneath a huge sky—a sky so big it seemed a little frightening to Jane. She had spent most of her adult life in cities, where she could be distracted by man-made objects. Her forays into nature as a child had all been west of the mountains where she had felt cushioned by green, growing things—trees and mosses and ferns like so much comfortable furniture for the eye.

In those surroundings, the sky and its vastness need never be confronted. Here, there was no place to hide and a scale that made her feel small and exposed. A landscape like this unrelenting prairie, she thought, was just the kind of place that would foster harsh religion. It was a place where a severe God who hadn't given you much in the way of decor, just a flat utilitarian surface to cultivate, could watch your every move and swoop down at you at any time. And the only station she could get on the car radio was indeed urging repentance, and quick before the whole thing went up in the flames of the Apocalypse. Jane switched it off, and hoped no little children had been frightened by it.

This was how the whole area would have looked if Ice

Age rivers hadn't gouged out channels in their rush to the sea, leaving behind islands like this, flat mesas of volcanic rock.

As it grew darker, the road went back down to the valleys again. It was night when she crossed the Columbia River right in front of the Chief Joseph Dam. This brilliantly lit structure lay like a jeweled necklace across the river's width. It was like something from a science fiction movie set on a barren colonial planet with a terrestrial installation looming up out of nowhere.

The state, she remembered from Washington State History, a graduation requirement at Roosevelt High School, had been transformed by a series of dams built during the Depression. They generated cheap power for factories and for the populated western part of the state, and they changed what had become a dust bowl east of the mountains to lush farmland in strips alongside the rivers, producing wheat and apples and other crops.

Woody Guthrie had come and written a song about it, "Roll on, Columbia." Jane had hated Washington State History, sitting in a stuffy classroom listening to that song on the soundtrack of a creaky old educational film flickering through the projector. She had hated Washington State too, and could hardly wait to get out of high school and out of there.

Her college junior year abroad was her exit visa to Europe, and she'd stayed for twenty years. Now, older and more easily moved by human optimism, she found the song rather moving. It came from a time when people had more faith in progress.

Watch it, she said to herself. Next thing you know, you'll be admiring heroic frescoes of people standing next to tractors or looking noble clutching wrenches. She turned on the radio to get the Woody Guthrie tune out of her head, and discovered a new station. She flicked on her high beams on the deserted road and listened to more sad country tunes about cheating hearts and honky-tonk angels.

Twenty miles later, she finally reached Pateros. It was hard to tell in the dark, but it seemed to be a nice-looking little town. The restaurant where Donna worked looked out over a bridge that crossed the Methow River near where it fed into the Columbia.

Inside, the restaurant was a big oblong-shaped room lined with the rec room paneling that seemed to be standard around here, and Western decor—a stuffed deer head, framed plaques with bits of antique barbed wire, wagon wheel light fixtures, and a sentimental picture of an Indian on a pinto pony, gazing out over the Scablands from high atop a mesa. From behind a salad bar there were the unmistakable sounds of the cocktail lounge—a Sonics game and voices and laughter.

In the deserted dining room there were a couple of women in white blouses and black nylon waitress skirts with white aprons over them. They were refilling red and yellow plastic ketchup and mustard containers. One was Indian—young, tall and dark with glasses, straight hair and heavy bangs. The other one was blonde and slightly plump with a tired face. She looked about forty, the age Donna's voice had sounded.

"Donna?" said Jane looking back and forth at both of them just to be sure.

"That's me," said the blonde. "You must be Jane." She gave her a quick, friendly smile, the kind good waitresses had, and Jane liked her immediately. "I'm just finishing up my sidework here," she said. "Sit down for a sec, okay?"

Her co-worker looked over at Jane. "Hey, it's okay, Donna," she said. "I'll do the salad dressings."

"Are you really sure?" said Donna, making sure the other

woman really meant it, the way women who work together do. She added, "I did the sneeze guard," as if to justify her bailing out.

"Sure I'm sure. Go on." The younger woman made a little shooing motion with her hand and gave Donna a reassuring smile.

"Thanks a lot, hon." Donna sounded relieved. "Listen," she said to Jane, "do you mind if we go have a drink as soon as I change? I've been on my feet a long time and I need to relax a little."

"Sure," said Jane. "I'll meet you in the bar."

"Oh not here," said Donna, flapping her hand in disgust. "I just pulled a split shift and I'm outta here. I don't want to see those same old faces. There's another place about ten miles up the road."

She hustled out of the room and Jane took a seat on an orange vinyl chair and exchanged smiles with the other waitress, who set about pouring French, Thousand Island, Blue Cheese, Italian and Creamy Ranch from stainless steel containers into giant bottles. A minute or so later, Donna reappeared. She no longer looked tired. Her hair was fluffed up and her mouth was now bright pink. Her ample figure, which appeared to be of the hourglass type, was packed into a pair of Wrangler jeans and a tight T-shirt. A change from waitress shoes to cowboy boots with heels had altered her gait to something more undulating, and she looked terrific and dressed for meeting new friends.

Jane wondered how long they'd be able to have a quiet drink and talk about Irene before the other customers started hitting on Donna. She didn't want to go in Donna's car, because she might not get out of there until closing time, but when Jane suggested they take her own car, Donna said, "Oh, why don't you just follow me? I like to be flex, and you probably do too," which was even better.

In the parking lot, Donna got into a dark car and Jane followed her taillights a short way up the road, pulling into the gravel parking lot in front of a new, rustic-looking building of peeled logs, bristling with neon beer signs. The place was isolated, surrounded by grassy, scrubby terrain.

Alan Jackson, singing "Don't Rock That Jukebox," blasted out the front door into the warm night. In the background, crickets chirped.

They went inside, and chose a small table in one corner. The place was about half full, and there was a small dance floor, but no one seemed to be dancing.

Donna sat down, ordered two beers, reached into her large purse for a Salem, lit it and leaned her chair back against the wall.

"So you're a private detective, huh? Sounds pretty exciting."

"Sometimes," said Jane, feeling like a fraud again.

"So I suppose you want to hear about this Irene character."

"That's right," said Jane.

"Well," said Donna, "since I talked to you last, I racked my brain for all the details." She wrinkled up her forehead to indicate deep concentration. "Thanks, Marilyn," she said to the waitress.

"And what do you remember?" Jane sipped her beer. It tasted good after a day of driving.

"Well, she came into the restaurant and this guy came in a little later. She had the patty melt, he had the chicken-fried steak."

"What did he look like?"

"Short dark guy. Foreign-looking. In fact, I think he had an accent."

"An accent? Could you tell what kind?"

"Not really. Maybe Mexican." She thought about that for

a second. "No, I don't think so. More like Dracula." Jane nodded. She supposed that Donna meant a Hungarian accent. As far as she could remember, Dracula was Transylvanian and Bela Lugosi, who'd immortalized him in the American consciousness, was Hungarian. But maybe the guy Donna had seen was Greek. Or Turkish. Or some kind of Arab or North African. He could have been anyone.

"But you'd never seen him around here?"

"I would have remembered him," said Donna. "He kind of stuck out. He had a gold tooth and a lot of cologne and he wore a suit. Around here, no one wears a suit except maybe for a wedding or a funeral. We don't even dress up to go to court. Anyway, they had kind of a tiff." She leaned over the table. "He said, 'You're bleeding me white.'" She said it just like Bela Lugosi.

Jane smiled. "Hey, that's not Dracula's line. He's supposed to bleed *her* white."

Donna giggled. "Well that's what he said. Sounded like they were fighting over a divorce settlement or child support. I've had a few talks like that about baby bucks myself."

Until now, and after talking to Dave Twentyacres, Jane had assumed Irene had only gone after a reasonably small amount. And she'd told him it was a one-time-only deal. But here was someone who said he was being bled white. It was crazy for Irene to go on *Jeopardy!* and advertise her name and location to her victims if she was bleeding them white.

"Did you see what he was driving?"

"No," said Donna. "I didn't see what she drove either. But I think they had separate cars." She thought for a minute. "I'm sure they did."

Jane nodded. "And how did Irene seem?"

"Scared I guess," said Donna.

"Anything else you can remember?"

"No. Not a thing."

Jane decided she'd better check with the local motels. Maybe she and this guy had checked into town at the same time. Neither of them were local. Maybe they arranged to meet in some place that was halfway between where they both lived. Maybe he arranged a rendezvous with his black-mailer somewhere where he wouldn't be noticed, and she made sure he didn't know where she came from. All of a sudden, Irene's little scam was looking a lot scarier.

"Think about it," said Jane. "Did they come in together?"

"No." Donna was sure on that point.

"Did they know each other?"

Donna thought a minute. "I guess I don't know, but I didn't know different if I thought it was a divorce thing they were talking about."

"Tell me more about the guy. How old was he?"

Donna threw up her hands helplessly. "I don't know. Maybe forty, fifty." She leaned over. "Do you think he kid-napped her or something?"

"She made it back to Seattle after their meeting," said Jane.

"But you are interested, right?" Donna was still leaning over and looking intense.

Jane made sure Donna thought her contribution was helpful. "Absolutely. We're trying to figure out if Irene might have been in some kind of trouble."

"Was she?" said Donna.

"She could have made some enemies around the state," said Jane.

"A lot of enemies?" Donna was clearly fascinated. "What was she up to? Running some kind of scam?" Her big blue eyes widened even further.

"Could be," said Jane. "Mostly, we just want to find her."

"Is her family worried about her?" Donna looked genuinely sorrowful now. A second ago, she'd just looked fascinated. A slow song came up on the jukebox. A couple was dancing—a big woman with black hair and a skinny man in a cowboy hat.

Jane turned a little in her seat and watched them swaying rather elegantly to the music with serious expressions on their faces. "She didn't have a family," she said. "Just some cousins."

"So who hired you to look for the poor thing?" said Donna.

"Her co-workers. She worked at a clipping service in Seattle." Jane wondered if Donna knew what that was, so she added, "She sat around all day clipping things out of newspapers, for clients who want to see what the press is saying about certain issues."

"At least she was off her feet," said Donna. "But it sounds pretty boring. No people."

"I guess she got all that second-hand. Through the papers," said Jane.

"Whatever she was pulling to get her in trouble, maybe it was related to that," said Donna, narrowing her eyes. "Sounds like she was shaking people down. How many people do you think she was victimizing?"

"I'm not prepared to say just what she was up to," said Jane, even though she'd have been thrilled to tell Donna everything and she seemed to have figured it out anyway. She was such an appreciative audience. But a private detective surely didn't blab all about her cases to everyone. It was just that Jane wanted to give people some payoff for helping her—a feeling that they'd done a good deed, perhaps, or in Donna's case, some juicy inside scoop. Instead she said, "Want another beer?"

"Sure," said Donna with a shrug. "Why not." She settled back and said thoughtfully, "I'd love to have your job, figuring out what people are up to. I already do that, but I don't get paid for it."

Jane didn't add that she didn't get paid either, not until the board reviewed everything and approved it.

"Most of it is pretty boring," said Jane. "I chase after stuff that doesn't pan out."

"Did you come from Seattle today?" said Donna.

"That's right. And I dropped by Coulee City on the way," said Jane. "I had a little errand there, then I stuck around for the rodeo."

"There's something about a man in chaps," said Donna thoughtfully, blowing out cigarette smoke, tossing her head back to avoid her own smoke, and rolling her eyes in a knowing way.

"They *were* pretty cute," said Jane. "But very young."

"So?" said Donna, laughing. "What's wrong with young?"

"Nothing," said Jane, who felt she and Donna had more in common than she would have liked to admit to just anybody. "Nothing at all."

Donna leaned forward again and lowered her voice. "Let's face it, guys get into middle age, a lot of them are kind of set in their ways. And a lot of them are out of shape."

"Not to mention married," said Jane.

"Yeah," said Donna. She warmed to her theme. "And they have bad haircuts and stuff. Younger guys take better care of themselves." She thought about it for a second. "Now bald, that's okay. They can't help that. It's genetic. Anyway, guys in their early thirties, that's ideal," said Donna. "I'm forty," she said and gave Jane an anticipatory look.

"I'm thirty-eight," said Jane. "Thirty-eight and holding."

"You're holding pretty good," said Donna, whose attitude toward life and love seemed to be that of a horse breeder. Jane herself, however, often had the same crass thoughts. "You could get a younger guy easy," said Donna appraisingly.

Jane wondered if Donna intended to recruit her on some kind of double-team stud safari. Trolling for guys was often a two-woman enterprise, and choosing a prowling partner was something a woman did fairly carefully. Ideally, they were at about the same level of attractiveness, discerning enough to evaluate the possibilities properly, trustworthy enough to divide up the spoils fairly, and discreet. Men were more smash-and-grab artists when it came to such things.

"That's nice of you to say," said Jane. "Actually, I'm not really looking." She shrugged. "But I have to admit I can't help noticing." She didn't add that sometimes she noticed to the point of extreme restlessness.

Donna nodded. "You don't have to be hungry to read the menu, and like I say, those rodeo boys are cute as pie." She gestured around the room. "We got some Sears and Roebuck cowboys around here. But in a little place like this, the merchandise gets kind of picked over right out of high school. Then it shows up later on the used market, after the divorce." Donna took another slug of beer and panned the room with her big blue eyes. "So you're single, I take it. If you're not, Jane, you're sure talking like you'd like to be. And I guess you're on the road a lot with this job." She winked.

Their second beers arrived and Donna fired up another Salem. The place was getting noisier and smokier. Jane thought about finding herself a motel after this next beer, taking a hot shower to get the driving kinks out, collapsing in front of CNN and getting a good night's sleep before the drive home tomorrow.

She'd come a long way to get some information she could have gotten over the phone, but she figured her time wasn't worth all that much. And she was getting a more vivid picture of Irene's activity.

She also thought about bumming a Salem from Donna. The best defense against barroom smoke was to fall off the wagon. She resisted the temptation. Quitting had been too hard. Donna was now calmly surveying two men by the bar.

Jane followed her gaze and immediately locked her sights on one of the men. Donna's patter must have been a bad influence, because all Jane could think of was what a perfect example of the classic American hunk this guy was—the kind of guy Jane had missed during all those years in Europe. He appeared to be in Donna's preferred age range, he had sandy hair and a tan, clean-shaven outdoorsy kind of face, jeans, boots, and a Western shirt with what looked like an Indian motif across the shoulders. He was laughing and pushing one of his companions a little. He had great teeth and he looked like he owned this place and any other place he might happen to be.

Under the table, Donna nudged Jane's foot with the toe of her boot. "Speaking of heartbreakers," she said in a low voice, "you're checking out the guy in the patterned shirt, right?"

Jane smiled. "I guess so," she said. She found herself seriously distracted. There was something entirely unself-conscious and free about the way he moved that she found tremendously appealing. Her only hope was if the guy had a weasely little voice. Jane was very partial to nice voices.

"He's a singer," said Donna. "He's got a real pretty voice."

Oh hell, thought Jane. The last thing she needed to be doing now was figuring out how to put some tasteful but effective moves on some good-looking cowboy with great pipes she'd spotted in a bar. Maybe he was really stupid with a dull look in his eye. That could ruin male beauty in an instant, as surely as a weedy voice.

"Him and his band, they've played all around," continued Donna. "They do the Omak Stampede every year 'cause he's local. His parents are in the apple business."

"Is that guy with him in the band?" said Jane, who couldn't care less about the man with him. She watched the heartbreaker run his hand through his hair. It was a nicely shaped hand.

"The guy on the left is named Carl," said Donna. "He manages the apple packing plant for the family. To tell you the truth, I hoped to run into Carl here."

Jane gave Carl a cursory glance, then allowed herself a survey up and down the length of the singing cowboy, who was in the act of putting one boot on the brass rail along the bar. As he did, he pulled a little on the leg of his jeans. She could see the side of his boot now, and there, tooled in leather, was a lemon yellow lightning bolt coming out of a cloud, exactly like the one Peggy in Coulee City had described.

Jane looked back up at his face, and discovered, to her horror, that he'd been watching her check him out. He had a quirky little sideways smile and a slightly arrogant, amused expression in his eye that Jane decided was absolutely charming, but he seemed kind of sweet too. He also looked far from stupid. Those eyes had some intelligence flickering behind them. She'd run out of reasons not to make an idiot of herself and she hadn't even met him yet.

She gave him a mysterious little sidelong half smile, what he'd just given her, but not so direct, and the same expression of amusement with a touch of the blasé. After all, she did need to ask him where he got those boots with the lightning bolts. It might give her some idea where to look for the blonde from Coulee City. This was strictly business.

15.

She realized, however, that if it were simply business, she'd just walk over to him and ask him where he got the boots, without worrying what he thought. The fact that he was the town heartbreaker and they'd exchanged a soulful glance across the room, however, brought her pride into play. She wanted to lure him over to her. She was rather disgusted with herself for acting like life was a high school dance, but maybe it was.

Donna was waving at his companion, Carl, who wore a black cowboy hat. For all her bold talk of young sleek things with washboard stomachs, it was clear she was willing to compromise. The guy she was waggling her fingers at while she goggled at him with her big blue eyes over her beer bottle had seen a good forty-five summers. Carl had the kind of leathery tan associated with hard work out of doors rather than tanning parlors or Club Med. The way he was sucking enthusiastically on his own beer was a vital clue as to how his stomach had blossomed out and over his big silver belt buckle. But there was a rascally sort of charm in the way he smiled back at Donna.

"Carl's wife left him last week," she said. Apparently, Donna wasn't waiting for the corpse of the dead marriage to cool off. A second later, he was over at their table, grabbing a chair and flipping it around so he could sit on it backward and lean on the back of it, a touch Jane found kind of phony. Then he beamed at Donna.

"This is Carl," she said, pointing at him with the base of her beer bottle as she tilted it back up to her lips. "And this is Jane da Silva. From Seattle."

From the corner of her eye, Jane watched Carl's hunky companion leaning against the bar facing the dance floor. They gave each other another look, just a millisecond too long to be accidental.

"Jane, huh. What brings you out here?" said Carl.

Jane was about to tell him she was a private detective. She may as well get used to it, and she supposed it was nice to be able to say something—it had been a while since she could say she was anything in particular. But Donna gave her a warning look, a frown and a barely perceptible shake of the head. Jane supposed the place was a hotbed of gossip.

"Just passing through," she said with a smile. Great, now she sounded like someone in an old Western picture. Carl didn't press her.

"I heard about you and Gail," said Donna, who managed to sound genuinely sympathetic and trampy at the same time.

Carl shrugged. "I guess it wasn't a big surprise," he said. "We've been struggling for a long time."

Jane wasn't in the mood to hear about Carl's marital problems. "I have to make a phone call," she said, rising. She'd sashay past the guy with the lightning bolt boots, hit him with a big eye lock, and give herself one more shot at getting him to make a move. Then she'd stop being silly and go up and ask him where he got the boots. He'd think it was a come-on, but she decided not to let herself care.

It happened suddenly, just like in the movies. Suddenly

was usually the way it happened for Jane, whether or not it actually turned into anything. As she walked past him she forced herself beyond the bounds of what little natural modesty she seemed to have left after a lifetime of successful flirting and gave him a great big bold stare and a shy, knowing smile.

Another song came on the jukebox—a kind of old-fashioned country waltz with a sweet, sad violin line. He didn't smile back, which made him somehow more interesting. He just gazed at her, straightened up a little at the bar, and said very politely, "Would you care to dance?"

"Sure," she said with a phony casual shrug that wasn't really meant to fool anyone. He put one hand around her waist and she put a hand on his shoulder and then their other hands touched and clasped and they began to dance. He held her decorously in front of him so they could look at each other.

"I noticed something from across the room," she said.

"Yeah? So did I," he said smiling now.

"I noticed your boots," she said. "With those lightning bolts up the side."

"A little flashy, but I guess they did the trick," he said. "You hustled right on over." He pulled her about an inch closer.

"I was on my way to the phone," she said in mock indignation, giving him the inch and adding a little something to it. He smelled like sweat and Ivory soap. She wished she didn't have to keep asking about his boots.

"I wondered where you got them. They seemed unusual."

"They are," he said. "Custom. I usually wear them onstage. I'm a musician."

"So you can write them off if you wear them onstage," said Jane, who had once been a singer and would have written off a series of slinky dresses if she'd made enough income to shelter.

"Actually, they were a gift," he said.

"From a grateful fan?" said Jane.

"I suppose you could call her that," he said politely, but with a kind of firmness that meant he wasn't going to talk about it anymore. "I've been on the road," he said. "I haven't seen you around here before."

"I'm from Seattle," said Jane.

"A friend of Donna's over there?"

"No," she said, wondering how much she should say. If she was going to pry out of him where the boots came from, it would be better not to say who she was. "I just met her. So what kind of a musician are you?"

"A little better than average," he said looking down at her from beneath his lashes. His eyes were kind of green with gold sunbursts around the pupil. Jane had heard eyes like that described as "American eyes."

She laughed. "That's not what I meant."

"We're what they call in the business a hat act," he said.

"As in cowboy hat?"

"That's right. We just kind of stomp and holler and make sure everyone has a good time, and once in a while we sneak in a nice slow ballad so everyone can dance close and sometimes we get a little bluesy."

Jane imagined herself dancing closer to him after an hour or so of sweaty stomping and hollering, with full frontal body heat transfer and her face against his chest. She tried to put the thought out of her mind, but discovered herself moving her hand from his nice level shoulder a little ways around to the back of his neck. She stopped herself when she felt his hair with her fingertips—it was smooth but kind of crisp—and slid her hand back onto his shoulder, a gesture that came across, she decided, more like a caress than the retreat it was intended to be.

The melody took off, soaring above them, and he took them into a deep spin, twirling her around the empty floor three times until she started to laugh.

When he saw her laugh, he started to laugh too, and twirled her around some more, with bigger, more swooping steps, so she got rather happily dizzy and when the music ended, he had to steady her a little with his hands on her arms, and they just stared at each kind of goofily for an instant.

"That was exhilarating," she said. "Is that the kind of music you play?"

"No," he said. "We're not that sweet. But it's great stuff. If you listen you can hear old Celtic reels back in there. Kind of haunting like." He stopped and gave her a look that she thought might cause core meltdown, then he said, "Want a beer?"

She pushed her hair back from her face. "Sure," she said, looking over at Donna, who seemed to be in animated conversation with Carl.

"Never mind about old Donna," he said. "She's fine." They sat at the bar and he gestured to the waitress. "So tell me about yourself. A new face kind of stands out around here." Beat. Disarming, confident smile. "Yours does, anyway."

"I used to be a singer too," said Jane. "Old standards. Gershwin, Kern, Cole Porter. Not much stomping and hollering."

"More torchy and swooning, I guess," he said.

"Something like that," she answered, repressing the urge to add "studied and corny." But maybe she was being too hard on herself.

"So where did you do this singing? In Seattle?"

"No, in Europe. I lived there for a long time." She wrenched herself away from his face to thank the bartender who had set down their beers.

"I spent some time over there," he said. "But one day I woke up and knew I had to come home. I needed more space. I felt crowded and hemmed in. Too many people."

"I know," she said. "But I got used to it. I think after all those years I started moving like them. Smaller, neater steps, you know. But what I liked about it was always being a foreigner. Some people feel more at home when they're away from home, and I was one of them."

"But you came back. Still singing?"

She shrugged. "In the shower. I finally figured out it wasn't a very stable life."

"And that's what you want? A stable life?"

"No. But that's what I think I should want," she said. "I came home to look after the family business."

"That's what I'll probably end up doing," he said. "It beats ending up in a trailer park somewhere with a sack of demo tapes and a liver like Swiss cheese. I'm kind of keeping track of things for a week or two now while my parents are in Japan."

"Japan?" said Jane. It sounded pretty exotic for a couple of farmers. Donna had said his family was in the apple business.

He gave her a sideways little smile. "My Dad's on a committee of apple growers negotiating with the Japanese to get our apples into their markets," he said. She hoped he hadn't guessed why she looked startled. He had.

"I guess you think we go out and pick them and put them in an old pickup and sell them by the side of the road. Apples are a global business. We sell them all over the world. The Japanese have a strong farm lobby of their own, getting good prices from Japanese consumers. They keep our apples out, making up a bunch of excuses about pests. Don't get my Dad started, or he'll be likely to grab a sledgehammer and bash in the windshield of some Toyota or Subaru. My mother and sister went along to take a tour of Japanese temple architecture. And I'm hanging out here in Okanogan County with my old friends from Omak High School, which is driving me nuts, to tell you the truth.

"So when I saw you, I thought good, there's an interesting lady to talk to, and I didn't go to high school with her. I don't know why she's here or where she's been or what her name is."

"It's Jane. Jane da Silva," she said, racking her brain to come up with some interesting rationale for her presence in this town and this bar. She didn't want to make herself sound too dull.

"Jack Lawson," he said.

"I'd never been east of the mountains, much, so I'm kind of driving around. It's beautiful country." Now she sounded sort of pathetic, taking in the scenery by day and drifting into bars by herself at night, after having failed as a singer and crawled back into some dreary family business.

Well, she wasn't here to sell herself, anyway, she reminded herself sternly, as she studied the bridge of his nose, which had a tiny little bump in it, and the plane of his cheek and the curve of his lip and the way his shoulder moved under his shirt. This was supposed to be business.

"While I'm here, east of the mountains, I suppose I should get some cowboy boots," she said, looking back down at his. "Did you say those were custom-made?"

"That's right," he said.

"So are they the only pair in the world?"

"No. There's one other pair," he said.

She looked up at him. "The woman who gave them to you. She had a pair made too?"

114

"That's right," he said after a pause. "I still have the boots, but I don't have her."

"Sounds like a country-western song title," said Jane, then, noticing that his expression had changed—to seriousness or wariness, she couldn't tell which—she said, "I'm sorry. I didn't mean to pry." Sometimes saying you weren't meaning to pry brought forth a confessional torrent.

Prying was, of course, just what she meant to do. The blonde in the boots from Coulee City was probably one of Irene's victims. But he didn't look like he wanted to talk about her. Not now anyway. Maybe after they got to know each other better.

"You're a fabulous dancer," she said, and he smiled, stood up and picked her up around her waist, lifted her from the bar stool like some cowboy lifting the new schoolmarm out of the stagecoach, and set her down again. "Let's dance some more, Jane," he said.

Jane, feeling a little guilty about Donna, looked over at their table. She made a sort of helpless gesture as she went out onto the floor, as if she were being charmed to dance against her will, which was actually partly true.

Donna just raised her eyebrows in a sort of congratulatory way and waggled her fingers before turning back to Carl.

"But after this," Jane said as Jack took her in his arms, "I've got to make that phone call."

"Oh forget it," he said. "Just relax. Call tomorrow. You must be exhausted from traveling all day. You started in Seattle, right?"

"That's right," she said, looking up at him. The song was slow and they took small, swaying steps. "It seems a week ago I was there but it was just this morning. I think I am exhausted."

"Just put your head on my shoulder and take a nap," he

115

said, touching her hair softly. "Like those marathon dancers they had in the thirties."

She decided what the hell, and melted against him in the kind of clinch the chaperones used to try and bust up in the Nathan Eckstein Junior High School gym.

"And after that phone call I really have to go check into a motel somewhere," she said into his shirt.

"I guess you know you better have a reservation," he said.

"Not really." She straightened up and looked at him to see if he was kidding.

"Oh, you'll never find a room tonight," he said with a smile. "Not with the big bass tournament up in Coulee City."

"You're kidding, right?"

"No. But you're in luck. You can stay in the guest house. And in the morning, we can saddle up a couple of horses and take a ride around the orchards and I can tell you how to grow the world's best apples."

"I don't think—" she began.

"And then I'll make you breakfast."

"I don't know . . ." she said, biting her lower lip.

"I know, I know," he said. "But you don't have to worry about a thing. I'm really a perfectly respectable member of the community. Ask Donna. She'll tell you how safe I am."

"She already told me about you," said Jane. "Said you were the town heartbreaker."

"She did?" He looked pleased. "Then you're even safer than I thought. If I'm doing that well, I don't need to go harassing houseguests. Trust me, it's very civilized. My mom keeps fancy soap there and coffee table books to look at if you can't sleep."

"It does sound great," said Jane.

"Of course, if you think the howls of the coyotes will scare you, you can sleep in the big house with me."

Jane looked a little skeptical and he said, suddenly serious, "Hey, I mean it. This is a legitimate deal. And the guest house has a bolt on the inside of the door."

Jane didn't tell him he might need a bolt on the inside of his door. The song ended and she disentangled herself from him slowly. "I'll think about it," she said. "But now I'll make my phone call, okay?"

She found the phone in a little alcove by the restrooms. But someone was using it. It was Donna. She didn't turn around, just patted her blonde hair with the tips of her candy pink fingernails and shifted her weight from one hip to the other while she talked.

Jane probably wouldn't have eavesdropped if she hadn't heard Donna talking about her. "This Jane da Silva was real straightforward about it. Seems like a nice gal. She's a private investigator. I give her the whole lowdown like we discussed, and I get a strong feeling this Irene person was blackmailing people around the state. Now what the hell are you mixed up in?" Donna sounded angry and worried. Jane had the feeling that she cared about whoever it was she was talking to.

"She says she's working for this Irene character's co-workers. Yeah? Well listen, I'll tell you all the details when you're ready to tell me what you're mixed up in," she said. There was another pause. "No, she doesn't know I'm calling you. How can she be? She's distracted by Jack Lawson."

There was another pause. "Well, I mean they're dancing and having a few beers and gazing into each other's eyes," she said impatiently. She listened for a second.

"How should I know?" she said, and then she snapped, "How in the hell am I supposed to do that. They're both over twenty-one and they seem interested in each other. Jane's very ladylike but she's a good ol' gal and she thinks he's cute. What's he got to do with it, anyway?"

Even from behind, Jane could see the body language changing. Donna's back was getting stiffer. Her free hand was tightening into a fist. Now she put one hand on her waist and cocked her hip. "You listen to me," she said in a tone she might use with a customer who got snippy about her refusal to make a substitute on the special, "I'm not helping you anymore until you tell me just what the hell you're trying to accomplish here." She slammed down the phone.

Jane stepped back into the shadows. She wasn't sure it was fast enough. Donna might have realized, or at least suspected she was overheard. Jane tried to act as if she were just coming around the corner to the phones.

"Hi!" said Donna, bright and perky and without any apparent trace of concern. She was a pretty good actress, thought Jane with admiration. "Having a good time?"

"Yes," said Jane. "I guess I am. I thought you and Carl might want some privacy so he could tell you his problems."

"Yeah, right," said Donna. "You're dancing with Jack Lawson all for me."

They both laughed.

"But listen, Donna," said Jane, "can I ask you just one more question?"

"Why sure," said Donna.

"I'd like you to take a look at a picture of Irene. Just to make sure she's the woman you saw."

"Okay," said Donna. She lowered her voice to a whisper. "Bring it into the ladies' room."

"There's nothing particularly confidential about this investigation," said Jane unsmilingly. "No need to sneak around. Let's go back to our table. The picture is in my purse."

"Oh, but this place is full of gossip," said Donna. "People would just ask a million questions."

"That's all right," said Jane with a smile, tilting her head back a little in a kind of challenging way. "The more the merrier. Maybe someone else saw her in town. Or that Dracula guy that was with her."

Donna was looking a little nervous now. Jane decided she'd better not crowd her anymore. She wanted to keep the door open. Donna was trying to help someone. But she was put out with whoever she was helping for not being more forthcoming. Maybe later Jane could use that.

"But I guess you don't want the hassle of explaining," said Jane warmly. "I'll go get the picture."

Donna looked relieved. Jane went to her purse, guarded by Carl, who was smoking a Camel with a serene expression on his leathered face. He gave her a little nod. She also passed Jack Lawson, who was chatting with a blowsy redhead at the bar. To Jane's satisfaction, his gaze followed her across the room and he was apparently ignoring the other woman. She gave him a little reassuring smile.

In the ladies' room, a tiny, harshly lit space with crumpled paper towels on the tile floor and crumbling plaster walls painted the color of Crest toothpaste, Donna was standing in front of a small mirror, reapplying mascara. Jane showed her the picture of Irene.

"That's her," said Donna confidently.

"Anything different about her?" said Jane.

Donna looked thoughtful. "I don't think so," she said. She looked at Jane for some sort of clue as to what the right answer was.

"Remember what she was wearing?"

"Something kind of plain," said Donna.

"I really appreciate your help," said Jane giving her a look of solemn sincerity. "This woman might be in some kind of danger. She might be dead. I'm worried about her, and I appreciate your help."

Donna looked startled and a little taken aback. Jane was pretty sure she looked a little guilty. And Jane was also pretty sure Donna had never seen Irene. If she had, she would have known that Irene's hair was a lot grayer than in the picture she just identified.

Jane didn't bother to use the phone. Instead, she went back to Jack Lawson. They smiled at each other and she said, "I'm so tired."

"We'll dance once more," he said, "but we don't have to talk."

She put her arms around him, put her head on his chest, felt the heat of him through the thin cotton of his shirt, felt his arms around her. It was as good a place to think as any.

Donna had been lying from the first phone call.

She'd never seen Irene March. Besides not having been able to say that Irene's hair was a lot grayer than in the picture, she'd said Irene drove. Irene didn't drive. Funny, even though Jane could believe Irene was a blackmailer, she couldn't see her driving without a valid driver's license.

The Dracula-like character was just the sort of thing Donna would come up with if she wanted to hook up Irene with some mysterious stranger. The whole description of that phantom conversation over a patty melt was telling.

Donna had been trying to point Jane in the direction of blackmail. "You're bleeding me white," Bela Lugosi was supposed to have said. Except for her corny description of the blackmail victim, Donna really had done a fine job. That little touch of thinking it was all about an alimony dispute, for instance, allowing Jane to reach her own conclusion.

It all seemed designed to point away from someone, from a real blackmail victim, no doubt. Someone Donna cared about. It might not be so hard to find out who Donna cared about.

She knew something else from eavesdropping on Donna's phone report. Whoever it was Donna had been talking to seemed to know Jack Lawson.

She made a decision. She knew she wouldn't have done it if she hadn't wanted to. It was just so convenient that it fit in with what she was supposed to be doing. She looked up at him. "That guest house invitation," she said, tentatively. "Are you sure . . ."

"I'm sure," he said. "No strings, Jane. I like you, and I'd like some company. I'd be grateful for just company, I really would." He meant it, she was sure. Nevertheless, Option B hung there between them, like the thick, sultry air of the bar.

16.

They said goodbye to Donna on the way out. Her third or fourth beer seemed to have kicked in. She was leaning way back in her chair, laughing a big whooping laugh and waving around a Salem with about an inch and a half of ash. Her lipstick was mostly gone and some of her mascara had reapplied itself beneath her eyes, with a pandalike effect. Somehow, while sitting in the bar in plain view, Donna managed to look like she'd been thoroughly ravished in the back seat of a car.

"Thanks for your help," said Jane, retrieving her purse. "I'll probably be in touch." To break you down, she thought. To find out who you're trying to help, who you're lying for.

"Sure, hon," said Donna. She looked back and forth between Jane and Jack. Her eyes narrowed, and she gave Jane a knowing smile.

Outside, the air was clear and clean and dry, and the sky was filled with stars. She turned to Jack, who seemed taller than she remembered. It occurred to her she was out of her mind to be going off with a stranger. "I'll need to phone Seattle as soon we get there," she said.

"No problem. Do you want to come with me? We can pick up your car in the morning."

"If I leave my car here it'll probably make page one of the *Pateros Daily Bugle*," said Jane.

"Ol' Donna already has the goods on us anyway," he said. "And she won't believe for a minute that I'm going to be a perfect gentleman."

"I'll follow you in my car," she said, finding herself suddenly trying to act brusque and nonsexual. A little late after she'd rubbed up and down the length of him on the dance floor, she thought, irritated with herself. Out here in the cool air she thought she'd overdone it. "This really is very kind of you," she said, trying to sound like a ladylike Audrey Hepburn gamine type.

"Just Western hospitality, ma'am," he said in a fake drawl with a nice little smile that reassured her immediately. He stretched and took a deep breath. "Nice to get out of all that smoke, isn't it?" Now he seemed even more sweet and wholesome. Jane's disquiet began to fade.

She went over to her car, parked next to Donna's Corvette. It was navy blue. Navy blue seemed a little restrained for Donna. Jane would have imagined she'd prefer fire engine red or candy pink.

Inside, illuminated by a sudden blast of green from the neon sign above, Jane saw a white nylon waitress apron in the back seat, and a few children's toys—a plush purple Barney dinosaur and a coloring book. She wondered where the child was. With Donna's mother, probably. Somehow, she didn't think Dad was in the picture. Now the sign flashed white, and Jane saw the upholstery was hot pink leather.

That made up for the subdued navy paint job. It was a very expensive car for a waitress. Maybe she blew a divorce settlement on it, or something. She had to find out more about Donna. Jack might know.

Jane smiled as she got behind the wheel. Donna might be a liar but you had to like her. There was something jaunty and charming about all that firm flesh packed into those jeans and teetering on those cowboy boots, and those big eyes with their sooty lashes.

Paradoxically, all that artifice seemed refreshingly honest. Which made Jane think that eventually she'd get Donna to come clean.

She followed the taillights of his pickup—a serviceable Ford—down the highway, then up a long drive past the ghostly shapes of apple trees and to a long, low house.

He opened the car door for her, took her bag. An owl screeched, startling her, and she instinctively stepped toward him. He took her elbow and led her to the house.

It was big and unapologetically sprawling and made of rough-hewn native rock and natural stained wood with big plate glass windows. It was dramatically lit, and appeared to be a nice enough piece of brash fifties or sixties architecture designed with the landscape in mind. A drought-proof garden of plants with gray-green foliage grew amongst more rock leading up to the tiled porch and big double doors.

Meeting a charming stranger in a bar and coming to a handsome place like this seemed a lot less sleazy than getting picked up in a bar and ending up in a trailer park, thought Jane. Money, deployed with a modicum of taste, took the taint off lust. It could have been a shabby realization, but actually it cheered Jane up.

Inside, there was a slate-lined entry hall. "You don't want to tuck in right away, do you?" he said. "You want a brandy or coffee or something?"

"Coffee," she said, thinking of Donna lolling around looking debauched with her panda bear eyes. Jane wasn't sure how the evening was going to end. She didn't want to wonder later whether a brandy had affected the outcome.

They walked through a big living room with a big fireplace and an unused look and into a kitchen to heat up water. "The phone's there," he said. "Or you can use the one in my dad's office."

"This'll do," she said. It seemed like a good idea to let someone besides Donna know where she was, who she was with. And to let Jack know she had. Although puttering around the kitchen making coffee he hardly looked like a psychopath.

She punched zero, then Calvin Mason's number, then her credit card number. His machine was on, which didn't mean anything. Calvin Mason, in his capacity as manager for a couple of apartment buildings, made himself elusive at night in case a tenant wanted him to go out and unclog a drain or something. Generally, he hovered around the machine, screening calls.

After the beep she said, "Hi, this is Jane. I'm in Okanogan County, between Pateros and Omak and I'm at—" She peered down and read aloud the phone number. "I checked on Irene in Coulee City." Jane looked over at Jack. The name Irene and Coulee City didn't seem to mean a thing to him. "And a witness places her down in Pateros too. I'll be in touch." Calvin would wonder why she was bothering to tell him all this. It was really for Jack's benefit. To see if he knew or cared about Irene in Coulee City and the woman with the boots like his.

She thought about calling her own phone for messages, but decided she'd wait until tomorrow.

"So what are you, you're some kind of a detective, or lawyer or something?" he said. He didn't sound wary at all. Just kind of pleased and interested. "Who's Irene? Somebody's wife who ran off with his best friend?"

"I can tell you are in the country music business," she said, ignoring his question. She leaned against the counter and looked over at the refrigerator. Fastened with magnets was a collection of photographs. One of them appeared to be a flyer for his band. A bunch of junior good old boys lined up against an old fence grinned into the camera. Underneath it read "Electric City."

"That's the name?" she said. "I like it."

"We named ourselves after a little town southeast of here," he said. He handed her a mug of coffee. "You want anything in it?"

She shook her head.

"Come on," he said, taking her hand. "Let's go in here. This was where I hung out when I was a kid. The living room seems too formal, and I guess I keep thinking Mom will come in and tell me not to spill anything on the upholstery."

Off the kitchen was a room that looked like it had evolved from a family room to an office. There was a desk with a phone and a computer and some file cabinets at one end, and a sofa with needlepoint pillows, some comfortable chairs, a big TV and bookshelves arranged around a big oval braided rug at the other. There was a fireplace here too, with a brace of family photos on the mantel and a big furry stuffed buffalo head on the wall above it.

"Very homey," said Jane, who half expected Jack's mother to appear in a June Cleaver dress and apron at any moment, offering them a tray of snacks and checking Jane out to make sure she was a nice girl.

Unless you wanted to indulge in some high school fantasy of heavy petting while your parents were in the next room, Jane thought, the fifties-looking room reeking of parental control had ratcheted down the erotic level about ten notches. All in all, this was probably a good development. Jane sighed and decided she'd concentrate on finding out about Donna and about the boots.

She sat herself on one corner of the sofa, slipped off her shoes and tucked her feet underneath her. He sat on the sofa too, about a foot away and put his feet in their boots up on the coffee table.

"So those lightning bolts on the boots, they tie in to the name of the band," said Jane.

He looked down at them. "That's right."

"And I suppose they refer to your own personal electricity too," she added.

"I don't know if there are that many layers of meaning," he said. "So tell me, who are you really, and what are you doing here?"

"I'm kind of a private investigator," said Jane. "I'm looking for a missing woman. Her name is Irene March. Ever heard of her?"

"No. Where does Donna fit in with all this?"

"She says she saw her here down in Pateros. Talking to some guy in her restaurant. So how well do you know Donna?"

"Donna." He scrunched up his eyes for a minute, as if he were phrasing his thoughts carefully. "Everyone knows Donna. She was the prettiest girl in high school, but real nice to everyone. She was a rodeo queen. She did some barrel racing too. Athletic and pretty. She'd have been a lot happier, though, if it weren't for her sister."

"Her sister?"

"Donna has a sister who's younger and a lot more ambitious. She found herself a rich husband and lives in Seattle, and I think Donna feels left behind in this little town."

"Is her sister prettier?" said Jane.

He thought about it for a moment. "No. It's not that. Her sister just looks a little more high-strung and sexy. You know what I mean? Kind of challenging you to make her happy."

"You mean kind of princessy? Men seem to like pretty women who are mean and demanding," said Jane, trying unsuccessfully not to sound a little mean-spirited herself. "I notice plenty of those women getting whatever they want."

"That's Donna's sister all right. Kind of tosses her hair around and pouts. I feel kind of sorry for her, in a way." Jane had a particular antipathy toward the narcissistic type he was describing. She'd seen a million of them. Seldom intellectual but always shrewd. Out for themselves. Jack was looking rather too forgiving talking about her, she thought.

"But they never seem to get what they want," he said. "They're never quite happy. There's a song there somewhere."

"The kind of woman I'm thinking of," Jane said, trying not to sound too irritable, "doesn't really like men. Too preoccupied with herself. So she's always sulky because she thinks she needs men to get what she wants. It's so unfair really, because men are sexually interested in her, ignoring nice warm, sweet women. It drives women nuts to see men get suckered by those princesses."

"Okay," he said. "I confess. I've been there and done that. In fact, this conversation is getting just a little painfully close to home."

She laughed, and tried to sound light. "Let me ask you something. Just a wild hunch. You got those boots from someone like that? Princesses aren't usually that generous."

He looked down at them and smiled. "Not unless they want something real bad," he said. He looked back up at her. "And what is it you want, particularly? Information? About Donna? Is that why you came here with me?"

"No," said Jane, feeling suddenly awful for interrogating him. "I came here because I liked the way you danced and the way you talked, and because I thought you were charming and I was too tired and miserable to look for a motel and I felt sorry for myself driving all day."

He smiled and reached over and touched her hair. "Poor Jane," he said. She smiled back and tilted her head toward his hand.

"I admit, I justified it in my mind by asking you about Donna, about her credibility as a witness," she said. She left out the boots.

"Sort of like talking a little business at lunch so you can write it off," he said. "Good work ethic, Jane. I like that." Now he traced the line of her jaw with his fingertips.

"Oh I have a lousy work ethic," she said, suddenly feeling too tired to try and remain in control. She leaned forward and her eyes widened and she said earnestly: "I'm hardly a real detective. I feel like such a fraud, really. I've just had a whole string of crummy jobs and my uncle got me into the family business. I'm sort of a nonprofit private eye and I'm not really sure I know what I'm doing." She smiled apologetically. "You seem like a nice man. I'm sorry if I was giving you the third degree."

"For a minute there," he said, "I thought you might have been employed by an irate husband or something, come to get the goods on me." He glanced down at his boots, then looked back up at her. "Luring me to confess."

She put a hand on his shoulder. "No luring. I promise. I should go out to the guest house and go to sleep," she said. "There is a guest house, isn't there?"

"Of course there is. There might be a few spiders and stuff out there, and the sheets are probably kind of damp and mildewy, but that's probably right where you belong," he said. "Unless I'm allowed to try and do the luring."

She laughed and withdrew her hand. "And what kind of information are you trying to pry out of me?"

"Oh, I don't know." He ran his eyes over her face—feature by feature, then put a fingertip on her lower lip. "I'd sort of like to know if you're a good kisser or not."

"I'm excellent," she said, deciding in a flash, at his touch, that life was short and there wasn't really any compelling reason she could think of to try and stop herself. "Everyone says so." She put her arms around him and let him draw her toward him and they kissed, slowly and delicately at first, then more and more greedily. She felt a huge physical sense of relief to be there against his chest, his arms wrapped around her tightly, desperately. He kissed her throat and her head fell back and she felt a delicious sense of surrender, and decided to trust him completely.

"Is this all right?" he said sort of muzzily through her hair, catching her around the waist and lowering her down onto the sofa. His face hovered a few inches over hers and his eyes looked glazed, but he still managed to undo the buttons on her blouse one-handed quite neatly. "I mean, if we can do this safely, is there any reason we should stop?"

"I'm sure there is," she said, as she felt his hand slide across her skin to her breast. "But right now, I can't think what it could possibly be." She drew in her breath quickly. "Or even how we could stop if we wanted to."

17.

It was later, but she had no idea how much later. She was lying beside him on the sofa, underneath a blanket, folded into the crook of his arm, warm and blissed out and feeling floaty, when the phone on the desk in the corner of the room rang. It was horrible and shrill.

"What time do you think it is in Tokyo?" Jack said in a lazy voice. "I'll let the machine get it." He kissed her forehead and shifted a little and in the half light she saw his eyes close. He looked very sweet and peaceful, but his face scrunched all up again with each of the subsequent rings. She closed her eyes too and waited for the ringing to go away and then a voice crackled into the empty room.

"Jane!" it said sharply. It was Calvin Mason's voice.

"Oh, hell," she said, sitting up and blinking.

"This is a message for Jane da Silva," he went on. The buffalo head stared glassy-eyed down at her and at the mound of shed clothing on the floor. The two cold cups of coffee sat on the coffee table. It felt very odd to be listening to Calvin's voice when she was stark naked with a similarly unclad man surrounded by this evidence of impulsive behavior.

"Who the hell's that?" said Jack, sitting up and looking just as guilty and nervous.

"That's just Calvin," she said. "Shhh."

Calvin's voice went on. "Sorry to call so late, but I just got in and got your message. Thought you'd like to know. They found Irene March's body. They say she fell down a hillside on a day hike. Where the heck are you and what are you up to?"

Jane fell back down on the sofa and Calvin mercifully hung up.

"Well he's getting in pretty late himself," said Jack, as if trying to justify Jane's cheating on Calvin.

"He's just a friend," said Jane. "Someone who helps me with my work." She sighed. "I suppose I knew she had to be dead. There really wasn't anywhere else for her to go. Poor, poor Irene."

"Did you know her?" he said softly.

"No. But I'm starting to feel like I did. I've been following in her footsteps." Jane suddenly felt a bleakness. "She was a sad person," Jane said. "I didn't think hearing she was dead would affect me this way, but I feel sad." It occurred to her that postcoital emotional vulnerability had made it worse. She wondered if she should really be here. If she should be gone by the cold light of day.

In the end, she stayed with him. She was comforted by his physical presence. There was nothing like a literal shoulder to cry on. He held her, rocking her a little like a child. She was sad that she was being comforted by someone she didn't know very well. He seemed to sense all this, and didn't talk much, just holding her and stroking her hair. If he hadn't been so tender, she knew she would have been devastated, and it frightened her a little.

In the morning she felt much better and she remembered her middle-of-the-night loneliness in an unsettling, shadowy way, like a dream. They made love one more time, with the morning light coming through the blinds, and he made her breakfast, scrambled eggs with salsa and coffee and toast, and she felt the shell grow over her again, like a sea creature building a new carapace.

After breakfast, Jane stood in the driveway while he brought around two horses. It was a clear, sunny day, and it was already getting hot. In the daylight she could see how elegant the garden really was, grayish plants set amongst the golden native rocks. On the horizon were more bare hills, and off to one side a swath of dark green orchard.

Jane put a hand to her hair in a slightly nervous gesture. "I haven't ridden much," she said. The last time she'd ridden Western was at Girl Scout camp.

"It's easy," he said. "I picked out a kid horse for you. She'll do whatever you say and put up with just about anything."

He got off his own horse, a tall Appaloosa with a silky mane. He took Jane's hand, leading her over to a little chestnut-colored quarter horse. "Here," he said. "We always do everything from the left. Now pat her and say hello. Her name is Hopscotch. My sister named her."

Jane stroked the animal's neck. It felt warm and damp. And she smelled the earthy, horsey smell, which reminded her suddenly of how much she'd loved the horses at camp, and especially a palomino named Missy. Hopscotch turned a little and gazed at Jane without much curiosity, blinking her big brown eye slowly, and twitching her skin to dislodge a fly.

Jack held the reins while Jane put a foot in the stirrup, grabbed the saddle horn and pulled herself up. She was startled and slightly elated to find herself so far up in the air. Is this what little girls liked about horses? Being tall and powerful? He took her left hand and put the reins in it. "Hold them like an ice cream cone," he said. She smiled down at him. He really was kind and sweet, she decided. Her instincts, thank God, had been right once again.

They rode silently awhile, along the road that bordered the orchard. The only noise was the rhythmic clop of hooves and the squeaking of the saddles. A small dog with black and white fur appeared and, apparently eager for a walk, joined them, trotting neatly at the horses' feet. "That's Betsy," he said.

"It's all so idyllic," said Jane. "Horses, a cute dog trotting along, a landscape to die for."

"This place was just dry rangeland before the dams and irrigation," he said. "I often wonder what it looked like then. The Caribou Trail used to run along here, and there were huge cattle drives coming through. My great-grandfather was in the cattle business. But then the dams and the water came and my grandfather planted some trees. Now we've got orchards and we own a packing plant too, and my father brokers apples. He just keeps a few beef cows around because he says he likes them better than CDs."

"So you're looking forward to running all this someday?" she said. She sensed a certain solid pride in the land in him, the kind of quiet confidence characteristic of landed gentry everywhere. They had a place for themselves, and they knew where they belonged.

He smiled. "I'm coming around," he said. "The saving grace of this business for me is that we've got customers in Europe, Asia, everywhere. That makes it more interesting."

She smelled damp grass. It grew between the rows of apple trees, whose branches billowed out in an agreeable way and whose long, irregular leafy branches cast moving dapples of shadow.

Situated as they were in such hot, dry terrain, these orchards seemed like oases of coolness. Jane imagined herself beneath the trees with a book on the dark green, tasseled grass full of clover.

The trees themselves were pristine—each leaf spotless. The fruits were perfect globes, green blossoming into a lip-sticky pink. Props of wood were holding up the heavier branches.

"What kind are these?" she said.

"Red Delicious. The best-selling apple in the world. But we're doing lots of new species too. Galas and Fujis. You have to keep ahead of the market."

"Apple trees in gardens in Seattle seem to get curly leaves and black spots on them," said Jane. "These are so perfect."

"We take real good care of them. But basically, it's too wet back there."

She looked over at him, watched the shadows of the leaves on his face. She smiled and he caught her glance.

"What?" he said.

"I was just thinking. I've never seen you in daylight until now."

"Oh no," he said. "Don't say you're full of guilt and regrets. Don't tell me that."

"No, I don't think so," she said. "It's a little late to get all coy on you."

"Why don't you stay for a few days?" he said. "Just relax and hang out."

"Maybe read books in the orchard," she said.

"And we can sleep in a real bed tonight," he said. "Not on the couch."

Jane laughed. "I keep expecting your parents to come home," she said. "I feel like a teenage delinquent."

Hopscotch lowered her head and chomped on some clover.

"Don't let her do that," he said. "She gets plenty to eat and it's too rich for her."

Jane, feeling harsh, yanked the horse's head back up.

"My folks'll be gone another week. But you can stick around and meet them if you want," he said. "You should at least stay for the Omak Stampede."

"The Stampede?" Jane imagined a herd of buffalo shouldering its way through the town.

"A rodeo. And the Suicide Race. A bunch of guys ride down a cliff, mostly Indians from the Colville tribe. Then horse and rider swim the Okanogan River, and then they pound into the rodeo arena. Tourists love it."

"Sounds hard on the horses," said Jane.

"They're bred to do mountain racing. They're like mountain bike horses. There are more injuries in flat track races. Those thoroughbreds are always being destroyed after breaking their skinny legs."

"I'm tempted," said Jane, who thought the idea of young men plunging off cliffs on horseback sounded thrilling.

"If not by me, then by the Suicide Race?"

"Mostly by you," she said. "But by the Suicide Race too."

"I'm not going to beg," he said. "But my band is playing the Stampede. They'll be joining me in a few days. If you're not here, you'll leave me open to the attentions of a lot of wild women, all liquored up and in a lather from watching men and horses and bulls stomping around in the dust. They'll be staring up at me while I play, and they'll have pure lust on their sweet young faces. Stay and you can keep me out of their clutches."

She laughed at his vivid description. "I can tell you write country-western songs," she said. "And I'd love to hear you play."

"You should catch the act before I end up full-time in the apple business," he said. "Let's cross the road and I'll show you some more."

They clopped across the two-lane blacktop that separated the orchard from the river and a complex of buildings.

"Ever wonder why apples are in the supermarkets all year round?" he said, as the horses picked their way around a huge stack of huge wooden bins, as big as sheds, painted barn red.

"Never gave it a thought," said Jane with a sideways smile. "But tell me anyway. Everything you say is fascinating. Nothing like an industrial tour to get me all excited."

"I'll have the Apple Commission in Wenatchee send you some material, seeing as you're so interested," he said sarcastically. "This is the CA shed. Completely air-tight."

Her horse had discovered a patch of clover and was back at it. She gave the reins a pull.

"What does CA stand for?" she said.

"Controlled Atmosphere. They suck oxygen out of the atmosphere and the ripening process is slowed way down. We put the very best apples in there and release them onto the market over the period of a year."

The big concrete building had a huge metal door, which looked as though it had been sealed shut with a bead of caulk around it. In the middle of the big door was a smaller one, with a thick glass porthole in it, a padlock and a warning in Spanish and English not to enter.

"Your pickers come up from Mexico?"

"They used to. Now they live here year-round more and more. Before Hispanics picked, it used to be hobos. Transient alcoholics I guess you'd call them today. They showed up at harvest time, picked and then left town." He gave her a kind of dreamy smile and said, "Just like you're going to do."

"I wish I could stay," she said. "I'd like to roll around with you in that damp grass under the apple trees."

"Bad for morale," he said. "It's pretty quiet here now, but

some guy running a forklift full of apple bins sees the owners fooling around with attractive women in the orchard,
they get resentful. You really can't stay?"

She took a deep breath. "I can't," she said. In the old days
she might have dropped everything for a lover, especially a
new one. Now, for a couple of reasons, she felt she had to sol-
dier on in the path old Uncle Harold had chosen for her.

They walked the horses back across the road, then had a
nice hard canter up to the house.

She went with him to the barn while he showed her how
to unsaddle and curry the horses and put away the tack, then
she stood in the sunlight right outside the door, watching
him in the shadows while he did a few more chores.

"I'm glad I decided to go out with Carl for a beer," he
said. "I really didn't want to, but I'm glad I did."

"I am too," she said.

"It seems about a week ago I first noticed those boots of
yours." She cleared her throat and gave him a steady stare. "I
wanted to find out where you got them because of Irene. A
witness says a woman wearing boots like that met with her
in Coulee City."

"Why didn't you tell me that before?" he said, giving her
a steely-eyed look. He came over to her side.

"I got distracted," she said, with a sideways smile. "By
you." She held out a hand to touch his arm. It didn't work.
He didn't smile back. The skin on his face seemed smooth
and tight like a mask. She pulled her hand back, horrified at
how quickly the mood had changed.

"Who the hell was this Irene, anyway?"

"She was a pathetic little woman who blackmailed people
for pathetic amounts of money," said Jane.

"So you think she was blackmailing the woman in my
boots?"

"Probably," said Jane, trying to sound businesslike. "Do you have any idea what Irene might have had on her?"

"What kind of a guy do you think I am?" he said. "You think I'm going to hand you some other woman because I slept with you last? So you can turn her over to her husband or whoever wants to get the goods on her? You can forget that, sweetheart."

"I'm not working for anyone's husband," said Jane.

"Listen, Jane," he said, getting close to her and narrowing his eyes. "I don't know what kind of a singer you were, but I think you should have stuck to it. Because what you're doing now . . ." He trailed off.

"Don't get self-righteous with me," she said. "I never said I was any good at what I was doing. I'm just doing the best I can. I'm not perfect, all right? I didn't intend to sleep with you. It happened. It seemed like a good idea at the time. It was unprofessional. It wasn't sensible. It seldom is. To be perfectly honest, at my age it's hard to think what you're saving it for when something like this develops. It didn't occur to me to ask you if you'd respect me in the morning, and I'm not sure I care."

"Jane," he said, with an exasperated sigh, "I can't tell you anything about her, okay?"

"Fair enough," she said. He'd sounded just a little bit apologetic, but it was too little, too late. She pushed her hair away from her face and decided she wanted to get the hell out of here and soon. She picked up her bag and started striding over to her car.

Over her shoulder, she added, "But I do seem to care that you think I'm a dishonest person. I try to be honest in all my dealings." What was she going on about, she thought to herself. Honest in all my dealings? It sounded like the Code of the West or something. And it wasn't particularly true, anyway. The thing to do was just to get in the car and get back to Seattle.

He followed her to the car door, stood by her elbow, annoying her a little by his closeness as she opened the back door and flung in her bag.

"Don't leave mad," he said. "I'm not mad anymore."

I'm sorry, she wanted to say. Instead she shrugged.

"Can I kiss you goodbye anyway?"

She gave him a peck on the cheek, but he put his arms around her waist and pulled her toward him. "Listen," he said. "Maybe we can start again. After your case is over. I'll be on the road for a while, but maybe I can call you in Seattle."

"Donna has the number," said Jane. If he really cared, let him work a little to get in touch. "But I might have to find out who your friend in the boots was. And it's nothing personal."

Later, driving down the highway back to I-90, Jane tried not to think about Jack. The first order of business was to find out if Irene had fallen or been pushed. If she'd been pushed, if there was anything suspicious about her death, Jane knew the police would take over.

And then, would there be any point in her finding all of Irene's victims? The police would follow up on what she'd found out so far.

In which case, she didn't need to find Jack's old lover. Jane had pieced enough of the story together to come pretty close to the truth there anyway.

Jack had given it away when he talked about Donna. In fact, when she'd asked him about Donna, he didn't talk about her at all, but about her sister. The one who married a rich guy but wasn't happy. The one who had that greedy, princessy air about her that drove men into groveling, nervous servitude. Jane hated her already.

She'd been too wrapped up in a cloud of pheromones to have put it together—what an idiot she had been—but she knew now. The conversation Donna had on the phone was a conversation between sisters if she'd ever heard one. Worry, concern, resentment at not being given the full story, and the kind of sharp scolding reserved for siblings.

So far, the list of Irene's victims included the church deacon who said he wasn't trolling for hookers, and probably the spoiled wife who'd become a country music groupie. (Not that Jane could criticize. After all, Jane had succumbed to his charms without even catching his act.) She'd eliminate Count Dracula, who was probably fictitious. And she wanted to check out the little girl who'd called. Amanda something.

After an hour on the road, Jane decided to check in with Calvin. In her zeal to peel out of Jack's driveway and get herself west of the mountains again, she'd put it off.

She stopped at a pay phone at a roadside rest on highway 17 with a panoramic view of geologic wonders, sage, deep gorges, wildflowers.

He did his usual lurking behind the machine, but picked up when she said, "Calvin, please pick up, it's Jane," in a nice but firm voice.

"Tell me all about it," she said.

"Found her at the bottom of a trail with a little backpack and her lunch. Kind of sad, isn't it? Down around Tiger Mountain."

"Somehow I didn't think of her as the outdoorsy type," said Jane. "More the type to sit inside behind drawn shades and smoke and read. Do they think there's foul play?"

"They don't know. It happened over the weekend so we'll have to wait for the autopsy. She's on ice down at Harborview for now."

"Listen," said Jane, "Irene told her co-workers she was

leaving her money to them. And there are those relatives—I wouldn't put it past Cousin Craig to find the will and destroy it if he hasn't already. Would it be filed somewhere?"

"Nope. It would be lying around or in a safe-deposit box or something."

"She banked at Washington Mutual. The downtown one," said Jane. "But can we get in there and check on it?"

"Sure," said Calvin. "We'll file an intestate probate and ask them to let us into the safe-deposit box if there is one or to search the house, all under the watchful eye of the court."

"Wonderful," said Jane. "I'd love to cut Craig and his mom off at the pass."

"I met them. They're pretty awful," said Calvin.

"Do you think they'll be able to tell if Irene was pushed or if she fell?" said Jane.

"Who knows. But I'll tell you one thing," said Calvin. "If this is a homicide you better back right off and find something else to do."

"I know that," said Jane, irritated.

But then, in a kindly way he added: "We'll find something else for you, or maybe a new angle on this thing."

"You really are very sweet," said Jane. "I'll call you when I get to town."

"Sweet. Great," said Calvin, and hung up.

18.

The next day, while Calvin busied himself getting the court to allow him into Irene's safe-deposit box (Washington Mutual confirmed that she had one), Jane set out to see if she could find Amanda Jenkins.

Calvin had provided her with a phone number, and an address. The phone call had been made from Shelton, a logging town on the Olympic Peninsula, a ferry ride and an hour or so west of Seattle.

The dark, cool, wet forest, muffled-looking gray skies and the mountainous terrain seemed like an entirely different planet after eastern Washington. The town itself looked a little tired. A reader board on the main street said, "Save a Logger, Kill a Spotted Owl."

The house was easy to find, a low ranch-style house on a short, quiet asphalt street. There weren't any sidewalks; just deep, grass-filled ditches to accommodate the heavy rains that fell around here.

There were two little girls in the front yard, underneath a big, black-looking, rough-barked Douglas fir. They were playing with Barbie dolls in the reddish dirt. Barbie's consort, Ken, lay forgotten a little ways away in the dust. He was wearing a human sock. It made him look as though he were wearing a straitjacket or a sleeping bag, but his pleasant expression seemed to indicate he was being a good sport about it.

The Barbies, clutched in dirty little hands, were formally dressed, and were having their platinum blonde manes combed by the serious-looking girls, who appeared to be about nine or so. One was thin and dark, the other a solid-looking child with freckles and straight bangs across her forehead.

Jane addressed them from one side of a tired-looking fence.

"Amanda?" she said. Both girls looked up at her, but the freckled one said "Yes?" She had blue eyes with thick lashes and beautiful dark brows above them. Her eyes looked intelligent, but they also looked shockingly mature—with an expression that seemed more than wary. It was the steely, resigned, grieving look of a child who'd seen more than she should have.

Jane had planned to insinuate her way into Amanda's confidence with some chat about Barbie and her dress. One look at those eyes and she decided that no matter how many adults she'd lied to, cajoled and flattered in the course of her work, she should be honest with this child.

"I'm Jane da Silva," she said. "From Seattle. You called me to help me find someone who was missing. Remember?"

"The lady in the newspaper," said Amanda. She smoothed out her Barbie's purple satin skirt and set her on the ground, rose and walked over to the fence. "Did you find her?"

Jane started to lie again, but she said, "She died."

"I'm probably going to die too," said the child, as if to say Irene's death was no big deal and Jane didn't need to be squeamish. "Was she sick?"

"No one is sure what happened to her. We want to know more about her. She came and visited you, didn't she?"

Amanda nodded. "I think she was one of the ladies coming to help for my fund-raiser."

"Fund-raiser?" said Jane.

The other little girl piped up. "She's getting a new heart transplanted in her."

Amanda looked solemn, and said, "I have an enlarged heart." Jane was startled to see she had a little hint of a smile. Jane thought it looked like a smile of pride. Was she proud of her bravery? Or her suffering? Was she pleased with the attention she must be getting? Was there any other way for her to cope?

Jane felt tears stinging her eyes, and resisted the urge to stroke her straight, shiny hair, or to tell her how brave she was. Instead, she smiled. "I'm sure a lot of people want to help you, Amanda.

"Are your parents home?" she asked. She wanted to know if the child really had seen Irene.

"My mom's home," said Amanda. "My dad's dead."

Jane opened the gate and started up the path, but first she turned to the little girl. "Thank you for calling me," she said. "It was good of you to want to help Irene."

"Who's Irene?" said the little girl.

"Irene March. That was the lady's name."

"I thought it was something else," said Amanda, frowning. "A longer name than that."

"Can you remember the name?" said Jane.

"No," said Amanda. She turned back to her Barbie.

Jane reached in her purse and took out the picture of Irene. She showed it to Amanda. "Is this the lady?"

Amanda looked at it for a few seconds. "Her hair was more gray. But it's her."

Could it be that while Irene was blackmailing the unworthy she was also dispensing largesse to the worthy? If that was the case, Jane had to revise her view of Irene. It didn't lessen her crimes, but it added a whole new dimension to her character. It changed Irene from someone who liked to know other people's secrets so she could compensate for her own feelings of inadequacy, to someone who took it upon herself to punish the wicked and reward the virtuous.

Amanda led Jane up two concrete steps onto the porch and opened the door for her. "Mom," she called out.

They were standing in a living room with a skimpy, inhospitable-looking sofa and chair. Over a Roman brick fireplace was a huge framed color portrait of Amanda, a little younger and rounder. She wore a frilly party dress all wrong for her solemn little face beneath its straight bangs, and held a prop teddy bear in her chubby hands.

From somewhere in the back of the house came a tired-looking woman carrying a plastic laundry basket full of sheets. When she saw Jane, she looked surprised, set it down heavily and self-consciously pushed a lock of light brown hair out of her face.

Amanda didn't introduce them. Instead, she watched her mother with those steely, grown-up little eyes, while she twisted the hem of her dusty dress in one fist in a squirmy, little-girl way.

Jane told the woman her name. "I was looking for a woman called Irene March," she said. "Your daughter says she was here. I guess she was helping with your fund-raiser," she added, so as to spare Amanda's mother the pain of having to explain.

"I don't know any Irene March," the woman said, glancing down at her daughter and back up at Jane.

Jane took the picture from her purse. "Maybe she was using a different name." She showed it to her.

"I don't think—" she began. Amanda interrupted her.

"She was here, Mom," said Amanda in a firm little voice. "I remember. She came and talked to you."

The woman looked at the picture again. "Yes, I guess so," she said. She flicked her eyes away from the picture to the side of the room. She was clearly uncomfortable. Jane's theory that Irene had been here to help was fading fast.

Amanda's dark-haired friend came into the living room, clutching her Barbie, now nude. Jane had forgotten how bizarre Barbie's body looked. Her legs were twice as long as her torso and her rocket-shaped breasts were obviously implants.

"Maybe the girls could play outside while we talk," said Jane in a firm voice.

Amanda looked stubborn and curious.

"Go outside," said the mother in a tone that had a fierce edge to it. Amanda's friend looked startled and started to go. Amanda followed, watching the two standing adults over her shoulder.

As soon as they heard the door close, the woman collapsed into a chair. Jane decided that was an invitation to do the same and sat rather stiffly on the edge of the sofa.

"This woman, Irene March, she died," said Jane. "Before she died she met a lot of people. I guess you were one of them."

"She was wrong about me and Amanda," said the woman. "She made up some lies."

"I can believe that," said Jane, gingerly. She thought of Dave Twentyacres. "Irene did sometimes imagine things about people. She tried to get money from them. What did she say about you?"

"She said Amanda wasn't sick," said the woman. She gave a harsh laugh. "Imagine that. The poor child has suffered so much, and she says she isn't sick. Last week her blood pressure was 108 over 88. She's had fluid backup problems, and she knows she might die. It's a damn lie."

"I'm so sorry," said Jane. "I never knew Irene but I believe she behaved very badly."

"I think someone should give me my thousand dollars back," said the woman. "She said she'd cause trouble for us, and I didn't dare let her. We're trying to raise money for an operation." The words started coming faster now, and tears slid down her cheeks. "They don't just give anyone a heart transplant, you know. Not just anyone. Even if you have a donor all lined up. I couldn't afford to let her say Amanda wasn't really sick. It would stop the fund-raising while I cleared our names, and even then, people wonder."

Jane agreed with her. A false accusation could cling forever, as if being accused in itself were somehow shameful.

Amanda's mother sighed. "The people in this town have really rallied around us. Times are tough here in the woods, but they love Amanda. The high school is doing car washes and the Kiwanis is raising money. One of the churches just gave me a beeper so I can know right away when a heart becomes available. People in these small towns are good people. That's why we came here."

"I'm so sorry," said Jane. She took out her checkbook.

"Make it to the Help Amanda Fund," said the woman, wiping the last of the tears away and sniffing. She seemed to pull herself together. "I couldn't believe anyone could be so cruel."

"After the thousand dollars," said Jane, leaving the check on the coffee table, "did she ask for any more?"

"No. She said I'd never see her or hear from her again. And I didn't." The woman looked as if she didn't believe Irene.

Jane leaned forward. "How did she get in touch with you?"

"On the phone," said the woman. "She said she was calling from the bus station. And that she was walking over to my house and I should have the money ready."

Jane couldn't bear to press her too hard. She said delicately, choosing her words, hoping the woman wouldn't cry again: "Why did she think you would give her the money?"

"She said she had proof Amanda wasn't sick. That we were stealing from people. Something about some newspaper where we lived before." The woman waved her hand impatiently. "You can't believe what you read in the newspapers. It's stupid. She was a horrible woman."

"Where is Amanda having her surgery done?" said Jane. "Who is her doctor?"

"Children's Hospital in Seattle," said the woman. "There's a whole team of pediatric cardiologists, and they're all plenty worried about Amanda, you better believe it. That's one brave little girl." She stuck her jaw out aggressively. "And I'm pretty stubborn. Nobody is going to stop me from helping my baby."

"Did she show you a newspaper clipping?" said Jane.

The woman's voice rose. It scared Jane a little. "It's all crap. There was nothing there." Her face was twisted into a scowl. "You sound just like her! Are you trying to kill Amanda too?" She stood up and came toward Jane. Her hands were in fists. "She's a walking time bomb. And I'll need easily two hundred thousand dollars to get her a new heart. But I'm not giving up."

Jane rose hastily. "I know you've been through a lot," she said. "I'm sorry to disturb you."

The woman sat down heavily. "You don't know what I've been through. No one can imagine. She's all I have in the world. It's just the two of us."

"I wish you both the very best," said Jane in a hushed voice. She let herself out the door.

At the gate, where the girls were playing, Jane bent down

toward Amanda. "Where did you live before, Amanda?" she said.

"We moved from Goldendale," said Amanda.

"Why did you move here?" Jane asked.

"I was supposed to go get an operation in Seattle, but it didn't work out, so we moved here instead," she said. She was walking her Barbie along in the dust. Barbie's tiny bare feet were flexed to accommodate tiny high heels so she looked like she was tiptoeing.

"Thanks for helping, Amanda," said Jane. She again resisted the urge to stroke her straight shiny hair, to treat her like a child different and more precious than other children.

19.

King County Detective James Walters, and his partner, Louis Hildebrand, stood on top of the hill near Tiger Mountain and looked down.

"The first thing I don't like," said Walters, "is that her pack wasn't on her back. It was at her side. Secondly, there's a few things missing. Like a key, wallet, money. Or cigarettes—the coroner said she was a smoker. Not to mention a vehicle to bring her here. There's a bus stop nearby, but how was she getting back without any money?"

"And thirdly," said his partner, "the fatal blow was on the back of her head and we found her on her back. I can't see her landing on a rock, then turning over to die."

"Let's see if we can figure where she might have landed," said Walters.

"Why did she have to be all the way down there?" muttered Hildebrand as the two men set off down the slope.

It was about a minute later that Detective Walters found the jagged, bloodstained rock. He knelt down and examined its edge, then stood up again and squinted over at the spot where Irene's body had been found. It was about five feet away, and, despite the number of people who'd been trampling around the scene, the grass between the rock and where they'd found the body was undisturbed.

He looked back up at the road. "I'd guess she and the pack and the rock all got down here separately," he said. "And none of them made it on their own."

Later that week, Calvin, Jane, two officers of the Washington Mutual Savings Bank to serve as witnesses as per the court's instruction, Monica Padgett and Clark Rafferty stood in the vault while the box was drilled and opened. Also present was Detective James Walters, whom Calvin had invited as a courtesy, and who seemed appreciative, as it made it a lot easier for him not to have to generate paperwork of his own for the bank.

The safe-deposit box was the small economy model. It contained a garnet necklace that appeared to be from the nineteen fifties and didn't seem to Jane to be particularly valuable, a tarnished silver christening spoon, a document of several pages with big letters across the top that said "Last Will and Testament," filled in by hand, and a pale yellow business-sized envelope.

Calvin placed all the items on a long table, then picked up the will, glanced at it quickly, clicked his tongue and said, "One of those do-it-yourself wills, God I hate those." His eyes flicked along the lines.

After what seemed like a heavy, ponderous silence, Calvin cleared his throat. "She leaves her entire estate to Monica Padgett, Clark Rafferty, Margaret Olsen and Norman Zimmer, to be divided equally. Real property on Argyle. Cash. Effects."

Jane squeezed Monica's hand and Clark allowed a small smile to cross his features.

"You think the will is okay?" said Jane.

"I really don't recommend these," said Calvin, shaking

his head. "But she seems to have filled it out all right." He flipped through the pages. "And she's got her two witnesses."

He read a little to himself and frowned. "There is also an additional paragraph in which Irene has added: 'None of my estate is to go to Wendy June Webber, my supervisor, who has treated me in a demeaning way since I began working for the Columbia Clipping Service, and who has shown her contempt for others by her arrogant and intrusive manner, listening to private phone conversations, forcing us all to take breaks simultaneously, denying us reasonable time off to go to the dentist or doctor, and showing a general lack of respect for our skill and expertise.' "

Clark snickered a little.

"I guess we'll send her a copy, since she was mentioned," said Calvin. Monica and Clark exchanged a smug glance. "I don't recommend these vituperative statements from beyond the grave, either. When they get too unpleasant they can provide the basis for a challenge based on sound mind or lack thereof."

"Oh, everything about Mrs. Webber is completely true," said Monica, her eyes big and dramatic. "I'll testify to all of it."

Calvin smiled at her. "I'm sure it won't be necessary."

"What's in the envelope?" said Jane.

Calvin opened it and extracted three clippings. He read them and passed them to Jane. The first was a short feature from a newspaper in Goldendale, Washington. It told the story of a fund-raiser for a little girl named Amanda Jenkins who needed a liver transplant. A donor had been found, but the family still needed eighty thousand dollars. A local committee was raising money for medical expenses. So far, the community had raised ten thousand. Donors were asked to send contributions to a bank account in Goldendale earmarked the Amanda Jenkins Fund.

The second clipping showed a picture of Dave Twentyacres looking serious in a suit and tie. "Westport Congregation Names Twentyacres Deacon," it said, with just a cutline below, saying that Twentyacres was a charter boat operator and had lived all his life in Westport.

The third clipping came from Woodinville, a horsey suburb north of Seattle. It appeared to be a feature about local classic car owners and showed a middle-aged guy with a paunch and a brimmed hat that was supposed to make him look like a sexy gangster but instead gave the impression he was bald and trying to hide it, leaning on the running board of an old black Packard.

There was also a shot of a pretty blonde lady in tight jeans sitting in a Corvette. "Angela Raleigh, wife of State Senator Hank Raleigh, shows off the hot pink Corvette she won as part of her national rodeo queen runner-up prize eighteen years ago."

Angela was quoted as saying, "I was just a little old country girl from Omak when I won that title. It was the biggest thrill of my life. I swore I'd hang on to the car forever. I still drive it in the Omak Stampede parade every year."

After a discussion of parts availability, the story went on: "How do spouses of these fanatics feel about the cars that get pampered and coddled like children? State Senator Raleigh says: 'We have a deal. I put up with that car, and she puts up with my hobby, collecting Western furniture and cowboy memorabilia.' " Presumably a rodeo queen was a top-notch collectible.

There wasn't much doubt in Jane's mind. Angela looked more than enough like Donna to be her sister. But she looked leaner and meaner, just as Jack had said. Jane thought it interesting too that both sisters drove vintage Corvettes.

Jane put the clippings back on the table. There was a small slit in the corner of each clipping, as if there had been a staple there. Dave Twentyacres had said Irene had brought him two clippings stapled together. She wondered if the police would notice that little slit, or attach any significance to it.

Later, after the others had left, she and Detective Walters had a cup of coffee in an old-fashioned kind of coffee shop that didn't serve espresso and allowed patrons to smoke. Jane went with him with a sense of nervous anticipation. Why had he specifically invited her?

"Was Irene murdered?" said Jane when they were settled in a booth.

"We haven't decided yet," he said. "But I think we can safely say her death seems suspicious. Were you a friend of hers?"

"No," said Jane. "I was trying to help her friends—the people at the clipping service—find her." She hoped he wouldn't probe too deeply into the reasons for her involvement.

James Walters was a nice-looking guy with reddish hair, younger than Jane imagined a detective would be. "I understand you ran an ad in the *Times,* trying to find her," he said.

"Yes," she said. "How did you know?"

"Missing Persons. Seattle Police Department. Guy there said he left a message on your machine but you never got back to him."

"I've been out of town," she said. And then she took a deep breath and said, "Following up on some leads I got from the ad."

He nodded and waited and took a sip of coffee.

"Irene March," she said, "was blackmailing people. For

small amounts of money. She found out nasty things about them from clippings and blackmailed them."

His eyebrows shot up, but his voice showed no surprise. "I see," he said.

Jane explained how Irene crossed the state on Greyhound buses and asked transgressors or imagined transgressors for a thousand dollars a throw.

She told him it had occurred to her that one of these blackmail victims, after seeing her on *Jeopardy!* might have decided to kill her. Then she decided to shut up and just answer the questions. Why draw attention to all her amateur detecting? So far, he just thought of her as a concerned citizen who was backing off now that the police were involved.

He spilled out the three clippings on the orange Formica table. "Know anything about these?"

She nodded. "This guy here." She shoved Dave Twentyacres's clipping over at him. "Someone using his name got picked up for soliciting a prostitute in the Tri-Cities. Irene read about it in another paper, and figured the deacon wouldn't want it known back in Westport."

He frowned. "I guess not. And have you talked to him?"

She nodded. "Yes. He says his nephew used his name in the Tri-Cities and that he didn't pay her a cent. He's very religious. He says he prayed for her."

Jane figured Detective Walters would be all over Dave like an old coat. If Dave wasn't telling the truth, the police could find out.

She reached over and pointed to the picture of Amanda Jenkins. "This one's a little stranger. It's about a little girl who's been raising money for an operation in Goldenale. It took me a minute, but what I think could have happened, or what Irene thought happened is that Mom pocketed all the money, took the child to Shelton over on the Olympic

Peninsula and started raising funds for another bogus operation.

"Unless there's a big mistake in this story. You see, this paper says she needed a new liver. Now they're working on a heart transplant. And the little girl told me she never did get that operation after they moved from Goldendale."

"So you spoke with them too?" he said.

"If they're running a scam, I got suckered myself," said Jane, watching Walters add masses of cream and sugar to his coffee and stir vigorously. "I gave them a donation. The mother really got to me. She gave me a bunch of medical details that rang true. I still think it might be true. She said Irene had come and harassed her."

"You met the little girl too?" Walters asked.

"One of those little girls with forty-five-year-old eyes," she said.

He sighed. "I meet too many of those," he said.

"In fact," said Jane, growing suddenly agitated, "if Irene was right and it's been a fraud, that little girl is being psychologically abused in the worst way. She thinks she's dying." She sipped her coffee and leaned back, trying to conjure up the heaviness she had felt in that house. "You know, whatever's going on, I think the mother believes it herself," she said.

"That's the secret to a good con," he said. "And sometimes, they do seem to be able to believe it. They're people who can believe two opposing things at once. We'll check into it. Now what's the deal here?" He pushed the third clipping over at her.

She didn't hesitate. After all, she really didn't know. She didn't see how this clipping could have anything to do with the fact that Angela had had an affair with Jack, which was presumably what Irene had on Angela. "I don't know," she said.

Let him check out the other two leads. She could spend just a little time on Angela herself before she decided if it were important enough to tell the police. What was the point of hassling Jack, Donna, Angela? So far, Jane wasn't sure Irene had gotten the goods on anyone. Why drag anyone else into an investigation?

And of course, the fact that she'd spent the night with Jack might come out too.

She'd devote just a little time to it herself. To make sure it was all right not to tell the police. But at the back of her mind she knew there was another reason she wasn't telling what she knew. She wanted to see if there was some shred of a hopeless case there. What she needed was the clipping that had once been stapled to the classic car story. And she had an idea where it might be.

20.

"Jane!" Calvin was frowning. "You said you'd turn it all over to the cops." They were sitting in her living room drinking the last of Uncle Harold's Scotch. Even after her redecorating—fresh paint on the walls in a light peach, and re-covering the dusty old mohair-upholstered pieces with celadon green—the room still looked a little too baronial for her taste. It was all that darkly varnished wainscotting, she imagined. It should be stripped. Maybe big bowls of white flowers would lighten the place up too.

"I turned over most of it," she said. "And I'll turn over this too, if I think I have to. Are you afraid the police will get on us for obstructing justice or something?"

"I hate to break it to you," said Calvin, rattling his ice cubes, "but they aren't going to be the least bit professionally threatened by your detecting efforts. They're just going to think you're an eccentric civilian who's seen too many TV shows, and they're going to just do what it is they do, putting one foot in front of another until they figure out what happened."

"So what's the big deal?" she said. "All you do is go in there, and bully that pale yellow envelope in the box from Irene's desk out of Mrs. Webber. Before the police get over

159

there and look around. She's apparently a bitch on wheels, and she's used to browbeating her employees. Just go in there and act like an attorney and she'll probably crumple. Nobody crumples faster than a bully."

"I don't have to act like an attorney," he said. "I am one."

She leaned back on the sofa. "You've been awfully irritable lately," she said. "And when people around me are irritable I always wonder if it's my fault. Is it?"

"No," he said. "It's Marcia's fault."

"Marcia," said Jane, sitting up a little straighter. "Who's Marcia?"

"Marcia's been my main squeeze for about five years now," he said. "She dumped me."

"A terrific guy like you?" said Jane. "Why?" As nice as she thought Calvin was, she could think of a dozen reasons. Five years, however, was the vital clue. Inability to commit to anything other than regular sex and a movie now and then, with both probably tapering off over the years, was no doubt the reason. But Jane always handled lovelorn friends with staunch loyalty. "Marcia is clearly out of her mind," she said with spirit.

"She said we had to break up because she just got engaged," he said. "She wants me to come to the wedding. Now I suppose I have to get them a gift. She's registered for everything. Crystal, silver. Down to bath mats and egg timers. She told me all about it."

"She probably would have dumped the guy in a minute if you'd proposed," said Jane. "Just had to change the groom's name in the computer down at the Bon Marché. Provided, of course, you like the china patterns and everything. Want that drink freshened up?"

He handed her the glass and ran a hand through his hair. "I don't think I had that option. The guy's a rich dentist. She met him at a class in investing. I never knew she was interested in investing. She never made that much as a beautician."

Men can be so dense, bless their little hearts, thought Jane piteously as she went over to the liquor cabinet. "She took a class in investing because articles in ladies' magazines tell you that classes is where to look for guys," she explained. "And presumably, if you want one with some disposable income, you go to an investing class. Very shrewd of Marcia, really."

"I never thought of her as shrewd," he said. "Just a lot of fun. And not very demanding. That's what I liked about her. She didn't seem to want to commit."

She added a little Scotch and an ice cube to his glass and handed it to him. He took a sip of his freshened drink. "Thanks. Not to me, anyway."

"You never told me about Marcia," said Jane, a little hurt. She had thought they were friends.

"You never asked. And I never asked about what you're up to in Okanogan County or wherever."

"Things do seem to pick up when I'm on the road," said Jane.

Calvin didn't seem to want to hear about her love life, which was just as well. "So why can't you just turn over what you know about that third clipping to the cops?" he said.

"Because it may be no big deal and it will mean they'll barge in and maybe wreck a marriage for nothing. Irene was putting the screws on some bimbo with an older husband who was fooling around with a younger man."

"You mean the babe in the Corvette? Mrs. Hank Raleigh?"

"That's right."

Calvin nodded. "Okay. I'll buy that. Some of my best

friends have been errant wives. It's interesting, though. Hank Raleigh is potentially a big deal."

"He is?" said Jane, who hadn't been back in Washington State long enough to pay much attention to state politics.

"He might run for attorney general next year," Calvin said. "He's been politicking around the bar association. And I wouldn't be surprised if he'd like to be governor someday."

"What's he like?" said Jane.

Calvin shrugged. "Seems nice enough. Old money. He's one of those guys born back east who come out here and act like real gung-ho Westerners. Lose those loafers and crew neck sweaters fast and get into wearing cowboy hats and stuff."

"His wife is an ex–rodeo queen."

"That figures," said Calvin. "Okay, so you want me to go get that envelope because you think it has the clippings that reveal Irene's blackmail secrets."

"I think it's a real possibility. Because the envelopes match and yellow envelopes are a little unusual," said Jane. "And because keeping them at work would have been safer for her than keeping them at home. Especially after her *Jeopardy!* appearance. Someone did search her house and they didn't find anything as far as I can tell, because they kept on searching."

Calvin nodded thoughtfully. "To tell you the truth, the thought of having something on the wife of a guy who might be the next attorney general or governor might be kind of a thrill. You'd be sitting in a bar, and whenever he came on TV, you could nudge the guy next to you and say, 'See that guy?' and tell him the story."

"That smug attitude is just what got Irene in trouble," said Jane. "Wanting to know the worst about people."

The phone rang.

Jane took her drink into the hall to get it. It was Donna from Pateros.

"Hi Jane," she said in her sweet voice brimming with the promise of girlish confidences. Jane reminded herself Donna had been lying to her from the beginning. "I just got curious about how things are going. I heard they found the poor woman you were looking for."

"That's right," said Jane.

"So, are the police checking into it?"

"They sure are," said Jane. "There's a good possibility she was murdered." She let that sink in, then added, " 'Suspicious' is the word they used."

"Did you tell the police about her? About her blackmailing those people?"

"You mean did I feed them the story about the stranger from Transylvania you told me about? The one who said he'd been bled white?" said Jane. She let the sarcasm come through loud and clear.

Donna was silent. Finally she said, "Well yeah, did you?"

"No, Donna, I didn't," said Jane in a kind of tired, fake-patient voice. "You know why? Because I didn't believe that story and I liked you and I didn't want the cops bugging you and finding out you lied. I believe you lied for someone you cared about."

There was another long pause. "That's fair enough," Donna said. "I appreciate it. I didn't know this was going to be such a big deal."

"I know," said Jane. "You thought you were covering for Angela, didn't you? Well, I didn't tell the police about her either. It's their case now."

"I guess I screwed everything up," said Donna.

"No you didn't," said Jane. "You were trying to be a good sister. But I don't think your sister told you everything."

"She's not a bad person," said Donna. "Not really. Hey, I

163

really do appreciate it. I'm sorry I tried to mess you up like that, I really am."

"Look," said Jane. "If you want to let me know what all this was about, call me. If you think I can help you, if you got in too deep. Maybe she asked you to do other things."

"No, no," said Donna. "Nothing like that. Just to lie to avoid trouble with her husband. Hey, I'd do that for lots of women, not just my sister."

"Okay," said Jane. "But be careful, Donna. Sometimes being too nice can get you in trouble."

"Boy, that's the truth," said Donna. "I gotta go, Jane. Thanks again."

When Jane hung up she realized Donna had sounded terribly relieved she wasn't going to have to trot out her story about Irene putting the squeeze on Bela Lugosi. But despite her cheery manner, Donna had sounded scared too. Jane thought there was a good possibility she was scared her sister had something to do with Irene's death.

21.

She came back into the living room where Calvin was scowling into his glass, thinking no doubt of the faithless Marcia.

Jane was thinking about Donna, and didn't feel like being sympathetic to Calvin right now. If he'd bothered to tell her about Marcia's existence, she'd feel more responsible for cheering him up. Maybe he didn't even want her sympathy.

But he looked so morose, she said anyway: "Let's go out to dinner somewhere festive. It will cheer you up. Or you can even wallow in it and tell me all about Marcia if you want. That might be fun too." For you, she added mentally, not me. Jane figured she'd spent more than enough of her life hearing about what went wrong with other people's love lives. Nine times out of ten she wanted to shake the victims and shout, "But they aren't good enough for you."

"I can't," he said. "I'm having dinner with Marcia. Sort of a debriefing. Like one of those exit interviews personnel departments have. I think it's where I hear how I screwed up, in painful detail." He sighed at the inevitability of it all and checked his watch. "So Marcia can get on with her life without a sense of unfinished business." He sounded as if he were quoting.

"Sounds like a million laughs," said Jane. While she hadn't really felt like cheering him up, she now felt paradoxically annoyed that he didn't seem to need her help.

When he had shuffled off to his doom, vowing to get the envelope out of Mrs. Webber's clutches in the morning, and as she was clearing away the glasses, the phone rang again.

"Is this Jane da Silva?" It was a man's voice. Relaxed, pleasant, with an unmistakable touch of New England. He sounded as if he were in his fifties. "This is Hank Raleigh. I wonder if we could get together and talk about Irene March."

It was a businesslike conversation and he stayed completely in charge. She didn't have a chance to ask him any questions, or feel him out. He simply requested that she come to his house in Woodinville tomorrow at eleven, and he apologized that it was far away, but assumed briskly that she would do as he asked. He gave her driving instructions, and said "Goodbye," very pleasantly.

She sat there in the hall for a minute after she had hung up. Here she'd been tiptoeing around, conspiring with Donna and Jack trying to cover for his cheating rodeo queen wife, and he summons her over in a brusque, brisk sort of way. There was no shame, no anger in his voice, no sense that he would demand the truth, no emotion at all. There was no explanation, either. No references to a delicate or unpleasant matter. And he didn't suggest they meet in any neutral place, away from his wife.

Jane could hardly wait to hear what he had to say. What she would say, was an entirely different matter. She decided she'd say as little as possible. He wasn't really entitled to know what she had learned. She had to remind herself that she was a private investigator, that her clients had been Irene's co-workers, and that her work was at an end now that the police were involved.

*　　*　　*

The house was a big Colonial with pillars, at the end of a long drive past a horse barn and a pasture with a tall palomino and a sturdy little quarter horse grazing side by side. Jane thought the pillars made it look too much like a bank, and the whole thing looked out of place here.

She rang the doorbell, big bonging chimes, and a tall man with white hair and a tan answered the door. He had extraordinary blue eyes and he wore faded jeans, plain brown cowboy boots, and a big oval silver buckle on his belt, emphasizing his narrow waist. This was a guy who could deck himself out in Western wear and not look the least bit silly.

His study, however, off a big bland living room with big poufy white furniture and lots of pillows in blue and rose and pale yellow, pushed the Western motif just a little closer to the cartoonish.

Jane found her head swiveling around to take in the details. There was a massive chair made of moose antlers and rawhide, a table with bits of bark clinging to the pine trunks that served as feet, a Navajo blanket on the floor and a desk that seemed fashioned out of two swollen burls, its slablike surface embellished with a collection of cattle brands. The mantelpiece featured a bronze of a cowboy twirling a lariat and there was a sofa and chair in red leather and hand-peeled fir with a kind of Arts-and-Crafts-goes-to-a-dude-ranch look that held her gaze the longest. Jane admired them for their simplicity and craftsmanship.

"You're looking at the best pieces in the room," he said. "Genuine Molesworth."

"Molesworth?" she said, her eyes flicking up to a cast-iron chandelier featuring the silhouettes of Art Deco buffalo.

"The Frank Lloyd Wright of Western decor," he said solemnly. "It's an early piece." He ran a hand along a row of metal tacks across the top of the sofa. "Star-shaped tacks are the tipoff."

He indicated a comfortable guest chair next to his desk (blue leather with burnt-in bow-legged cowboy-and-cactus motif), and climbed behind the burl desk and sat in his own chair (steel gray and chrome Italian-looking model without any Western content, designed to save middle-aged backs), moved a Georgia O'Keeffe skull onto some papers he'd been working on and sat back, placing the tips of his fingers together.

"I understand," he said, "that you were looking for people who had some contact with Irene March."

Jane sat there with a pleasant expression despite the implied question mark at the end of his sentence.

Her silence didn't faze him. In fact, he smiled. "I know this from my rather giddy sister-in-law, Donna MacLaine, a nice enough woman who adores shabby intrigue."

This time Jane gave him a little nod and a sympathetic half smile.

"Now that it has come out that this unfortunate March woman has died, I want to know whether you will continue to pursue your inquiries into her activities."

He sounded like a lawyer all right.

"The King County Police have a homicide investigation going," she said. "I was looking for her. She's been found. There's no need for me to look for her anymore."

"I'm a little confused," he said. "I haven't been able to find that you have a private investigator's license in the state of Washington."

"That's because I don't," she said.

"But you are representing yourself as such," he said. "And presumably accepting money from clients."

"No," she said. "I don't accept any money from clients. I am acting pro bono. Or I was."

"And now, presumably," he said, "you are cooperating with the police." He nodded as if she were expected to do so, to be a good citizen.

"To an extent," she said. What was he getting at? Did he know what his wife was up to? Did Donna confide in him? Did his wife?

"I understand," he went on, "at least my charming but giddy sister-in-law tells me, that Irene March was a blackmailer."

He leaned forward and put his forearms on the desk. "I'll be honest. I live in the public eye. I don't want any unsavory attention, especially not right now. The road to public service has become a goddamned gauntlet. Nowadays, people think they have the right to know whatever they want. About me and my family."

"It must be awful," said Jane.

"Can you understand my concern?" he said. "If there's no reason for the police to know that my wife and Irene were mixed up in some silly way, is there any reason you need to tell them?"

He picked up an envelope from his desk and held it lightly in his hand. She tried not to notice it.

"You're asking me to withhold something from the police," said Jane. No point telling him that was her intention all along. For Jack's sake. For her sake. And she felt sorry for Hank Raleigh too. What good would it do for him to have to let the world know his younger wife was stepping out on him? Did she really want to be the one to break it to the world? Jane had been around long enough to know that marriages were as different as people, and for outsiders to judge them all to one standard was just naive.

Jane sighed. "I don't want to make anyone unnecessarily miserable. I'll be frank. If I thought Irene was anything more than a petty chiseler, I might feel duty bound to tell the police she was blackmailing your wife."

He cleared his throat. "I had intended to offer you something. A consulting fee. A retainer. Whatever you want to call it. Maybe a client fee to take the case and drop it." He handed her the envelope. "I didn't realize your work was pro bono. Perhaps you'll make an exception. For my peace of mind."

He handed her the envelope. She started to refuse, then it occurred to her that it might be handy to have some proof that he had tried to bribe her.

Jane rose, looked down at the envelope in her hand. She handed it back, using the tips of her fingers. "I don't think that's necessary," she said.

He grabbed it firmly and held it back at her. "Give it to your favorite charity," he said. "Really, it will make me feel better all around."

"All right," said Jane. She put the envelope in her purse and offered him her hand to shake. His hand was moist. The guy was nervous. He hadn't seemed nervous at first. His hand had been firm and dry when she touched it before.

"I am sorry," said Jane, meaning it and feeling wretched about carrying away the envelope, "that you've been through all this unpleasantness."

"I'm not a jealous man," he said looking at her with those remarkable blue eyes, as if hoping for some understanding. "Not anymore. But foolishly perhaps, it suits me to have Angela believe I am." He paused. "I feel privileged to be her husband. I love her very much and I'll do anything to protect her."

He led her to the door, saw her out with a kind of courtliness. Watched while she pulled around the driveway and headed back out. He wasn't what Jane had expected. There was a quiet dignity about him she'd liked.

In the field next to the drive, she saw the palomino horse, now saddled up and bearing a rider, galloping alongside the fence. The rider was a blonde woman, sitting straight and beautiful. Jane slowed a little, so as not to startle the horse, and the woman waved at her, motioning her to stop. She was the woman in the clipping. Angela.

Jane stopped the car and, curious, rolled down the window. Angela walked the horse over to the fence and bent down low over the horse's neck so she could speak to Jane.

"Jane da Silva, right?" she said.

"Angela Raleigh," said Jane with a smile.

"That's right," she said, absentmindedly stroking the horse's neck. "I guess you just spoke to my husband. I wonder if we could talk too."

"Why not?" said Jane.

"Meet me in an hour at the Bellevue Mall. By the elevator that leads to the museum."

"All right," said Jane. Mrs. Raleigh was just as officious and sure that Jane would make the meeting as her husband had been. Jane was beginning to find them a little overbearing. But she was very curious to hear what Angela had to say.

22.

"So you're the lawyer who's handling Irene's estate, huh?" said Mrs. Webber, with an elegant curling of her lip.

"Yes," Calvin said, "but I didn't draft the will." He wanted to make that very clear, after that unflattering paragraph Irene had inserted. Mrs. Webber really was a pretty good-looking woman, he thought. He wondered what she'd look like if she smiled.

"I wasn't surprised at the nasty things she wrote about me," said Mrs. Webber. "When it comes to ungrateful employees, when it comes to poor attitude, nothing would surprise me."

"Employees don't really understand the challenges faced by management," said Calvin solemnly.

"That's for sure," she said with feeling. "You know what it's like running this little zoo?"

Calvin looked out through the glass panels onto the work area where the readers sat bent over their desks like a quartet of Bob Cratchits on their high stools.

"This is a tough business," said Mrs. Webber. "So it hurt when I read those lies in her will."

Calvin leaned across the desk. "May I say something personal," he said. Then, without waiting for her permission, he plunged on. "Has it occurred to you that Irene March may have been jealous of a successful, attractive professional woman such as yourself?"

Mrs. Webber smiled. It really was a nice smile. Calvin decided he may as well lay it on with a trowel. Mrs. Webber looked like she needed cheering up.

"You know," he said, "when I walked in here I thought to myself, here's a woman who looks a lot like Grace Kelly. Poor Irene. I bet no one ever thought that about her."

Mrs. Webber simpered a little, then leaned over the desk with a conspiratorial air. "That's the trouble," she said. "They're all jealous of me. I can tell. I can't really afford to pay them much. Naturally they resent me. But it's not like *I* have such a great life."

Calvin murmured "Oh?" and Mrs. Webber looked alarmed, as if she'd revealed too much. Calvin, sensing vulnerability, dove in, partly because of his general smarming-up campaign to get her to turn over the envelope, partly because he really wanted to know. "You don't?" he said, registering surprise.

"I'm still adjusting to my divorce," she said with a little wave of her hand and an embarrassed smile. "To tell you the truth, I didn't realize I'd have to earn my own living. It was kind of a shock. My ex-husband ran off with his secretary. It was really very sordid."

"A long-term relationship of mine just broke up," said Calvin. "She found someone else. It's rough, there's no doubt about it."

Mrs. Webber straightened up and brushed back the hair at her temples in a tense little gesture. She was clearly uncomfortable with the intimate turn the conversation had taken. "How can I help you?"

Calvin cleared his throat in a businesslike way. "As part of settling Irene's estate, I'm here for any personal effects she might have left here."

"Personal effects?" Mrs. Webber looked vague. "I think we already cleaned out her desk. There might have been a bottle of hand lotion somewhere. And I know she had a personalized coffee cup over by the sink."

"Her co-workers tell me you collected some things in a box. From her storage area."

"Yes, I guess I did," said Mrs. Webber, looking around the room. She went over to the box on the shelf above the radiator and peered into it. "Just some odds and ends," she said. "I thought there were some keys there but I don't see them now."

"Fine," said Calvin, stepping over and swooping up the box.

Mrs. Webber frowned. She didn't seem to like the idea of his taking it away, but couldn't come up with any reason he shouldn't. "I guess that's all right," she said.

"Of course it is," he said. He cast a quick, appreciative and what he presumed was a subtle eye down her body. "I've enjoyed meeting you," he said. "In fact, I wonder if I might call you. Maybe we could have lunch or something."

It was somehow typical of Bellevue, the suburb across Lake Washington from Seattle, thought Jane, that it should have its art museum on top of a multistoried shopping center. Having burgeoned in the fifties, the whole place was built for the car, with multilane streets connecting malls.

In fact, Jane had read about a celebrated case in this very mall where one Bellevue lady had run her car into another in a fight over a parking space. The victim had been standing in the disputed spot, trying to save it for a friend's car. The perpetrator's defense for vehicular assault was that she needed the space more because she was late for a nail appointment.

Jane, however, did find a parking space, and walked from the parking lot on a concrete walkway to Nordstrom. She cut through the store, with a quick lateral visual sweep of the shoe department. A pair of gray suede pumps with a lovely sculptural heel called out to her, but she kept moving, also fending off a beautiful boy who looked like Rudolph Valentino as he tried to spritz her with a new scent. Jane thought it smelled like gin with a touch of tuberoses.

Where Nordstrom spilled out into the mall itself, she found an espresso cart and picked up a coffee and a cookie with pink, almond-flavored frosting. She figured it would take Angela a little while to stable the horse and drive down from Woodinville, so she settled herself on a white wire chair and watched people walk by.

Angela joined her about twenty minutes later. She must have flown down the freeway. Jane got a better look at her. While Donna's hair had been bright blonde, Angela's was a natural-looking dark, streaky blonde. As she sat down, she pushed it away from her face rather fiercely and let it all fall back into a perfect cut. Instead of candy pink, her nails were a milky white.

Angela hadn't bothered to change. She was still wearing her jeans and a soft cotton knit V-necked sweater in a buttery sort of beige that showed off a triangle of tanned, firm skin and a necklace of flat diamonds. Jane thought snobbishly that the necklace was a little vulgar with the simple, pretty sweater, and made Angela look more matronly.

"What can I do for you?" said Jane.

"Donna told me about you," she said. "She said you were an investigator, looking into the disappearance of Irene March. And that you learned some stuff about me."

Angela looked mean and sulky, which put Jane off immediately. Looking sulky was poor strategy on Angela's part, she thought.

Jane kept her own demeanor noncommittal. "That's right," she said with a little nod.

Angela glowered at her and seemed to be expecting an apology.

I can be a bitch too, Jane thought, and I hardly ever exercise my option. She tossed her head back a little and added, "So?"

"So it makes me nervous," said Angela. "What did my husband want?"

"He wanted to know if I was going to tell the police what I found out," Jane said. "They're kind of curious, about who might be irritated with Irene, seeing as it looks as if she could have been murdered."

"So what have you told them?" demanded Angela.

"Nothing," said Jane. "From what I can tell, she hit you up for money because she found out something unpleasant about you." Jane shrugged and decided to spill it all. "Probably that you had an affair with someone from your hometown whose initials are Jack Lawson. I didn't tell them that, because it's not their business, and it isn't mine either, really. I didn't even tell them you and Irene rendezvoused in Coulee City last year."

"Why didn't you?" said Angela.

Jane noticed that the woman's hands were in tight little balls. Angela caught Jane gazing at her clenched fists, and she blushed a little and opened her hands and folded them loosely on her lap in a self-conscious way. Suddenly, Jane started to feel a little sorry for her.

"They didn't ask," said Jane. She leaned over, and told Angela Raleigh what she had told her husband. "I don't really care about any of it. I was just looking for Irene. Now she's been found and it's a police matter. To be honest, I didn't see any reason to put you through a lot of scandal over something like this." Jane leaned back and said in a different tone, "How much did Irene stick it to you for? The usual thousand?"

Jane had now positioned herself on Angela's side in the transaction. Angela relaxed a little. "A thousand bucks," said Angela. "Pathetic, isn't it."

"Look," said Jane, "I never would have found out about you in the first place if your sister hadn't called with that stupid story. I'll just forget all about it, unless the police ask me directly, which they won't."

Now Jane was annoyed because she expected some show of gratitude from Angela, and it wasn't forthcoming. Not even a smile. Instead Angela's eyes narrowed and she said, "Donna told me you went off with Jack Lawson. Did you, or did she just tell me that to upset me?"

Jane shrugged. "We spent some time together. He's a nice guy. I wanted to find out about his boots, because I had a witness in Coulee City who said Irene talked to a woman with cowboy boots like his. But why would Donna try to upset you? Does Donna do things to hurt you?"

Angela pushed her hair away from her face again and leaned back in her chair. "She's jealous. She thinks things worked out so great for me. She thinks I've got a rich husband who's crazy about me and I don't have any reason to complain."

"Do you?"

Angela sniffed. "Rich people like my husband, they never are really totally crazy about you. They're suspicious all the time. The second thing they say after 'I love you, marry me' is 'Let's get the prenuptial drawn up.' She looked over across the mall where a bunch of teenage girls were pushing each other and giggling, and clicked her tongue impatiently. "I don't know. I guess life is okay. I try to be good to Donna. I give her some of my clothes and things. And she takes them and then seems to resent it."

"Well, she tried to help you," said Jane, wondering just what Angela was up to here with these revelations. Was she trying to get sympathy? "Frankly, Mrs. Raleigh, I am a little curious about all of this. I take it you saw my ad about Irene, and asked Donna to call me."

"I wanted to find out who you were and what you wanted," said Angela. "And I guess I wanted you to think Irene was blackmailing some strange guy and maybe he did something to her. In case she'd been killed, you'd suspect him."

"And why did you want me to think that?"

"Because," said Angela, "I was afraid my husband killed her."

"Did your husband know you were being blackmailed by Irene?" said Jane, sitting up suddenly, and trying not to reveal by her demeanor that what Angela had just said was rather startling. Hank Raleigh *had* said he'd do anything for her.

"I was scared. When Irene first called, I told Hank. He went with me to Coulee City. Watched me hand her an envelope in a restaurant. After all, I didn't know who would be there. Maybe some big scary guy. Later, he saw her on *Jeopardy!* He got her name."

"Do you still think he could have killed her?" said Jane.

Angela's mouth tightened. Her eyes slid to one side. "No," she said. "He was back east when she disappeared. In Boston. When I realized that, I was sorry I got Donna involved. But I wanted to find out what you were doing."

"How did your husband take your little hometown fling?" said Jane.

178

ELECTRIC CITY

"Oh, he still doesn't know about that," said Angela with a sly smile. Jane wasn't sure that was true.

"He doesn't?"

"Nope." Angela looked very pleased with herself. "He thinks it was something else entirely."

"Like what?" said Jane.

"Shoplifting at the new Wal-Mart in Omak." Angela rolled her eyes, as if to say, "Men are so dumb." "He bought it. And later I told him that I got Donna to tell you a story about my having an affair, so you wouldn't find out about the shoplifting conviction. He figures that as a politician, he could live with the unfaithful wife thing, but as attorney general, he couldn't have a wife who'd broken the law." Jane was reeling. Irene had blackmailed Angela about the affair. Angela had told her husband that Irene was actually blackmailing her over a shoplifting conviction. Then Angela told her husband she'd planted the story through Donna that it was all about an affair. Jane was beginning to have more and more respect for Angela's machinations. The way she'd set it up, if Jane did tell her husband the truth, he'd assume he was hearing disinformation.

Angela looked pleased with herself but her smile faded fast. "What did Jack tell you?" she said.

"Nothing," said Jane. "Your name never came up. I asked him about those boots that matched yours and he told me a woman gave them to him. So I figured it out by myself. But he never said one word about you."

Angela nodded. Jane could have told her more. She could have said "We had a fight about it," but she didn't. She decided that if Angela had the nerve to ask her if she and Jack had slept together, she'd lie. She didn't want this woman to know anything about her. In fact, she wanted to be far away from her. There was something repellent about her.

"So listen," said Angela in her strange, deadpan voice,

and Jane realized what it was about her that was so off-putting. Angela wasn't trying to be charming or nice or ingratiating or pleasant the way almost all women did almost all the time. She didn't care what Jane thought or whether Jane liked her. The dead inflection in her voice, the eye shifting around the mall, they were arrogant little signs that Angela wasn't even going to bother to establish any rapport. Jane could have been a piece of furniture. Presumably, Angela was different with men. Unless Jane had missed something and there were guys who found near autism sexy.

"Listen," said Angela now. "How come you aren't telling anyone?"

Jane shrugged. "Because I don't care enough," she said.

Angela reached into her bag and pulled out a checkbook. "Just in case you start caring, how about I write you a little check? Like in case someone wants you to check up on this Irene some more you won't lose any money."

Jane's eyebrows rose. Exhibit B. To be filed next to her husband's envelope. "Sure," said Jane. "If you want."

Angela smiled a superior little smile. Jane assumed she was relieved Jane could be bought. "Say like five thousand?" she said.

"Say like five thousand," said Jane. That was more than the thousand Irene got. Angela had handed her a lot of information too. But how much of it was true?

Back in town, Jane gingerly opened Hank's envelope and found it contained seven one-thousand-dollar bills. She decided to leave both the envelope with the cash and Angela's check with Calvin. She wanted to be able to say later she hadn't really been bought off.

23.

"So," said Jane, putting her feet up on Calvin's sofa. "You tell me about your blonde witch and I'll tell you about mine."

"Wendy isn't really a witch," said Calvin.

Bells clanged in Jane's head and she swung her legs back on the floor and sat forward with her hands on her knees. "What?" she said. "You have something nice to say about Mrs. Webber? Who, according to my friends at the Columbia Clipping Service, is practically the Antichrist?"

"Maybe she comes across a little severe," said Calvin, "but I think she's just frustrated."

"Sexually frustrated?" said Jane.

"Maybe that too," said Calvin thoughtfully. "Do you think so?"

"There's a pathetic touch of hopefulness in your question that I find very alarming," said Jane.

"Hey, I had to be nice to her to get what you wanted, and she was quite pleasant back. I bet no one bothers to be pleasant to the poor woman."

"If only little Liza had been more pleasant to Simon Legree," said Jane. "Did you get what you went over there for?"

"Yes I did," he said, handing over the squashed box. Jane plucked out the pale yellow envelope and shook three clippings out on Calvin's coffee table. There was a staple in the corner of one, and the characteristic slit in the corner of the other two.

"Fabulous," she said, smiling.

"Maybe the police should see them," said Calvin.

"Let me read them first," said Jane.

The first clipping, from the Tri-Cities, gave a list of men who'd been rounded up soliciting a policewoman dressed in a metallic push-up bra and a spandex skirt. One of the names was David Twentyacres.

The second clipping showed a picture of Amanda Jenkins staring solemnly into the camera. The story said that Shelton High School was having a car wash to raise money for her heart transplant.

The third clipping, dated about a year before, was tiny. Ella Mae Tinker, eighty-two, of Electric City, had died in the early-morning hours of internal injuries sustained in a hit-and-run accident at two A.M. One witness said he'd seen a bright pink car careening around nearby shortly before Tinker left a neighborhood tavern.

"Where the hell is Electric City, exactly?" said Jane.

"Up near the Grand Coulee Dam," said Calvin.

Detectives Walter and Hildebrand said goodbye to Amanda's mother, one Maureen Louise Jenkins, and walked out into the front yard. They looked over at Amanda, who was playing there under the fir tree. She and her thin, dark friend were dressed in some old sheer curtains, which swathed them like shawls.

The other little girl was wearing a lot of costume jewelry and a pair of adult high heels. Amanda had on an old purple beach hat and carried a big navy blue handbag, much too big for her. She opened it up and removed her Barbie, three crayons and a Hello Kitty change purse.

"The kid *looks* healthy," whispered Hildebrand.

"Mom said her condition isn't apparent," said Walters. "But we'll check with Goldendale. What the hell county is that in?"

"I'm not sure," said Hildebrand. "Maybe Yakima or Wahkiakum?"

"Anyway," said Walters, "if it's some kind of a scam, she should be stopped. And that da Silva woman was right. Besides fraud, it's child abuse. We'll notify CPS too. Get a social worker to check out the kid."

24.

Electric City sounded like some comic book city—Metropolis or Gotham City, all skyscrapers and neon. Instead it was a skimpy collection of mostly tired-looking small businesses facing the two-lane highway, with some surrounding residential areas vaguely reminiscent of Dogpatch.

There was a hairdresser, a few industrial businesses in corrugated metal, and a white stucco grocery store with a balloonish false front, a strange melding of streamlined thirties and the Old West.

The Electric City Tavern had similar architecture—low-rent Bauhaus, white stucco encrusted with old air-conditioning units punched into one wall. Nearby were a couple of establishments with weathered old siding and overhangs onto the wooden sidewalk—a kind of instant Old West strip-mall look, unmistakably of recent vintage.

Curious, Jane drove off the highway left toward Banks Lake. On the strip of land between lake and road, she found a nest of side streets arranged in lazy curves full of small bungalows from the thirties. Some of them looked neat and cottagy, others were listing with peeling paint and barking dogs chained in the yards. It was the kind of neighborhood where morning glory vines entwined the carcasses of old cars, where horsetails poked through the gravel and grew out from beneath old sheds patched with galvanized metal, where the insides of clothes dryers served as jolly planters for nasturtiums or weeds—a place where, due to human neglect or exhaustion, industrial relics and the biomass became intermingled. In its own cheesy way, it had some of the same poignancy the Victorians tried to capture with their fake ruins covered with ivy.

Cadillac Drive led down to the man-made lake. Its cluster of small boxy houses gave it the look of the tourist court motel Clark Gable and Claudette Colbert checked into in *It Happened One Night*. Nearby was a big, modern motel with a parking lot full of four-by-fours and boat trailers.

The whole place looked as if it weren't zoned in any way. Some streets were paved, some were dirt roads. The lots were all higgledy-piggledy and at odd angles to each other, as if the place just sprang up organically.

Some of the little houses were surrounded by old rose bushes and lilacs, overgrown fruit trees and huge poplars that gave them a shady, spooky look. Dusty old mobile homes from the fifties, that hadn't moved since then, with plywood and tar paper additions growing out of their sides clustered nearby. There was a church that offered "Hope in a Hurting World" on a big plywood sign, a garden full of stacked old tires, halfheartedly painted white and filled with dirt and planted with geraniums.

On the other side of the road, things seemed to have been platted, or at least to have sprung up less hastily. In the background, looking like the set of a Hollywood Western, was a flat-topped wall of rock. It was streaked with rust-colored and acid green lichen, giving it an industrial look to match the detritus of the town.

Past the collection of trailers and old bungalows, on streets with the names Diamond, Pearl, Gold and Silver, was the fancier part of town—a collection of suburban-looking ranch-style houses in pastels. They were surrounded by meticulous landscapes featuring colored gravel, junipers and driftwood arrangements. Beyond that was the desert—sage and bunchgrass.

Jane went back to the main street and pulled up in front of a store with a sign that said "Gifts" and seemed to specialize in painted plaster seagulls. On a flatbed truck in the front, a ceramic painted seagull sat on a chunk of wood wrapped with rope to represent a piling. Inside, there were tons more birds perched on driftwood and in various attitudes—flying, resting, even dead. Lining the walls were more of them in unpainted form. It looked like the seagull equivalent of an unpainted furniture store—U-Finish Seagulls, maybe, or a factory outlet.

The owner seemed busy on the phone. He sounded cheerful and optimistic. She sidled over closer to where he was. "Everyone loves seagulls," he was saying. "Hey, we're doing great. I just got a big order for Portland." Apparently, they were moving the stuff by the gross. Now that she thought about it, she had seen the things around, on suburban mailboxes she thought.

He seemed deep in a big transaction, so Jane abandoned her plans to buy a seagull and chat with him, and went next door to a store that looked like it might once have been a gas station.

There was an ancient metal Texaco sign nailed to the building over the window. Stenciled in green paint were the words "Antiques. Treasures. Baseball Cards. Collectibles." It was a big jumble of a place, with its contents spilling out onto the gravel shoulder of the road, a collection of objects that seemed to have sprung forth like mushrooms.

Jane moseyed among the tables, which appeared to be giant wooden cable spools and barrels with plywood set on them, and surveyed the grim inventory. Used rusty shovels and farm tools, old horseshoes, beat-up aluminum lawn chairs with frayed webbing, the frames of baby strollers, hubcaps and old bicycles, tires, washtubs, wooden containers for Pepsi bottles, Sears appliances in no-longer-fashionable avocado green, harvest gold and copper.

Feeling like an archaeologist, she found the original old gas pumps in the middle of it all, surrounded by concrete pads cracked by the weeds that had pushed their way through them.

She paused for a moment at a collection of old fruit baskets and milk cans. A woman of about fifty with a big knot of silvery hair on top of her head came over. She was wearing a T-shirt and a pair of shiny stirrup pants and flats and she carried a cigarette. She smiled and gestured toward the baskets and cans.

"You could paint those and use them for dried flowers," she said.

"Yes," mused Jane, getting into character right away. "I think I saw something like that in *Family Circle*. You can paint them teal blue or white and tie cute little checked ribbons around them. Maybe do some decoupage on the milk cans. Kind of a country look for a foyer or something."

"Exactly," said the woman. "I can see you're really artistic. Most people have no imagination."

"I kind of like to look at old things," said Jane, omitting that she had no desire to tart them up for a foyer, and that the feeling most of this old junk evoked was bittersweet if not absolutely depressing. She looked around at a nest of old milk bottles, a beat-up old galvanized tub and a rural mailbox that looked like a pickup truck had careened into it. "You sure have a lot of stuff here. Been doing this long?"

"I bought this business last year," said the woman. "Put

in my twenty years as a state employee in Spokane, then retired early and put my retirement money into it."

Jane resisted the urge to grab the woman, shake her and say, "You'd have been better off with CDs or a passbook savings account. How can you throw away all those years on a bunch of rusty shovels!" Jane herself had once been involved in a disastrous retail venture that involved a pointless little store selling baskets, sachets and paperweights.

"I go to a lot of estate sales, and now, the word's getting out and people bring me stuff," the woman said happily. Sure, thought Jane. These country slickers probably get this stuff in truckloads by the side of the road and out in the desert and bring it here for some quick cash from the city sucker. She could just see the locals, a gleam of greed in their eye, unwinding blackberry vines from old rusted bedsprings in ditches.

"I guess you get a fair amount of traffic along here," said Jane.

"More or less." The woman frowned and crushed out her cigarette with her pointed shoe. "If we could just get some civic spirit going. These merchants along here don't want to do anything to promote the place. Me personally, I'd like to see it become an artist's colony or something. What we need is one or two famous people to get the ball rolling. From Hollywood or something. And I'd like to see a dozen gift shops just like that along here."

She gestured toward the seagull shop. For the first time Jane noticed a big pile of old computer gear—printers, monitors and keyboards sitting in a big pile between the two stores. So this is where old computers go to die, she thought. Electric City. It seemed appropriate. Maybe they'd end up as nasturtium or geranium planters someday.

"Not too trendy, though," added the woman hastily. "That would spoil it."

Absolutely, thought Jane. Don't let them put a Gucci here in Electric City, no matter how hard they beg.

"I wish they'd all fix up their stores in a Western theme like Winthrop up on highway 20," continued the lady with the topknot. She was on a roll now and there was a zealot's glow about her face. "They made the whole place look like an old Wild West town with a saloon and everything. The tourists love it. And Leavenworth over in the Cascades. They did a German thing, you know, a Bavarian mountain village with bands and lederhosen and edelweiss. Real cute. Even the Safeway has those old-fashioned German letters. They've made a mint with a theme like that."

"So who lives here?" said Jane, squinting out into the sunny, dusty road as if seeing the charm of the place for the first time. She tried to look like somebody famous, or at least someone who knew some famous people looking for an artist's colony. "Who lives here now, I mean," she added, as if she were planning to arrange for an immediate onslaught of beautiful people, all eager to buy old washtubs and milk cans to decorate their rural hideaways.

The woman shook her head sadly, as if the present citizens left much to be desired. "The bikers left last year. I think they ended up down in the Tri-Cities. We've got some people on disability and stuff. They just pull a check and they can live here cheaply. They tell Labor and Industries they have a bad back or something." She arched a skeptical eyebrow. "Of course, there are some nice families, but the place isn't anywhere near its potential."

Jane nodded sympathetically.

"And," continued the woman, tilting her head to one side, and looking prissy, "there seem to be a lot of retired people who've been here forever. They tell me some of them were pretty wild but old age slowed them down."

"Wasn't there an old lady who got run over around here," said Jane. "Ella Mae Something?"

The woman didn't find anything odd about Jane's knowing this. "Yeah, that's right. Ella Mae Tinker. She used to spend a lot of time at the Kilowatt Tavern over across the way. She was going home from there one night and someone ran over her. I guess it was bound to happen sooner or later, the poor old thing staggering around at two A.M."

She didn't sound too sorry. Jane guessed Ella Mae hadn't fit in with this woman's vision of Electric City as it could be when its full artistic and commercial potential was realized.

"Did you know her?" Jane was beginning to comprehend that here was someone who answered questions without wondering why they were being asked.

"Oh, yeah. She sold me a couple of things. Old kitchen stuff. People collect that Depression stuff with green handles. Eggbeaters and whisks and strainers and stuff. She was about eighty or so, but her language could get pretty salty." Jane imagined Ella Mae telling this woman what she thought of her offer on her old kitchen utensils.

"And," continued the woman, "she had two bright circles of rouge on her cheeks. When ladies get older and their eyesight goes, they don't always know how bright their makeup is." She clicked her tongue critically.

So Ella Mae was one of those overrouged old ladies sitting on bar stools until closing time, chain-smoking unfiltered Pall Malls and grousing in a gravelly voice about crooked politicians and people who didn't have the sense God gave hens. Jane had met a few of those old ladies and there had been times in her life when she'd wondered if that wasn't how she would end up herself. It wasn't an entirely unattractive prospect.

She tried to pump the woman for more, but she didn't seem to know more. Jane felt somehow obliged to buy something, so she ended up choosing a battered aluminum tray.

She stepped inside the store to pay. It was dark and cool in there, with rows of old bottles and stacks of *National Geographic*s sitting around.

On a pink dinette table, next to a collection of Melmac coffee cups and some junk jewelry, she saw an old-fashioned green-handled eggbeater. It had a price tag of twelve dollars. Maybe this racket wasn't so pathetic, after all.

"Was this Ella Mae Tinker's?" she asked.

The woman handed her her change and looked embarrassed. "Yes, it was," she said. Why had she sounded ashamed, wondered Jane. Maybe because the woman was dead. People were often squeamish about dead people's houses and effects. Jane imagined the woman's topknotted head bent over boxes of potholders and napkin rings and old shoes, as she rummaged through them at estate sales.

It was good to get back out into the sun. Jane left the tray in her car, mentally consigning it to her curbside recycling bin back in Seattle, and made her way across the street to the Kilowatt Tavern.

It was an old clapboard building, with peeling blue paint. Where there had once been a big front window, there was a sheet of buckled plywood. A reader-board sign surrounded by a row of light bulbs said "Kilowatt Tavern."

Inside, back in the gloom, the air was heavy with the smell of fried chicken, a powerful disinfectant of some sort, and cigarettes. An old swamp cooler air-conditioning unit sucked like a wheezing asthmatic at the stale air.

The place was lined with more of the fake wood paneling used to make basements into do-it-yourself rec rooms, and there was a bearskin and a collection of antlers on the walls. The floor was covered with red and black tweed shag carpeting and there was a row of harvest gold Naugahyde-covered bar stools along the stained Formica bar. One of the stools was occupied by an old man. In the center of the room was a pool table, dramatically lit like an altar.

A man in his thirties, very thin, with a goatee and a T-shirt that said "Princeton," was scraping some carbonized material off the grill while a few baskets of French fries spattered away in hot fat.

He looked up and Jane gave him a friendly nod. They exchanged hi's, and in answer to his vaguely questioning, can-I-help-you? look she said, "I was wondering if you would have happened to know a lady named Ella Mae Tinker. I hear she used to hang out here." She had made up a story as she came through the door. It was getting easier and easier to lie. She was going to say she was writing some tear-jerker newspaper feature about senior citizens who'd perished in hit-and-run accidents.

"She was a reg'lar," said the man. "But before my time. Charlie here can prolly help you." He turned his attentions to the fries.

Jane sidled down toward Charlie and gave him a nice smile. He gestured to the stool next to him.

"I knew Ella Mae real good," said Charlie. He was a grizzled old guy, with long gray hair coming out from under a greasy leather-brimmed hat lashed together with a thong—Jane vaguely remembered the style from crafts fairs of the sixties. He had a silver beard and a red-veined nose.

"Oh yeah?" said Jane, insinuating herself next to him on an adjacent bar stool. He looked like somebody's sidekick in an old Western movie. It took some effort for her not to address him as "Old Timer."

"We were drinking buddies I guess you might say," said Charlie. "And we used to shoot pool. Ella Mae was a real fine pool player." He didn't look at Jane directly, but addressed her image in the mirror that ran along the back of the bar.

"Tell me about her," said Jane, looking back at his image. "Tell me about Ella Mae." He didn't seem to need her backup story about the newspaper feature. Actually, she thought, she really didn't need to know anything about Ella Mae anyway.

It probably didn't make any difference. Ella Mae could have been anybody. But Jane wanted to know just who it was who'd been struck down that night in Electric City, who might have set off a long series of complex events just as surely as Helen of Troy had launched all those ships.

Charlie looked pointedly into his glass, and Jane lifted her hand. The bartender came back down and filled Charlie's glass with whiskey and set down the fries next to him. Breakfast, she imagined.

Jane was surprised the Kilowatt Tavern had a license to sell hard liquor. In Washington State, only restaurants could have a bar. Taverns sold wine and beer. Maybe the fries counted, or maybe the inspector didn't make it here very often, or maybe Charlie got a special deal.

The bartender raised an inquiring eyebrow at Jane. She nodded and he gave her a glass too, and she asked for a coffee back. It was a little early, but she didn't want to insult Charlie.

Charlie looked like he needed to maintain a constant level of booze in his bloodstream to remain functional. An IV drip kind of alcoholic. It was something about the businesslike way he sat at the bar at one in the afternoon, face forward, without any pretense of festivity or any ragged sense of being on a bender.

"Ella Mae," he said, thoughtfully selecting a fry and looking down at it as if it were a fine cigar, "came out here when the dam was built back in the thirties. A lot of men came to build the dam. It was hard times, and they'd hop a freight and show up with maybe a dime and a sandwich their mother gave them wrapped up in a big old handkerchief. There was work here. There wasn't nothing else here but a mess of rattlesnakes and some Indians, but there was work here." He took a sip. This was going to take a while, but what the hell, Jane had a while.

"Soon after the men came," continued Charlie, "a lot of women came too." He frowned. "Like I said, times was hard. Ella Mae wasn't more than fifteen I bet when she showed up here. A camp follower I guess wold be the polite way to say it. She did what she had to do, I guess.

"She was from somewhere down south, judging by her accent. And she liked Southern food. Biscuits and gravy and funnel cakes. She never talked about being a kid, except to say she grew up on a farm and things were pretty bad.

"Anyway, she ended up here and she had plenty of stories to tell about the old days. How they all lived in tents and shacks, with oil lamps—they didn't have any electricity, which is kind of ironic. Every once in a while, a fire would tear through those old shantytowns."

Charlie leaned back happily. "She'd tell about how the men diverted the river and then got down on their hands and knees and polished the granite floor of the riverbed by hand. And how the men were always whooping it up, busting up saloons and all that, a regular Wild West kind of scene."

He smiled. "I got a big kick out of Ella Mae. I guess she was getting to the point in life where you kind of reminisce and all. She liked to talk about the old days. She was here when Roosevelt came to check out the dam. He made a little speech and all; said they were making good progress, I don't know. She saw him. I think it was the biggest thrill of her life. They've got the wheelchair he used in the museum over at the Visitors Center. Ella Mae loved that. She was a big Roosevelt fan and a lifelong Democrat. She always voted."

"What happened after the dam was built and the men left?" Jane asked.

"Ella Mae had some kind of old man for a while, I know. I think he worked for the Bureau."

Jane looked puzzled.

"The Bureau of Reclamation," he said, as if that explained everything. Jane supposed they were in charge of reclaiming the desert by irrigating it. Claiming it would be more apt.

"I guess he died or took off or something," continued Charlie. "She was a waitress later, and she scraped by somehow, I don't know. She used to hustle a little pool once in a while, I know that. Nobody figured a little old lady for a pool shark." He laughed. "She was living on Social Security when I met her. Thanks to her old pal, FDR, huh. This isn't a bad place to do it. Rents are pretty cheap." He grinned. He had one blackened tooth. "And electricity is cheaper than anywhere else in the world. That was the whole idea behind this town. It was supposed to be the city of the future. All modern and electric." He laughed, and sipped delicately at his whiskey.

"So did you come here when the dam was built too?" said Jane, regretting it instantly. After all, it had been sixty years. Charlie looked around seventy. "No, of course not," she said. "You'd be much too young."

"I sure would have," he said. "I would have been minus ten years old. I'm only forty-eight." He turned away from the mirror and looked at her straight on. "I'm your basic baby boomer," he said, looking at her as if he were challenging her to tell him how old and worn-out he looked. It was hard to imagine him as a crew-cut kid watching *The Ed Sullivan Show* with his parents every Sunday night. She smiled at him a little nervously and he said, "But it's not the year that counts, it's the mileage, right?"

Jane laughed and took a sip of her drink to be friendly. It tasted raw and harsh. This stuff would make her look like Gabby Hayes or Hoot Gibson too, and in short order, she thought.

"So no one ever found out who hit poor Ella Mae," said Jane.

"Naw." Charlie looked back into the mirror. "There was just one old guy said he thought he saw a bright pink car tearing up that street that night. It's a little dirt road that led up to her place.

"A pink car kind of sticks out, you know. Some other people saw a pink Corvette that night in town. But no one saw it actually hit her or anything. Anyway, the old man's dead now himself. Stroke.

"She was walking home from this place right here. She lived just around the corner. It was a dark, rainy night. Next day, they found her in a ditch. She'd been knocked over flat. They say she probably never knew what hit her. And because of the rain, there weren't any tracks or anything." He shrugged. "They'll never find out who did it."

After a minute he turned to her and said, "Wanna see where it happened?"

"Sure," said Jane.

He knocked back his drink and left his fries on the bar. "I'll be right back," he said to the bartender.

Jane took a deep sip of the coffee, slid off the bar stool and paid on her way out.

She followed Charlie around the corner. He was a short man with a brisk step. He led her down a gravel road to a dirt one that led into it. There was a ditch there, full of dusty horsetails and someone's old muffler. "Here's where they found her," he said. He stepped back. "She lived right there." He pointed over a picket fence into a little over-grown yard. "She kept it real neat. It's gone downhill since she died."

"Anyone live there now?" said Jane.

"Nope. The owner says he's going to make some repairs and sell it. See, she rented it for thirty years or so. The owner died and then she paid the owner's kid. Some guy in Seattle. He never raised the rent but he never fixed nothing neither. I helped her out a little."

It was a grayish-looking little nondescript place with green indoor-outdoor carpeting running up the sagging steps and along the front porch.

At the bottom of the porch was a collection of homemade whirligigs, garden ornaments like little windmills made of found objects. They were the only things in the composition that moved, circling slowly, apparently catching an imperceptible breeze.

The first one was made out of an old fan, the blades painted hot pink, an old grate, painted turquoise, serving as a kind of counterweight. Another one was a series of teaspoons in alternating red, white and blue attached to a child's tricycle tire painted yellow. The third had an aluminum coffee pot for a top and a row of old funnels painted green on the inside, peach on the outside, to catch the wind. There was something brave and cheerful about those garden ornaments.

She coughed to clear her throat. "Doesn't it make you mad that they never found out who did it?" said Jane. "It sounds like you and Ella Mae were pretty good friends."

He nodded solemnly. "She was good people. She woulda given you her last ten bucks, she really would have. But maybe it was better that she went like that. Real quick. Not in a home or anything. She was too independent for that." He looked uncomfortable and turned back toward the Kilowatt Tavern. "The guy was probably drunk anyway. He didn't mean nothing. Could've been anyone."

25.

The dam seemed to have spawned a trio of little towns. Besides Electric City, there was, down the road a piece, Grand Coulee. Compared to Electric City it looked considerably less like a husk of a town, but there were a few odd bits and pieces of the past among the new buildings at the side of the main road—a stucco city hall with a neon sign and an old drive-in hamburger place with a plywood teepee on the roof.

There didn't seem, however, to be anywhere to stay. Jane was tired and she wanted a clean, anonymous motel where she could collapse, shower, sleep and think before heading back the next morning.

She drove through Grand Coulee and on to the next settlement, Coulee Dam. But before she got there, she encountered the dam itself.

The scale of the thing rendered everything else around it toylike. It was a big wall of concrete, looming up five hundred feet or so, with about a mile of road spanning the top of it where tiny cars winked in the sun. The dam sealed off a huge chasm, leaving a still, blue lake above it, and below it a deep plunge into a basalt-lined gorge. There were some outcroppings of utilitarian buildings along the top, and on one side, the dam's flat, smooth walls seemed to grow up out of a mass of real rock.

Overhead, power lines led away from the dam, strung on huge metal structures that resembled giant robotic devices marching over the barren hills to where the people who wanted the electricity lived.

The town lay below, straddling both sides of the gorge, the two halves connected by an old-fashioned little Erector Set bridge. It was by far the prettiest of the towns around here, thought Jane, as she drove down streets dark from overhanging shade trees. Genteel little white houses sat back from the sidewalk in well-tended, lush gardens. Jane imagined that fifty or sixty years ago, while the dam was being built, respectable engineers' wives started those gardens in the desert soil. The weaker women probably went mad behind fluffy white curtains, weeping in letters home about the dusty outpost where they'd been banished, while Ella Mae and her friends were ripping and roaring in a shantytown full of whores, whiskey and rattlesnakes and the coyotes in the hills howled at the moon.

Jane checked into a motel near a little city park. She thought it would be quiet there, and she spent an hour or so lying on her bed and staring at the cottage-cheese ceiling and the big light fixture made of orange plastic that looked like a cluster of half-sucked candies. A baby was crying in the next room. She tried to nap, but instead she thought about her case.

Angela had come up with a couple of versions of her blackmail story. The one Donna had told—a mysterious, accented stranger being bled white for some unnamed offense. Then there was the story she had told Jane—an affair with Jack Lawson, solemnized with custom cowboy boots. After that, there was the story Angela said she'd told her husband, and the one she said he'd bought: Angela caught shoplifting at the Omak Wal-Mart. But Irene's two clippings told another story.

Irene hadn't had much to go on. The article mentioned someone who'd seen a pink car. And he was dead. Anyone who'd been around the Kilowatt Tavern at closing time, though, would probably be a geriatric drunk and a questionable witness.

Presumably there was some sort of physical evidence. No clear tracks, according to Charlie. But maybe some chips of paint or something. And couldn't the police have done some sort of computer run on pink cars? At least in the surrounding geographic area? Poor old Ella Mae. It wasn't likely anyone would be pressing too hard for a solution to who had struck her down.

What Jane still couldn't figure out was why Irene had gone ahead and made the leap to put those two clippings together. There had to be something Jane hadn't seen yet.

Some insects batted against the screens at the windows and a slight breeze lifted the curtains Jane had drawn. The baby was still fussing, but now a male voice was barking and a female one snapping back. She couldn't make out what they were saying, but she presumed he wanted her to make the baby be quiet, and she was explaining that she might not be able to.

Jane wished she had a copy of the clipping about Angela's pink car with her. What had it said, really? That she had won it as part of some rodeo queen pageant. And that she drove it in the Omak Stampede parade every year.

Jane got up from the bed and walked across the shag carpet to the phone on the dresser. Next to it, she found a tourist guide—a newsprint magazine-sized thing with a picture of an Indian teenager in a prom dress on the cover and ads for motels and restaurants and frozen yogurt parlors and insurance agents all jumbled in with maps of the dam and essays on Indian culture. It was there all right, in a long listing of events. She wasn't sure about last year's dates, but this year the Omak Stampede took place this week, the same calendar week that Ella Mae died last year.

She scrabbled around a little more and found a map of the area. Omak was definitely within striking distance—maybe an hour away, in the middle of the land belonging to the Colville Indian tribe. The reservation, according to the guide, began in the middle of the cute little bridge that ran over to the other side of Coulee Dam.

So that pink car was probably in the neighborhood at about the right time. Was that what set Irene off? Jane thought about it for a while. Irene didn't have to be right. All she had to do was contact Angela and see if she was right. If she was wrong, as she had been with Dave Twenty-acres, she really didn't have anything to lose. The fact that Angela Raleigh had paid up would indicate she was right. But what was Angela doing up in Electric City at two in the morning running Ella Mae Tinker into a ditch? One thing was clear. Here at last was something worth killing Irene March about.

Wouldn't Angela get rid of the car? Just in case there was some paint or something that could be matched up? Jane thought she knew what had happened to the car. It wasn't just old clothes she handed down to her big sister. A navy blue paint job, and she'd turned over the Corvette too. The upholstery, however, was still pink. Jane wasn't sure that was too smart. Presumably, there was still pink paint underneath the blue. She wondered just how smart Angela really was.

It hadn't been smart to sic Donna on her with that bogus story. If she hadn't, Jane wouldn't have known anything about her until she put the clippings together. She'd just drawn attention to herself. And if she'd run over a little old lady with her car, was it smart to paint it and give it to her sister?

Jane looked down at the phone and called for her messages. There was one from Calvin Mason. "My crack sources at the King County Sheriff's Department tell me they finally got the autopsy report," he said. "Looks like homicide. Call me for juicy details."

The second call was from Donna. "Hi, Jane," she said rather plaintively. "Could you call me? I'm sort of worried about something." Jane jotted down her number.

She called Calvin back first. The story he told was simple. It looked very much as if someone struck Irene with a rock, pushed her over the edge, tossed the rock after her (the rock, with blood and hair and a distinct pattern matching the wound, was some feet to the right of Irene) and left her to die down there.

"What do they know about who did it?" said Jane.

"Right-handed. And, this is interesting, about the same height as Irene—who was five feet five inches. Give or take an inch."

"So maybe a woman," said Jane.

"That's right," said Calvin. "I gave them the three clippings we retrieved from Wendy."

"So they can find out what I found out," said Jane. "Which is that it looks like Angela Raleigh ran over a little old lady up here and Irene was blackmailing her. Angela Raleigh is about five five." She sighed. "I can see her doing the deed too. Irene should never have gone on *Jeopardy!*"

"It'll be pretty spectacular news if it's true," said Calvin. "Politician's beautiful wife gone bad. This could be like a TV Movie of the Week kind of thing."

"Yeah, well there's nothing there for me, I'm afraid," said Jane, who wasn't sharing Calvin's enthusiasm for the story's newsworthiness. "I guess I'll just spend the night here . . ."

"Where's here?" said Calvin.

"Coulee Dam," said Jane. "Ever been here?"

"No, but I understand they have some kind of a laser light show there every night. They use the dam itself as a giant screen."

"How bizarre," said Jane. "It is a rather strange place. I think because there's something off about the scale. The dam is so huge and the gorge is so deep and then there's this little puny town at the bottom. It looks like a movie set or something."

She took a breath. She felt defeated and tired and frustrated and rather puny and weak herself. "So I'll just come back, tell the police what I know and look for another case. The board is quite specific. It has to be something the police can't or won't bother with."

"Presumably the possibility of a high-profile homicide conviction will rouse the police from their lethargy," said Calvin. "Can't you tell the board you gave the cops some good leads or something?"

"I don't know." The baby next door let out a piercing scream. Jane pulled her hair away from her face and looked at herself in the mirror above the dresser as she spoke into the phone. She looked tired. Her eyes looked old today. "I'll have to think about it." Not for the first time she reflected on how ridiculous her position was. Scrambling around trying to please a lot of rich old men who'd never had to worry about anything beyond replacing their divots on the golf course.

It did occur to her not to return Donna's call. What was the point, now that the police were involved? And what had Donna ever done for her, besides lie? But she called her anyway, because, basically, she liked Donna, and because of that plaintive note Donna had sounded on the phone. And because she was very curious.

Donna got to the point right away. "My sister, Angela," she said. "She's disappeared."

"What?" said Jane, whose first thought was that Angela had taken off one step ahead of the law.

"Her husband doesn't know where she is. He showed up at the Stampede all by himself. At first he made up some excuse, but when I bugged him about it he said he doesn't know where she is. It's not like her. I have a feeling she's in some kind of trouble and hasn't told me about it. She's my baby sister and I worry about her and I wondered if you knew what she was mixed up in."

Donna sounded choked up and as if she were about to lose it. Jane spoke to her in a firm sort of voice. "I'll help you find her," she said. "I'm pretty close. In fact I'm in Electric City. Well, Coulee Dam, actually." Jane shuddered at the thought of getting back in the car and driving on to Pateros. "How about if I come to Pateros tomorrow. Maybe if we put our heads together we can figure out where she is."

Maybe, thought Jane, I can get the truth out of you about Angela. And your car. Maybe you'll be scared enough to tell me. And maybe I can snatch a little victory out of this whole thing by finding Angela before the cops do. Maybe there was some hope here, after all. "Do you want me to come over now?" said Jane. Maybe she shouldn't dawdle.

"I'm going on shift pretty soon," said Donna. "We're real busy 'cause of the Stampede. But if you want to come today, I guess you could stay at my place. There's no rooms in town right now, the place is packed." She paused. "Unless you want to stay with Jack again." She said it in a nice way.

"I wouldn't want to impose on his hospitality more than once," said Jane. "I'll come by in the morning and we can see what we can do. Is Angela's husband worried?"

"I think so. He seems like he's worried but he doesn't want to let on, you know?"

"I know," said Jane, imagining his stoic New England demeanor, and his face with those sad bright blue eyes. Angela Raleigh was one of those sulky, selfish people who nevertheless attracted devotion and so caused heartache; rings of trouble emanating from a stone splashed into the water.

After she hung up, Jane took off her clothes and tucked in between sheets smelling vaguely of antiseptic, and slept.

When she woke, it was because the phone was ringing. Why, she wondered crossly, wasn't it next to the bed? She went over to the bureau and picked it up on the third ring. "Hello," she said. There was a pause and whoever it was hung up. A wrong number, she supposed, seeing as no one knew where she was.

She was surprised to feel so refreshed. She couldn't remember her dreams, if she had had any. Now she was hungry and she wondered vaguely what to do about that. She had lost her sense of time. The bright light coming from the edges of the curtains was slanted in a way that made her think it was evening.

She took a tepid shower, lathering herself up with Lifebuoy soap and rinsing off for a long time until she felt completely awake. Then she dressed in a T-shirt and a cotton skirt, searched for a while for the room key, and went outside. Her car was sitting there and she decided she couldn't stand to get back in it. She'd walk until she found a restaurant somewhere.

Walking felt good. She hadn't been getting any decent exercise lately. Her path took her down quiet residential streets until she came to the main road through town. Across it was a riverfront park, a strip of green lined with pines, the dam looming overhead.

The place seemed to be jammed with little concession stands, as if some festival were going on. She crossed the road and went down a path. It was cooler down here. There were a lot of people, families mostly, in shorts and T-shirts.

She bought some noodle and beef mélange at a Thai stand and sat down in the grass, eating it with a plastic fork from a paper plate that kept buckling under the weight of the food. Maybe, she thought, she could get her energy level back up and drive on to Pateros. There was still the problem of a place to stay, however. Better to stay here. Which filled her with a kind of restlessness. What would she do, now that she was awake again? She wondered if the TV in her room had cable and regretted the fact she hadn't brought anything to read.

She watched a family go by, little kids, teenagers, an old lady in a wheelchair getting a bumpy ride over the grass. Who were all these people and what were they doing here? There was a sense that they were waiting for something. Perhaps it was the laser show Calvin had talked about.

She heard the sounds of a band setting up. Twangy guitars, scratchy mikes, screeching feedback. On the hill behind her, a zigzag path led up to a group of buildings. She remembered from a sign coming into town that this was the Visitors Center, presumably with old photographs of the dam's construction and models of turbines or something.

Dumping her fork and paper plate in a trash container and wiping her hands on the inadequate clump of shredded napkin and ditching it too, she decided she'd walk up that path, and maybe go further, up to the dam itself and look down into the gorge. The thought made her vaguely dizzy, but she needed a little project with a goal to keep herself from feeling melancholy. She had noticed that of all the people milling around at crafts booths and eating snacks, she was the only one alone. It wasn't that their lives appealed to her particularly, but something about the slanting rays of light and the dwarfing dam above and her own apartness all conspired to make her sad.

The band started playing. A walk out of the area was definitely in order. This was, she decided, the world's worst country-western band. They had just launched into a creaky cover of "Achy Breaky Heart" that was indeed heartbreaking.

The walk up the zigzag path, where little boys bolted to rush over the steep side of the hill, crashing through foliage despite their mothers' warnings, proved to be the beginning of a real workout.

By the time she made it to an upper parking lot, which seemed to be wall-to-wall Winnebagos with some big cruisemobiles and a clutch of Harley-Davidsons, complete with lounging old bikers with grizzled pony tails and their ill-nourished-looking tattooed women, the band had softened to the point where she just heard the throbbing bass and a reedy baritone voice. She hoped Jack Lawson and Electric City were better than that.

She stopped for some water from a fountain—there was a big piece of bright pink bubble gum in the basin—and kept on, climbing up the road to the dam itself, breaking a sweat and feeling the dust stirred up by the passing cars flying against her damp skin.

The scale had fooled her, and it was a longer walk than she thought. She glanced over her shoulder and discovered that she wasn't the only person alone.

Behind her, looking purposeful with his hands in his pockets, was a man in jeans and sneakers and a sweatshirt. She realized she'd seen him out of the corner of her eye when she was eating her Thai food down below. He made her vaguely uncomfortable.

26.

By the time she got to the top of the hill, he'd lagged back some and she was less nervous. She got up to the dam itself, decided the pump generator plant sounded boring, and headed the half mile or so to the center of the dam.

She quickened her pace and caught up with a huge family. In an increasingly familiar Pacific Rim scenario, some were white, some seemed to be Southeast Asian, and there were some Eurasian teenagers and babies. They were speaking both English and a language that was probably Vietnamese or Cambodian.

Beyond the streamlined steel rails, there was galvanized fencing that reached above her head most of the way. Still, Jane found herself walking over on the curb side of the sidewalk to avoid the feeling of being sucked down into the gorge. It looked about three hundred fifty feet down to the curving blue-gray Columbia. Jane tried to imagine it before the dam, when it was full of white water, churning its way to the Pacific.

On either side of the river were desolate strips of land: pale, rock-strewn shores. Beyond, on the left-hand side, was the bright green irrigated wedge of riverfront park, and on both sides were the two halves of the little town full of dark green trees, connected by the little bridge. The whole vista was surrounded by tall brown stone walls, like castles. Above, the huge sky was now turning pinkish as it grew darker.

At the center of the dam, underneath a sign marked "Spillway," the galvanized fencing was gone. Now there was just a brushed-steel Art Deco–looking rail that came to about Jane's chest but still seemed inadequate.

The family was taking pictures. A pretty young girl with reddish black hair and green almond-shaped eyes, carrying a baby sibling on her hip, strayed close to the railing, and peered down. A small Asian woman in a black sweatshirt emblazoned with the Chanel logo said in accented English: "Don't stand there with the baby, you're making me so nervous." Jane knew how she felt.

The group moved further along to where the dam turned at an angle, toward another squarish building, the right power plant. It was breezy walking the three tenths of a mile or so over to it; Jane felt more comfortable near them and there were people around there. She was aware that the man who'd walked up here after her was still behind her, leaning against the rail—something Jane's vertigo would never allow her to do—and smoking a cigarette.

When she got there, a few visitors were getting into their cars and driving away. The family had pushed through some heavy glass doors into a lobby, their voices echoing against the black-speckled terrazzo floors and plaster walls.

A glance over her shoulder told her the man was now headed her way, stopping for just a second to flick his cigarette over the dam. She saw its glow making a perfect arc in the dusk as it flew over the side.

The wide elevator doors were closing as she approached them. She pushed the button frantically, but the doors just kept closing.

She hoped the man hadn't changed his pace and she'd be able to catch up with the family, whom she now felt were somehow her saviors.

She took a deep breath and willed the elevator to make it back quickly. There wasn't any logical reason she should be fearing the man with the cigarette. Maybe she was being paranoid, shook up by the vertigo she had felt on top of the dam, by its monumental scale, which had left her feeling small and weak, by what she had learned in Electric City about random violence. Ella Mae Tinker minding her own business and ending up in that ditch.

The elevator arrived and took her down one floor. The doors opened to reveal another lobby with shiny black floors speckled with white, all shiny and waxy, and walls of beige, one on the left, another door on the right, and straight ahead, a wide archway leading to a room lined in a deep turquoise blue. The whole dam was apparently riddled with rooms and passages. From behind the door on the right, she heard footsteps coming down stairs.

There was a red phone next to the archway, but what excuse did she have to pick it up? Was it for emergencies? This wasn't an emergency, was it? Would anyone answer it after hours? If someone were stalking her and found her on that phone, would he leave her alone?

She went past it into the archway, which had looked so welcoming, but when she turned into the passage, she found it sealed off by a barred gate, padlocked shut. Beyond it she could see an interminable tunnel, with eerie lighting at intervals. It led deeper into the concrete of the dam.

She got back out, rolling as silently as possible on the balls of her feet across the noisy tile. She could hear the footsteps just outside the right-hand door now. She fled through the other door, which led to a ladies' room.

Here were more handsome marble walls and a tiny

frosted window. She tiptoed into one of the stalls, and stood crouching on one of the toilets. She heard feet thumping along the terrazzo floor toward the dead end arch she had discovered.

A second later, the feet came back. The door to the ladies' room opened. Hunched over with her arms wrapped around her knees, she saw a pair of men's shoes. Now she knew she had reason to be frightened. She was sure he could hear her heart pounding in her chest, sure he'd check the stalls, grab her, throw her down on the hard tile. The shoes bounced there for a minute, like a basketball player full of energy deciding which way to pivot, and then he left. She heard the door slam and the other door off the lobby creaking open.

She supposed she should stay where she was, but she felt cornered. Her choices—vertigo on top of the dam, claustrophobia within it—were both horrible. The thing to do was find other people.

She climbed off the toilet, crept back out into the hall, summoned the elevator, waited what seemed like forever until it came, then got inside and pushed 1, clearly marked "Top of Dam."

But it was too late. Someone had already called it down one more floor. It churned into action, making ominous hydraulic sounds. Going deeper into the dam wasn't what she had in mind. She eyed the elevator phone and toyed with the idea of picking it up. No, she'd see if he was there when she arrived. Grabbing the phone then might deter him if he really meant her harm.

He wasn't there. Neither was anyone else. She took a deep breath. To her right was another archway, trimmed with some pretty ceramic fluting. This one wasn't sealed off. It was the opening to a round-ceilinged tunnel, and sloped down, the whole passageway lined with more blue tiles—these lighter ones of aquamarine, which gave them an underwater look. The tunnel was lit with a long strip of fluo-rescent lighting down the middle of the ceiling.

Did she want to go down, or turn around and go back up in the elevator? Or find the stairs and go up that way? No, not the stairs. Alone in a stairwell sounded the most omi-nous.

She thought she heard voices at the bottom of the tunnel. That made her decision for her.

She worked her way eagerly toward those voices. On the way down, she told herself to get a grip. Perhaps she was imagining she was being stalked. Like that nutty English-woman going berserk in the caves in *Passage to India*. If any-thing happened, she'd scream. (She wasn't sure she could bring herself to do this, but she told herself to give it a try.) With all these incredible surfaces—tile, terrazzo, marble—the place was a regular echo chamber.

She felt the tunnel closing in on her and experienced a surge of relief when it ended. Now she was in a nice open, airier space lined with beautiful rosy pink marble. Really, they built quality back then, no doubt about it. She heard the voices, English and that other language, behind a shiny black door.

She opened the door and there they were in a dim room. Black walls with lit-up display cases featuring masses of ar-rowheads. She made out the mom and dad, and a grand-mother and somebody's boyfriend and the Eurasian teenager with the green eyes and the baby. She felt like embracing them all, but instead she smiled a little greeting and feigned interest in the backlit displays of Indian artifacts lining the walls and on a central table. Her eyes tried to adjust.

The family began to file out and she, calm now, and chalking her feelings up to some sort of panic attack, lin-gered just a little so they wouldn't think she was stalking them.

As the last of them filed out and the door gently closed, she gave herself a beat to go after them. Then he stepped out of the shadows of the room.

Somehow, he'd found the darkest corner of that dim room. Now they were alone. She lunged toward the door but he put out a hand a few inches in front of her. She froze, not wanting to let him touch her.

"Hey," he said. "I just want to talk."

"Sorry," she said, wondering if this was just some clumsy pick-up attempt. Somebody should tell this oaf that stepping out of dark corners wasn't the best way to initiate a conversation. She got a better look at him now. Maybe thirty. Crisp dark red hair. Moonlike sunburned face. Stupid grin. A big guy, powerfully built with a barrellike chest and short tree-trunk legs in faded jeans. The kind of guy you'd want as the anchor on a tug-of-war team.

"I have to go," she said. The door opened and an elderly couple walked in. Jane slipped out behind them and the man got momentarily tangled up with them.

She just made it into the elevator with the Eurasian family as he followed her out of the artifact room. She saw his face, red and angry, as the doors closed, and caught just a brief glimpse of him turning to race up the ramp.

He wasn't waiting at the top of the elevator. She walked out the upper lobby with the family. There were so many of them they didn't seem to notice her. But as they all emerged with her from the lobby, to her horror, she realized they were all piling into some squarish, green vehicle. Where had that come from? Maybe they'd parked it here before. And now she was about to be alone with someone who knew she was afraid.

As soon as the big family pulled away, he came out of the glass doors and smiled at her.

27.

She found herself smiling nervously back. Was it a reflex? But what else was she to do?

"I just want to talk to you," he said.

"What about?" She stepped back a pace, then, deciding that fearful gestures were unwise, she straightened up and stood tall with her feet planted apart, her arms relaxed at her sides.

"You have some money that doesn't belong to you," he said.

"I do? You must be confusing me with someone else."

"Nope." He crossed his arms across his chest. "You took some money for dropping a case, and now you're up here still messing with it. Unless you're here to check out the laser show tonight, which I seriously doubt." He said this last in a kind of simpering, smart-alec tone that made her want to smack him.

"Who sent you?" she said. The breeze came up again from the gorge, lifting up her hair and blowing it into her eyes. She brushed it away with an impatient gesture. "Look," she said, "I'll be glad to discuss this with whoever sent you." Who *had* sent him? It had to be either Mr. or Mrs. Raleigh. "I'm sure we can work this out. If they want, I'll be glad to return the money." She avoided saying "to him" or "to her." "I didn't really earn it," she added, giving him a level gaze, "so I'll be glad to return it."

"Good," he said.

"I don't have the money with me," she added.

"Bad," he replied.

"Hey, I'll take care of it," she said.

"Bad for you." He smiled again. There was a little gap between his front teeth.

There didn't seem to be much more to say. She realized that he was the one who had called her in her motel room. It was pretty easy to find someone in Coulee Dam. Just call the handful of motels and ask for a guest named Jane da Silva.

But who had known she was in this town, in the first place? Only two people. Calvin Mason and Donna Mac-Laine. She'd told Donna she was in Electric City, then corrected herself and said Coulee Dam. A big mistake. She was always telling Donna too much.

"How do you want to handle this?" she said, trying to make it sound like a simple, routine transaction. Like returning something to a store.

"You're the one who screwed up," he said, stepping toward her. She held her ground, even though she didn't like being this close to him. "You'll have to figure it out," he said with that same irritating simper.

She gave a little female tongue click that signaled impatience and derision. She knew at once that he didn't like that at all. He made his hands into fists and scowled. He had a stupid face, a pumpkinlike sort of face with wide cheeks sprinkled with the remains of some adolescent acne.

"I can arrange to have it sent by Fed Ex," she said.

A look of incomprehension flitted across his face. She guessed it was because he didn't know that "Fed Ex" was short for Federal Express. Why should he? He didn't look like the kind of guy who stepped out of his office and said, "Madge, could you have this Fed-Exed to the East Coast?"

"Have like a messenger service send it," she said, trying to sound less educated and therefore less irritating. Americans denied it, but they had speech patterns and accents denoting class just like everyone else.

"They can get it here real fast," she added. "Or direct to whoever wants it."

"My instructions were to scare you real good first," he said, as if he were going over his orders and savoring them. "Real good."

He stepped forward and took her by the forearms.

"Hey!" she said with a nervous little laugh. "You don't need to do that. I'm already scared. Okay? I'm giving back the money. I can go back to town and make a phone call and we can get it all arranged. Then I'll drop the whole thing. Tell them that. I'll drop the whole thing. For real." She wasn't really lying. She would drop the whole thing. After she told the police everything she knew.

She was talking too much and too fast. She tried to shake him off, but he just tightened his grip. His face was very close to hers right now. She saw what seemed like every pore in his face. He had the beginnings of crow's-feet—white lines in his florid skin radiating out from small blue eyes.

"I noticed you don't like heights," he said. "When you were walkin' along here, you kept pretty far from that railing." He pulled her closer to the railing now, away from the curb. She felt her stomach lurching, like in an elevator.

With a puff of exertion, he adjusted his arms, pinning them around her in a bear hug. He was using much more strength than he needed. She was being squeezed slowly but tightly. She felt his breath on her face. He clearly enjoyed bullying her.

He dragged her an inch or two closer to the railing.

She swiveled her head as well as she could to see around her. There was no one nearby. Just a little knot of tourists further away.

From that vantage point, she imagined they looked like some cute couple playing around. It was just the sort of sadistic horseplay in which courting couples sometimes indulged.

He held her so her face looked down the gorge. She screamed, an involuntary shriek, and he laughed. Which just added to the perception of a couple of crazy kids fooling around. She didn't like her scream. It sounded flighty and helpless. She wished she could come up with a serious Wagnerian scream that would startle him and get everyone's attention. She wasn't a good screamer.

Instead, she took a deep breath and said, "If you kill me, I can't pay up, can I?" She tried to will her shoes to cling to the pavement. He was pushing her the final few inches to the railing, lifting her a little to eliminate drag, as if he were muscling an unwieldy package around a loading dock. She felt her toes grazing the cement beneath her and then got her back smashed against the rail. She felt a jolt of impact, then the cold, smooth metal.

"If I fall," she said, "you'll go to prison."

"I'll tell them I was trying to stop you from jumping. I'm a local boy. I was just walking around up here for some fresh air." He was speaking to her through clenched teeth now, and she heard the anger in his voice and felt it in the arms pinning her own arms close to her body. Her breasts were smashed against his chest. Why was he so angry?

"I see this crazy lady tourist from Seattle," he continued. "She comes up here all by herself. To end it all. Maybe she's in love or something."

"Please," she said. "Leave me alone. I'll do whatever you want."

He was lifting her now. She tried to hook her feet over the bottom rail, but she lost her footing. He lifted her some more, then he let go of her with one arm and tilted her backward over the rail.

Instinctively, she clung to him with her arm that was now free, and curled her head forward, toward him and away from the gorge.

"Don't do that," he said. "I want you to put your head back." He tilted his own head back just a little to demonstrate. He sounded like a lover, making a tender, wheedling request in an intimate moment.

Tears formed in her eyes. Her throat was constricted. "I can't," she said.

"Relax," he said. "I won't drop you. Trust me."

Maybe if she did as he asked he'd let her back, away from the rail. Slowly, trembling, and now, perversely, clinging to him, she tilted her head backward so that her hair tumbled down, away from her face into the emptiness.

"That's right," he said with satisfaction.

The blood rushed to her head. He inched her up just another inch. She decided she was ready to fall, wondered how much consciousness she would have on the way down. She wished she could scream on the way down. Suicides never screamed, did they? Then he'd be held responsible.

But who would hear her?

"Please," she said, trying to keep some dignity in her tone—hoping that some dignity in her would allow him to find it in himself to treat her with respect.

"Say it again," he said, like a cruel child. "Say pretty please. Pretty please, Travis."

"Pretty please, Travis," she said, like someone learning a language, pronouncing each word carefully, hoping to God he would like the way she said it.

A second later, just as she thought she'd mercifully faint

and slip from his grasp without consciousness, he lifted her up another inch, then slammed her down hard on the balls of her feet, her shoulder blades against the railing.

He let her go, but to her disgust, she clung to him for an instant longer until she was sure she was on firm ground.

He shrugged her off, and looked at her with disgust.

She felt a sudden wave of nausea, and began to slither back down the rail to his feet.

He yanked her back up. "Go back to your motel room," he said. "I'll call you there in an hour or so. We can work out the details." And then he turned and walked away.

28.

You must, she told herself, pull yourself together. She was shivering and there was a bitter taste in her mouth. She felt like collapsing, sinking back down—partly to be as close to the ground as possible until her vertigo went away (she wasn't sure it ever would go away) and partly to let her body get back to normal. Fear had covered her in a coat of stabbing, crawling little prickles.

But she forced herself to stay standing and took deep breaths as she watched her tormentor walk away with a jaunty little gait. He paused for a second to light a cigarette, then resumed his strolling.

She couldn't remember ever having felt hate surge within her as it was doing now. In fact, it seemed to be replacing the fear.

Strength was all a person like Travis could understand. If through some miracle she had the strength right now, she knew she would enjoy his fear as much as he had enjoyed hers. But she wouldn't torture him. She would just pluck him up and throw him over the railing and watch his burly body becoming smaller and smaller, a tiny silhouette, arms extended, until he was driven into the cement and his broken, bloody body bounced into the steel blue water and drifted lazily downstream. She knew if she could, she'd do it in an instant.

But she couldn't. She would instead have to think very hard. Like some crafty, weak little animal. Which, she reflected, was exactly what she was when facing someone like Travis—a big, cruel animal whom nature had messily and unfairly given the strength to humiliate and do harm.

She began to pace a little, staying where she was, still watching him walk away from her, wanting to do nothing to decrease the distance between them.

She supposed she should call the police. She didn't want to, though. For one thing, it would take an inordinate amount of time and require long explanations. And even if she managed to get them to arrest him, he would be let out, pending a trial.

Secondly, he would see her as weak still. As someone working through channels that he didn't need to bother with because he had not only the strength to terrorize but the will, even the desire. That was the aspect of the whole thing that had made her gag, that had given her the feeling of nausea: the cloying overtones of lust, the hideous intimacy, his bending her back over the railing as if part of some erotic passage from the tango, his mastering her completely.

The only thing a beast like Travis would understand was another beast, humiliating him. She must arrange it.

In the end, she didn't have to walk back to her motel. A pickup truck with a crest on the door came by. It seemed to be part of the Bureau of Reclamation that ran the dam. There was a young woman in some kind of uniform at the wheel, and Jane convinced her that she had turned her ankle and managed to get a lift.

At first the woman had looked dubious, as if she thought there would be reports to fill out, and somehow her department would be accepting some kind of liability, but Jane reassured her, saying it was an old injury that had kicked up. "All right, get in. I'll run you down to the Visitors Center," she said. "But it's not official or anything."

"I really appreciate it," said Jane, who leaned way back in the cab as they passed Travis on the way down. She didn't think he saw her and she was glad of a head start.

Back at the motel, Jane went immediately to the office.

The owner, a plump lady with a squint in one eye, came out from her lair to the front desk. Jane got a glimpse of the room from which she had emerged. Rows of Reader's Digest Condensed Books and a plaster statue of the Blessed Virgin Mary, as well as a TV and a sofa with a crocheted afghan on it. The kind Irene March might have run up on the bus to work.

"I need my room changed," said Jane.

"Well it's kind of a hassle for us," began the woman. "What's wrong with your room?"

Jane thought of complaining about the baby, but couldn't bring herself to do it because she liked babies and in any case decided she'd better come up with something more solid.

"The room's fine," said Jane. "But my husband's coming up to join me and he's very superstitious. He'll never be happy in 213."

The woman looked irritated, so Jane added, "I keep telling him that a good Catholic doesn't need to be superstitious, but that's just the way he is."

Jane could sense the woman softening a little, but to hurry things along (she wasn't sure how long it would take Travis on foot) she slapped down a twenty-dollar bill.

The woman pushed it back. "That won't be necessary," she said. She handed Jane another key.

Jane thanked her and added, "I may be getting a phone

call, but I hope you won't let anyone know my room number. I'm a little nervous on my own." She allowed her hand to flutter helplessly over her breastbone for a second. "I'll be glad when my husband arrives. Give him another key, all right? You can't miss him. He's a real big guy. A Samoan. You know, like a big Hawaiian?"

She made quick work of her move and flung herself into her new room. It was on the second floor again, thank God. She could imagine Travis and his big fists plunging through the aluminum frame windows on the first floor with horrifying ease.

She figured she had an hour to make it all come together. She put the chain on the door, which looked flimsy and hollow, and then, even though she knew it was ridiculous, she pushed the bureau laboriously over to the door, dragging it across the heavy, spongy carpet.

It took time she could have used, but in a strange way the physical exertion allowed her to take some of that angry energy that was still coursing through her, and focus it on one simple task.

That done, she went to the phone, and started to work.

First, she called the local airport, then she called Boeing Field in Seattle. After a few more calls there, she called Calvin Mason, praying that he was home as she heard the phone ring. Her prayers were answered. He didn't even hide behind the machine as was his craven habit.

She started out defensively. "Don't ask, please," she said. "And don't lecture me. But please, just do what I say as fast as you can. I'll explain it all later and make it well worth your while."

The seriousness of her tone seemed to work. The hardest part was asking him to put together a duplicate of the envelope she'd taken from Hank Raleigh.

"Seven thousand!" he said. "That's a lot of cash."

"Yes, but you'll be holding the original cash in its original envelope. I want you to hang on to it because I'm sure his prints are on it. His hand was all clammy. And then I can prove he tried to bribe me if I have to."

"Jane," he began ominously. "Since when are you an expert fingerprint technician?"

"I'm doing the best I can," she said. "Please don't give me any grief."

"Okay, okay," he said. "What about the check?"

"Xerox it," she said. "Keep the copy, and put the original in a large manila envelope with the other envelope." Jane was going to throw all the Raleighs' money back at them. It didn't seem prudent to keep it after what she'd been through. But she didn't want to give it to Travis. She'd return it in person and let them know she wasn't going to cover for them anymore. Not after what she had learned in Electric City.

And when she'd given them back their money, she would tell the police everything she knew. Whether it was enough to connect them to the deaths of Ella Mae and Irene, she wasn't sure, but she was very weary, and she felt ready to call the police and retire from the fray—defeated for now.

"I'll call you back when I know what I want you to do with the package," she said. "Are you going to be around for a while?"

Calvin said he would, and she thanked him and tried Bob Manalatu's number and his beeper number. He called her back after twenty minutes. She explained what she wanted him to do.

"Okay," he said calmly. "This guy messed with you real bad. I can hear that in your voice. We'll take care of the problem. There's only one part I don't like."

Please, she thought. Don't go squeamish on me now. "I

really don't think the guy will be a problem," said Jane. By which she meant Bob outweighed him about two to one.

"I'm not worried about some weenie who picks on girls, shit!" said Bob. "The thing is, Jane, I really hate to fly."

She took a deep breath. "An extra thousand." She was counting on the fact that he was still behind on his gym bill. "And we can rent you a car to drive back in if you want."

"No, I gotta get back 'cause our band is playing at a wedding," he said.

"Have you ever flown before?" she said.

"Sure. How you think I got here from Samoa? They wedged me in that little seat and it was white knuckles the whole way, I gotta tell ya."

"You weren't more scared than I was when he dangled me over that dam," she said.

"He scared you pretty good, huh?"

"First he scared me. Then he made me madder than I can ever remember being. So I called you."

"Okay," said Bob. "An extra thousand. I fly."

She told him to stay by the phone while she got the last details nailed down and called Calvin back.

"Okay," Calvin reported. "I cleaned out my trust account, so we must get everything back in there in a reasonable amount of time. Guys have been disbarred for pulling this stunt."

She reassured and thanked him and then she said, "Can you pack it all up, deliver it to Bob and take him to Boeing Field?" She gave him the charter information. "And could you do one more thing?"

He sounded wary.

"Send along a bottle of booze with him. Hard stuff."

"No mini-bar in the room?" he said.

"It's not for me," she said.

He sighed heavily. "Want to tell me what you're doing?"

"I think it might not be legal," she said.

"Then don't tell me. I'll deliver Bob, bucks and booze to Boeing Field. And you can fill me in later."

She wondered if she had been driven mad. Surely what she was planning now wasn't what Uncle Harold had wanted for her.

"Jane, you'll tell me as soon as you can, won't you?" he said. And then he added with what almost sounded like a little jolt of anguish, "I trust I'm not doing anything that will cause you to come to harm."

"You'll have to let me decide for myself what's best," she said.

"All right," he said. "What kind of booze do you want? I'll stop by the liquor store on my way. All I've got is a case of Rainier."

"Tequila, I think," said Jane.

29.

She lay down on the bed and, not for the first time in her life, prayed for God to let her get away with something that was wrong. Just this once—I won't ask again. Which she knew was a lie. She felt a jittery sort of peace for a moment, and then the phone rang.

It was Travis, who didn't bother to introduce himself.

"When can you get the money?" he said.

"It's on its way," she said. "About an hour and a half."

"I'm in the parking lot outside your motel," he said. "I'm watching your car so you can't leave."

"I'll find you there when it arrives." She hung up on him. She certainly wasn't going to coo "Bye, bye" into the phone.

Jane went to the window. She didn't want to let him see a flicker of curtain so he'd know what room she was in. The curtain was already open a crack. She placed herself in front of the mirror, and was able to see him this way. He was standing in a phone booth and talking on the phone.

He wasn't talking to her anymore, so she imagined he was reporting back to his employer. She imagined it was the male half of the Raleigh ménage. For one thing, Donna had said Angela was missing. Presumably, Donna had told her brother-in-law where Jane was.

Or had that missing Angela story been a ruse? Jane felt that Donna's real loyalty lay with her sister. After having met both of them, Jane thought it was more Angela's style than her husband's to employ some crude jerk like Travis. And he had said he was local, which also pointed to Angela, who had grown up around here. Maybe he was some inbred cousin or something.

In the mirror she saw Travis leave the phone booth and walk over to a pickup truck. She wished she had the license number in case Travis bolted before she had a chance to find out who sent him.

Then she collapsed back on the bed and stared at the cottage cheese ceiling some more, while outside the light changed to darkness.

She heard the key in the lock about two hours later, according to the digital alarm clock on the bedside table. She rushed to the door, fearing for a mad moment that the woman at the desk had given the key to Travis. The door was open now, the chain taut. She got a glimpse through the open door: satiny brown skin, black hair, a flash of perfect white teeth.

"Hang on," she said, believing Bob was perfectly capable of yanking the chain off by its screws. She wrestled the bureau away and let him in. He was wearing a hot pink T-shirt and voluminous black and white plaid shorts and carrying a canvas satchel. His calves looked like bowling pins.

He came inside and she locked the door after him. He sat down on an upholstered chair, billowing over onto the arm rests.

"How was the flight?" she asked.

"Not so bad. I thought it would be worse. Definitely worth a grand." He flashed her a smile and set down his satchel.

"And they had the courtesy car waiting for you?"

"Yeah. Big old Buick station wagon. Nice big car. So where's the guy?"

"In the parking lot."

"Chevy pickup? Kind of orange hair?"

"That's right."

Bob nodded. "I checked out the area. We're right up against a little park, and there's a dried-up creek behind it. Tell me exactly what you want."

She took a deep breath. "I want him to be scared."

"No problem," said Bob. He was rummaging around a little in his satchel, then handed her a manila envelope and a bottle of tequila.

"And I want him to tell me who hired him to scare me," Jane continued. "I figure it's one of two people. I want to know which one."

"Okay." Bob looked thoughtful and produced a can of Spam and a loaf of bread from the satchel. "You can ask the question. But if you think he might lie, the thing is to go slow. Make him real eager to tell you. Like you don't care if he gets hurt instead of telling you." Bob was now wielding a can opener. "They never have the kind of food I like in places like this," he said.

Jane watched as he made himself a sandwich. Pacific Island people were notoriously crazy about Spam. Maybe it went back to prerefrigeration days when boats brought this stuff to them and weaned them off taro root or whatever they had been eating up to then. "Want some?" he asked.

"No thanks," she said.

Jane removed the check and the envelope from the larger envelope and replaced them with the tourist guide to the Grand Coulee Dam area. The originals, she slipped between the mattress and the box spring.

"Anyway," said Bob, eating contentedly, "I figure we can muscle him down to that creek bed. As good a place as any."

Absurdly, she hadn't figured out where they'd terrorize Travis. Clearly her room wouldn't do.

Just then, a huge voice boomed through the window.

Bob killed the lights, went over to the window and pulled back the curtains.

"Wow," he said. "Take a look at that."

"But he's out there," said Jane.

"He can't see a thing when we have the lights out," said Bob. "Look." He pointed to the dam. She hadn't realized they had a spectacular view.

The spillway, which had been bone-dry earlier, was now gushing a wall of white water. She could hear its roar. It was all lit up, almost as if from behind, so it served as a giant screen. "Fresh!" said Bob appreciatively, polishing off the last of his snack.

"I am the Columbia," intoned a godlike voice, as images projected on the rushing white water depicted stylized waves and fish and animals of monumental proportions. The voice of the Columbia, which, besides sounding like God also sounded like an old-time announcer from the golden days of radio, named all the tribes who had lived along his shores. It was the sort of thing, reflected Jane, that they would only think of doing here in America. The effect was sort of like a giant drive-in movie showing an outsized, animated educational film.

"That should keep everyone in town busy," said Bob. "Let's go."

"No marks," said Jane.

"No marks," he agreed.

She took the bottle of tequila and put it in Bob's canvas bag with the envelope. In the parking lot, Travis was clearly taken aback to see her in the company of a man who looked like a sumo wrestler. He flinched a little behind the wheel of his truck.

Jane went up to the window, which he cranked down.

"Come on out and I'll give you the envelope," she said, flapping the tourist guide in its envelope in his face.

"Just hand it over," he said with a scowl.

"You heard her," said Bob. He reached over and yanked on the truck's door handle, opened the door, then grabbed Travis by the collar and pulled him out.

He came tumbling out from behind the wheel, landing on his feet and bobbing a little for a second. Jane scanned the parking lot nervously. There didn't seem to be anyone around.

"Hey," said Bob. "Let's go for a little stroll."

"Just wait a sec," said Travis.

"You want to come easy or hard?" said Bob. He didn't wait for an answer. Instead, he pinned one of Travis's arms behind him and gave it a little tug.

Travis gave Jane a look that could kill.

"Don't look at me," said Jane with a helpless gesture. "I can't always control the big guy."

Bob was now frog-marching Travis across the parking lot, across the street and over a ditch into the little park. Jane had to trot to keep up.

"The lady says you tried to scare her," said Bob. She liked that, his adding "tried." Bob really did have lovely manners and a lot of tact.

Travis didn't say anything. Jane noted with pleasure that he looked resigned. His head was down a little, like a dog that knows it's going to get kicked.

They crossed a green strip of lawn and passed a tennis court with a sagging net. From beyond some locust trees they could hear the laser show rumbling on.

There was a little gravel path that led from the park. As Bob jerked Travis toward it, Jane could see Travis begin to panic, thrashing around as if he suspected he was going to be killed.

"Hey!" barked Bob. "If you do what the lady says, I'll only hit you once. Think of that as something to work towards. A goal like."

Travis looked as if he might dissolve into a whimper any minute now. Bob fell silent and so did Jane. The silent treatment ought to soften him up a little.

They went across a path that led to a little foot bridge, where their feet made a wooden blonking sound that echoed down the little creek bed below. Once they crossed it, Bob left the path, dragging Travis down so that they stood beneath the bridge.

As her eyes adjusted to the dark, Jane saw none of the bright green she'd associated with the irrigated land around her, nor the desert vegetation of sage and bunchgrass. Here there was a thick, prickly profusion of strange shrubs and tall grasses and wildflowers, growing out from among boulders and sandy soil. This must be what happened naturally when a spring or a creek appeared in the desert landscape. The place also seemed to be teeming with insects.

Bob let Travis loose for just an instant, then, to Jane's horror, he drew back one of his big glossy arms and backhanded the other man, sending him tumbling backward against one of the supports for the bridge, then falling over into tall weeds.

"We need to know something," he said.

Travis got up slowly, looked into Bob's face, then stepped back a pace. His nose was bleeding. He dabbed at it with the back of his hand. He examined the scarlet streak there, snuffled a little and tilted his head back.

"What is it you wanted to know?" he said.

"Who hired you?" said Jane. "Who wants their money back?"

"What's the big deal, anyway?" said Travis, rubbing his face with his other hand.

"Just a simple question," said Jane.

"Hey, you want to work me over, go right ahead," said Travis. "I can take a lot. My old man started me really early. Toughened me up. Okay?"

"Don't be stupid, Travis," said Jane. "Why not tell us sooner rather than later?"

"I had a deal with the guy," said Travis. "A deal's a deal, right?"

"The sniveling picture of you, trying to do the right thing and pretending you know how to behave honorably is really pathetic," said Jane, who, thanks to Travis's choice of noun ("the guy") was now pretty certain she knew who had hired him.

"Don't be as stupid as you look, Travis," said Bob. "How'd you like a couple of bleeding ears to go with that bloody nose?"

"So you're just going to keep hitting me?" said Travis.

"Nothing messy," said Jane, who was beginning to wonder if she had the stomach for revenge. She couldn't deny, though, that she had enjoyed seeing him down in the weeds.

"I got something else in mind for Travis," said Bob. "Something that won't leave a mark."

"Yeah?" said Travis. It was almost as if he had a professional interest.

"You play football in high school?" said Bob.

"Yeah," said Travis looking up at him warily.

"Well, we had this game with Garfield," said Bob. "I tackled this big guy and messed up his arm and shoulder real bad. Turns out I dislocated his shoulder. Popped it right out. Like a ball joint kind of thing."

Bob advanced on Travis and stroked his shoulder. Travis brushed it off, looking disgusted. Bob didn't get mad, though. Jane imagined Bob never actually got mad. He didn't have to.

"So," he said, continuing his narrative, "the guy was laying there screaming. Big tough guy, he's been through a lot, but I swear, if he had a gun he would have killed himself to end the pain. Until the doctor popped it back in."

Travis gave Jane a calculating look. He was wondering, she imagined, whether she had the stomach to let him do it.

"He's got the technique down pretty good," said Jane. "It's kind of his specialty. Just wrench a little, then bam. You're in agony."

"It's all in the wrist," said Bob, lowering his velvety lashes modestly. "At first I just kind of pulled at it and twisted it. That's not the same thing. You tear up ligaments and stuff. But now I got it down real good. You just lay there screaming, like I said. And when you manage to tell us, like between screams, what she wants to hear, then I pop it back in for you.

"And you know what, Travis? It's funny, but after I do that for you, even after what I did before, you'll think I'm the greatest guy in the world."

"If I scream, someone might come," he said.

Bob laughed. "Then we'll tell them what you were up to at the dam. Get you booked for felonious assault or something. Then you go to Walla Walla where some of my friends are. And we mention how sad it was you fell off the bridge and dislocated your shoulder. Of course then you'll have to wait for the ambulance or whatever they got here. It'll be faster if you let me pop it back in."

"Well hell," said Travis, "if she's so dumb she doesn't know who she stiffed—"

Jane stepped forward. She wanted to slap him, but Bob got there first. "I'll do the left, Travis," he said. "That way, if there's any permanent damage it won't be so bad. You are right-handed, aren't you? If you're left-handed I'll do the right side."

"Fuck!" said Travis. "You guys are fucking nuts. It's Raleigh. Hank Raleigh. Okay? But if he asks, I'm telling him I didn't tell you nothing you didn't already know."

Jane took the tequila out of her bag. "Have a drink, Travis," she said.

30.

Travis took the bottle and took a swig. "Look," he said, "if it's okay with you, I'd like to go."

"Sorry," said Jane. "You've got a lot of catching up to do. Have some more."

"No," said Travis, handing her the bottle. "I just want to get out of here. You can understand that, can't you? I told you what you want to know."

"She wants you to drink some more," said Bob.

Travis shrugged and took another sip.

"You'll have to do better than that," said Jane. "We're not leaving till you're on your lips."

"Hey, why don't you just let me go?" said Travis, a whine creeping into his voice. "I'm sorry I scared her. Let's just forget about it."

"I'm not forgetting what you did," said Bob. "I wanted to teach you a lesson about picking on women. She wouldn't let me. But if you ever come near her again, if I hear you ever pulled anything like what you pulled today, I'm coming after you. Me and some guys I hang with. And we're going to squash you like a damn bug on a windshield."

Travis nodded as if he were getting a lecture from a traffic cop in lieu of a ticket.

"You're not drinking fast enough," said Jane.

"I'm disappointed," said Bob. "A big tough guy like you. You should be able to chug that whole bottle in just a few seconds."

He stepped toward him and put Travis in some kind of a head lock and poured tequila into his mouth. Travis sputtered and coughed and seemed to be getting about half of it down. Then he started to gag.

"You might choke him," said Jane. Bob set him loose. Travis took the bottle and went over to a rock and sat there drinking it as fast as he could with his eyes screwed shut. He gagged again, and Jane told him to take it easy for a few minutes, and he set the bottle down. It was half empty and Travis was red in the face. He began to bat at a cloud of mosquitoes.

"How about just a little more?" said Jane.

Bob advanced toward him and he took a few more sips hastily, ducking down so Bob wouldn't hurt him.

"We can't let him drive," said Jane.

"Keys," barked Bob.

Travis, his movements now fluid, his head bobbing, dug in his jeans pocket. Jane took the keys and with a rather jubilant feeling pitched them as far as she could into the darkness. About twenty feet ahead of her in the dark, she heard a jangle and the rustle of weeds as they landed.

Travis, listing now, didn't even bother to look at which direction she was throwing them. His eyes were at half mast.

She turned to Bob. "This way I figure he gets slowed down, and if he comes up with any story about us, he's hardly a credible witness. They'll probably find him here in the morning. If he doesn't crawl out on his own."

Travis seemed to be weeping now. Jane watched him drink a few more swigs, then followed him with her eyes as he slipped off his rock and into a fetal position in some tall grass. She prodded him with her toe. He seemed semi-comatose. She picked up the bottle and sprinkled some more of its contents over his body, then wiped it off with her sleeve and lay it beside him.

She and Bob went back across the bridge and through the quiet little park. "I guess we missed most of the laser show," said Bob, sounding disappointed.

"We can probably catch some of it," said Jane.

They left the little city park, went down a few curving lanes and entered the big riverfront park. Here, they were surrounded by families wrapped in blankets and sitting on lawn chairs.

They found a spot on the damp lawn and looked up at the screen of rushing water and saw colored line drawings of turbines and running water and apples being irrigated and Roosevelt and Lincoln and American eagles. They learned how the dam generated enough electricity to help Boeing back in Seattle build bombers and help the Allies beat the Axis. Jane looked over at Bob, who was studying the screen with rapt attention.

At one point, it became filled with abstract shapes, like early computer graphics, and the godlike narrator's voice went away, replaced by twangy electronic music. It was an odd juxtaposition of heroic thirties imagery and seventies high tech. Bob started to laugh. "Meanwhile, back at the disco," he said.

"Is that true?" she whispered. "Did you dislocate some guy's shoulder in a game with Garfield?"

"No," he said. "I changed it a little. Actually, it happened to me. It really hurt bad. But I don't know if I could do it to someone else. To tell you the truth, it's never come up." He looked over at her. "I hardly ever have to hurt anybody. I didn't have to hit him, but I felt like it after you told me what he did."

Jane thought about Travis. Passed out. Being eaten by mosquitoes. In the morning he'd have a horrible hangover. His mouth would taste like tequila and wool and his head would pound.

"You think he'll be okay?" she said.

"He got off pretty easy," said Bob. "The thing is, there's guys that have no respect for ladies. And guys like that, the only way to put the brakes on 'em is force. It's the only thing they get. The only thing. Forget restraining orders and that shit. I can guarantee you, he'll never mess with you again."

The laser show came to an end, and the tourists streamed back up from the river to their cars and campers. There was a little traffic jam on the main road through town as the place cleared out, but by the time Jane had said goodbye to Bob, thrown out the fake envelope, retrieved the real one from under the mattress, checked out and set out for Pateros, things were quiet once again.

The drive to Pateros took about an hour. Jane got behind a big semi and followed its lights most of the way. From there, it was a short run south on 97 to the restaurant where Donna worked. And, according to the dashboard clock, she was due off shift in about twenty minutes.

The navy Corvette was parked outside. The dining room was dead, but there were a few people at the counter, and there was a lot of noise coming from the bar. Jane found Donna there, polishing glasses.

She went and sat at the bar, and caught her eye.

"Wow," said Donna. "You made it. Listen, Jane, I would have called you back but I wasn't sure where you were."

"Oh, really?" said Jane. She decided not to tell her about

Travis. If she knew he'd been sent after her, let her guess what happened.

Donna's eyes widened. "Listen, Jane, the reason I wanted to call you is to tell you my sister showed up again. Want a beer or something?"

"Sure," said Jane.

Donna yanked on a spigot and plonked down a foamy glass in front of Jane. "She finally called. Said she had a spat with her husband." Donna had lowered her voice for this last revelation and was leaning over the bar. "I'm going to see her tomorrow at the royalty breakfast over at the Elks."

"Royalty breakfast?" said Jane.

"Well, ex-royalty too," said Donna. Jane had a flash of a roomful of pretenders to various European thrones, leftover Romanovs and Hapsburgs, in white tie and tails, bristling with moth-eaten egret feathers and tarnished tiaras, all working their way through hash browns with ketchup and greasy fried eggs on long Formica tables down at the Elks Club.

"Ex-rodeo royalty," said Donna. "We're all having a sort of reunion. Angela said she'd be there. I shouldn't have panicked but I worry about her." She flitted off sideways and slammed another couple of beers on the bar further down, then flitted back and picked up where she'd left off. "Because of all this weird Irene March stuff and all."

"Yeah," said Jane. "Things have been weird." She wasn't about to tell Donna she thought her sister might have killed Irene. That she was the right height and she had a strong motive. She'd let the police handle all that. Nor was she about to suggest to Donna that her sister might previously have killed Ella Mae Tinker with her pink Corvette.

"Listen," said Donna, "did you come all the way out here to try and help me?"

"That's right," said Jane. Finding Donna had been her

last, pathetic attempt to find some wrong worth righting. Now Jane would have to face the fact that she was simply going to hand over all her suspicions to the police and back out of the whole thing.

"Gosh, that's real nice," said Donna. "And here you came for nothing. Listen, you want to stay at my place? I can get the kids to double up. There's really nowhere else around here at Stampede time."

"Thanks anyway, Donna," said Jane, who wasn't about to accept her hospitality the night before she turned in her sister. "But I'll work something else out." And besides, Jane didn't want to get any children involved. What if Travis roused himself and came after her? Or Raleigh sent someone else after her? Besides, she thought she had a few more questions for Jack.

Jane just asked Donna one thing. "I saw your car out there," she said. "It's a great car. Didn't your sister have one like it?"

"That's the same one," said Donna, folding a bar towel so it had a new clean side facing out. "She painted it blue, then decided she didn't like it and gave it to me. I would have liked it the original pink myself, but hey, I can't complain."

"So how long have you had it?" said Jane.

"Almost a year," said Donna. "She drove it in the Stampede parade last year and about a month later I get this phone call. Her husband is leaning on her to get rid of it because she didn't like the new color or something." Donna gave a shrug that seemed to indicate her sister and brother-in-law were eccentric rich people.

"So why did she paint it?" said Jane, who thought she was on dangerous ground but wanted to see if Donna reacted.

Donna shrugged again. "Who knows? It would have been worth a lot more with the original paint. And cuter too." Then she laughed a bitter little laugh. "Maybe she wanted to make sure it wasn't so cute when she passed it on down to me."

She frowned and wiped off the bar. "I'm just kidding," she said. "Angela's tried to be good to me. Really. I guess she just likes to redecorate. She's always been like that. Nothing's ever been quite right, you know?"

Jane went out to the phones next to a bank of noisy video games with a huge sense of relief. She knew Donna was capable of lying for her sister, but she was so calm and unflappable talking about the car, Jane couldn't believe she knew anything about a hit-and-run up in Electric City. She'd hoped she didn't. Because Jane had thought that Donna might have been behind the wheel herself. She didn't realize until now how much she didn't want Donna to be involved.

Jack's parents were in the White Pages. And he answered the phone. "It's Jane da Silva," she said.

"Jane," he said. She loved hearing that lazy baritone. She wondered if he were busy. Curled up on the sofa with some fan, maybe.

"Look, I hate to call this late, and I am sorry to do this at the last minute, but, um, that invitation for the guest house during the Stampede? Is that still open?"

She immediately felt like an idiot, and started backtracking. In fact, she found herself leaning against the wall and twirling her hair with her free hand, a nervous habit she thought she'd managed to give up around age seven. "I'm in town, but just tell me if it won't work out—"

He laughed. "Come on over," he said. "I'm really surprised to hear from you. Really nicely surprised. You remember the way?"

She remembered the way. She turned off the main road at the cluster of concrete buildings that was the family packing plant, then up along the side of the orchard to the big glass and stone house.

She managed to get herself quite swoony imagining him kissing her and touching her and carrying her off to somewhere with nice crisp sheets—not the rec room with the glassy-eyed buffalo this time, she thought—and blasting her free—body and soul—of all the mental and physical strain she'd gone through the last twenty-four hours.

She knew, of course, but completely suppressed the thought, glazed over by desire as she was, that everything could blow up horribly. That he could turn on her out of loyalty to Angela. That she was about to hand over his ex-lover to the law, and still had to return a bribe to her and to her husband. But she decided to forget about all of it until morning. And even then, she had decided to let Calvin, as executor of Irene's will, be the one to actually tell the police about the Electric City clipping and Angela's possible involvement in a hit-and-run.

But for now, none of it really mattered, did it? Because all she knew was that a night with Jack would do her no end of good.

31.

"I've missed you," he said to her at the door. And then she put her arms around him.

"I wasn't sure I'd see you again," he said. "I mean, when you left, it got kind of cold right there at the end. Want to talk about it?"

"Absolutely not," she said between little kisses. "Too much verbal communication can be disastrous."

Calvin Mason was sipping coffee in the Madison Park condominium of Wendy Webber. She was leaning back in a corner of the sofa in a languid manner. Calvin couldn't decide if the pose was meant to be seductive or if it just indicated fatigue and ennui.

"This is wonderful coffee," he said. The evening had been borderline disastrous from the get-go. Calvin wished he could chase after women he found physically attractive but actually disliked. Like this one for instance. It would make life a lot simpler.

But he didn't have it in him. Wendy Webber, he had decided, was simply a whiner. She hadn't liked the table in the restaurant. It was too close to the door and it was distracting to have the door opening and closing so close to her all the time. She hadn't liked her dinner. The vegetables weren't all cooked to the same degree of firmness and she felt cilantro had really been done to death. She seemed to think Calvin should do something about all these problems, but all he could bring himself to do was agree with her.

She certainly hadn't liked her ex-husband. Calvin had heard a lot about Mr. Webber's shortcomings. ("He was emotionally unavailable. He wasn't there for me. And besides, he was screwing his secretary.") Calvin had clucked sympathetically throughout the meal and nodded thoughtfully. Somehow, Wendy had managed to make him feel that all this was Calvin's fault too, through the taint of maleness.

Now, although he had contemplated beating a hasty retreat at the door (elaborate checking of the watch, exclamations of "Gosh, it's almost ten o'clock and I have to get up really early tomorrow"), he had chickened out and was now drinking coffee and crème de menthe—not one of his favorite liqueurs. It reminded him of mouthwash.

Wendy was now complaining about her employees. "They all stop talking whenever I enter the room. It really hurts my feelings. I never know what they're up to. And I don't see how I can manage them without knowing what they're up to."

"Mmm," said Calvin, who was absentmindedly admiring her arms. She was wearing a sleeveless navy blue linen dress and had creamy white skin.

"I'm glad you agree," she said. "I think Irene tried to make me feel guilty about monitoring the occasional phone call." She wet her lips with the tip of her tongue. "I wouldn't want *you* to think I was out of line." This was the first indication Wendy had given that she gave a damn about what Calvin thought of her.

"I suppose there's a time and place for that sort of employee surveillance," said Calvin. Although he couldn't

think what it could be, with the possible exception of a dishonest plutonium factory employee using the office phone
to sell nuclear materials to terrorists. If Calvin ever had a
boss who listened in on the phone, he'd be tempted to
knock his or her teeth down his or her throat. But Wendy
had certainly piqued his curiosity.

"You know," he said, "in this case, something you might
have heard could be very important. Because Irene received
a personal call the Friday before she disappeared. I suppose
the police didn't ask you about it?"

Wendy began to squirm. "It was a little awkward," she
said.

"Not everyone would understand you were monitoring
their communications for the good of the office," said
Calvin. "But as the attorney for her estate, you can give me
the information and I can pass it along without your being
bothered in any way."

"You can?" said Wendy, looking a little confused.

Calvin leaned forward intensely. "I know you've been
through a lot of stress lately, Wendy," he said. "I'd like to
help you avoid more pressure." He cleared his throat and
gave her a sincere look, removing his glasses and allowing
his voice to catch a little. "I'd like to be there for you."

He saw her visibly melting. He figured she'd not only tell
him what he wanted to hear—he knew Jane would be interested—but if he played it right he could get her to bed too.
Which was sort of flattering and reassuring after Marcia and
all, but, even after factoring in the ego gratification, it was
still a dismal prospect. As soon as he got the information,
he'd give her a dose of what Calvin believed repelled all but
a few saintly women: a litany of his worldly failures and pre-
carious finances.

*   *   *

Jane didn't want to get out of bed the next morning. In fact, she would have been glad to spend a mindless week or so there with Jack. "If you can sing country songs the way you do this," she told him, "Garth Brooks better watch out."

"Well it helps to have fabulous material to work with," he said, pushing away damp strands of her hair to kiss her neck once more. "Classily arranged," he added, running his hand down her side.

"It goes against all my instincts," she said, closing her eyes and gritting her teeth, "but I am going to get up, take a shower, get dressed and take care of a little leftover business from my last case."

He pulled her over on top of him and kissed her.

"I think I better make that a cold shower," she said.

"I think," he said solemnly, "that we are extremely sexually compatible."

She laughed. "Tell me something I don't know." She slithered out of his embrace. He didn't ask her, thank God, what business she had to finish. She was grateful for that.

Before she left, they arranged to meet again. His band was arriving and he invited her to a rehearsal. "Forget it," she said. "I don't want to hang around like Yoko Ono while you work."

He looked a little relieved. "Okay," he said. "Let's meet for the Suicide Race. I can get us a great spot down by the river. Meet me at the rodeo ticket office at three. You sure you'll be all right? You can amuse yourself?"

"I can probably make it without you until three," she said. Out in the fresh air she even felt a little relieved to be alone again. She was afraid he might be addictive.

It wasn't hard to find the Omak Elks Club. There was a collection of cars and horse trailers outside, and inside, a collection of women of various ages mingling in a gentle, animated way, a buffet with fruit—berries and melons—on skewers and cinnamon rolls, and a sweet-looking lady pouring coffee.

Along the wall were blown-up portraits of girls around eighteen or nineteen from various eras, wearing cowboy hats trimmed with wraparound rhinestone tiaras. The sizes of the crowns and brims seemed to have waxed and waned over the years, and the fashions in hair had changed too, but all the young women seemed to have had a wholesome, outdoorsy, open, Western look about them.

Besides the Omak Stampede queens, there were portraits of various Indian princesses, pretty girls with smooth, glossy black hair, from the Colville Tribe, wearing traditional beaded buckskin dresses.

There was a big portrait of Donna from the seventies, looking young and innocent and kind of tomboyish, and another, a few years later, of Angela, who had a big perm exploding out from under her hat. The label said she'd gone on to represent Washington State at a national rodeo pageant.

Jane grabbed some coffee, because she thought she needed it, but seeing as she was crashing this event, she laid off the food. She stood in a corner, watching the women mingling and greeting one another. Some of them were current queens and princesses decked out in hats, tiaras, satin-fringed sashes over glitzy shirts and the currently favored loose-cut Wrangler jeans and black lace-up Roper boots. They looked young and shy.

There was visiting royalty from around the state and from Canada fifty miles away to the north, more young girls with sashes from places like Penticton and Tonasket, Kelowna and Wenatchee, Chehalis and Spokane, here to drum up business for a brace of roundups, rodeos and festivals.

And there were older women who'd had their year of youthful glory, traveling around the state with their horses to wave in parades, attend civic dinners, flirt with cowboys and sell the Omak Stampede.

A tall woman with dark gray hair and an aristocratic bearing wore a sash saying she'd reigned in the mid-thirties. Jane could imagine her still looking fabulous on a horse. A few had put on at least fifty pounds, but some still fit into their original costumes. A queen from the forties was wearing knee-length orange buckskin culottes with contrasting suede laces that Jane found herself coveting.

Sipping coffee and scanning the room for Angela, Jane eavesdropped on two queens from the sixties, who were laughing about how hard it was to get into the tight jeans of the period. "I remember lying on my back in the trailer with a pair of pliers trying to get that zipper pulled up," one of them said.

"It was nearly impossible getting on your horse in those tight jeans," said her friend. "God, I was so embarrassed. I had one outfit that ripped right down the back seam when I swung my leg over. It was at the Calgary Stampede too, of all places."

"I can believe it," said the first queen. "Do you remember putting your feet in plastic bags so you could get the boots on?"

"I just remember sleeping on those rollers," said the other one, patting her hair and cringing with remembered pain. "People think rodeoing is hard on the animals—heck, it's hard on the women."

Angela was definitely not in attendance, but after a moment or so, during which Jane was afraid someone might ask her just what she was doing there, Donna came in. She was wearing her sash and the same red cowboy boots and jeans she'd worn when Jane had first met her.

Jane watched her greeting an old lady who chatted with her for a while holding her hands, and with one of this year's runners-up. "Cute outfit," said Donna approvingly to the girl, who blushed behind her freckles. Then Donna spotted Jane, looked startled and went over to her.

"What are you doing here?" she said, her eyes wide.

"Looking for Angela," said Jane.

"She's still not here? I'm late 'cause I couldn't find my damn sash."

"No. You did speak to her?"

"Yes. On the phone. She said she'd be here. They're taking a group picture of all of us, and she promised she'd be here. Then we're going to be in the parade."

"What did you have to do to be a rodeo queen?" asked Jane.

"Not fall off your horse," said Donna. "Smile a lot. Not let the judges hear you swear or see you smoke. I had a blast. I love horses and I loved traveling around. Those chaperones loved to use up the royalty budget on the road. We always had fabulous steak dinners. It was terrific."

She looked around the room. "Some of these girls went on and married cowboys and rodeoed with their husbands until they had kids."

"Rodeoed?" said Jane.

"Ladies' barrel racing. It's the only ladies' event." Donna sighed. "I was a pretty good little barrel racer and the cowboys were neat. I always liked the steer wrestlers. They're bigger guys, about two hundred pounds. I almost hooked up with one of them and took off on the road. Thinking back, I should have done it. Instead, I married my high school sweetheart."

"So how did Angela meet her husband?" said Jane.

"Oh, he was a big rodeo fan. He saw her at the Ellensburg Rodeo after she won the state title. She was planning to go on to Washington State on a rodeo scholarship, but after the national pageant he just swept her off her feet. Him and his million bucks."

"There she is now," said Jane.

Angela came in, wearing a cowboy hat, sunglasses and a gold lamé outfit.

"That's her old costume," said Donna. "It was that kind of disco era. She was really great. I remember her wall ride when she finished up at the state pageant. She looked like a million bucks, really confident, just cantering around the arena smiling and looking completely relaxed." Donna was waving at her sister.

Angela stopped, looked clearly taken aback to see Jane, and came over to them. She put her arm around her sister. Donna squeezed her shoulder. "I'm so glad to see you," she said.

"What the hell are you doing here?" Angela said to Jane in a loud whisper. Meanwhile, she smiled and waved at someone across the room.

"I wanted to return something to you," said Jane.

"Jack Lawson, by any chance?" said Angela out of the corner of her mouth. She leaned over to Donna. "Would you be a doll and get me a cup of coffee?" she said.

Donna looked a little taken aback. "I'm off shift," she said in a hard voice, "but I guess maybe you want to talk to Jane."

She left them.

"Look," said Jane, "I just want to give you back your check. I never should have taken it in the first place. There's no reason I should have it." She touched her purse.

"Don't give it to me now," said Angela. "Not in front of all these people. Just tear it up or something. I don't care." She took off her sunglasses and stared at Jane. "How come you're hanging around in my life? Talking to my husband.

251

Messing around with Jack Lawson, from what I hear. Now you show up here. You really are starting to give me the creeps. It's like you're stalking me or something."

"I'm leaving now," said Jane, who found herself somehow withering under Angela's monotonic barrage. Angela apparently said whatever she wanted to anyone. Without her sunglasses she looked very different. She had a lot of makeup on, orangey foundation and old-fashioned-looking eyeshadow and a lot of mascara and a big streak of blusher. But close up like this, with her sunglasses off, the skillful makeup job didn't quite conceal the bruise under her eye. It was definitely faded. It had a yellowish cast. But it must have been spectacular a few days ago. Which would explain why Angela had been out of circulation for a few days.

32.

Jane made her way to the door in the general confusion as the royalty was rounded up for a group shot. Sitting right outside in a mud-spattered Range Rover, wearing a cowboy hat, a black shirt, jeans and a big turquoise bolo tie and reading a newsprint rodeo program, was Hank Raleigh. Apparently, he was waiting for his slightly battered wife to finish her photo opportunity.

Jane felt herself tense up with anger, and she went over to the curb. "Where the hell do you get off sending that scummy little thug Travis to terrorize me?" she demanded in a voice she tried to keep from ascending into the higher registers.

He looked startled and opened his mouth but she went on. "I'll give you your money back. You just had to ask. I told your wife the same thing. I didn't earn any of it. I don't want any of it."

"Fine," he said. "Considering the circumstances."

"Don't you want to know what Travis did?" she said.

"To tell you the truth, I don't," he said. She thought he looked a little squeamish.

"Well I won't tell you what I did to Travis, either," she said.

Now he looked genuinely appalled. Maybe Travis had been improvising quite a bit on his own.

"Here," she said, handing over the bulky envelope with his cash and his wife's check as well. He looked nervously around—a politician's instinct perhaps when receiving large amounts of money on the street—and glanced inside her envelope. Then he reached into a beautiful cowhide briefcase that lay by his side on the seat, snapped it open and put it inside.

He blinked slowly. "I don't know what I was thinking about," he said. "I guess when it comes to Angela, I'm not quite rational. I told you, I'd do anything to protect her from unpleasantness. When Donna told me you were up at the dam, still prowling around—"

Jane was tempted to tell him that if men were rational when it came to Angela, she would have spent every Friday night of her life since the onset of puberty home alone with a romance novel and a box of chocolates, and the phone would have sprouted cartoon spider webs. After her last encounter, Jane had decided Angela had no redeeming characteristics, and she couldn't stand the sappy way her husband was talking about her, so she said, "Then I guess it wasn't you who gave her that shiner she tried to cover up with makeup."

He ignored that detail. "I'm glad it's all over," he said. "To be painfully honest, I was worried that Angela might somehow have been involved. I had tried the carrot to get you to stop pursuing it, and you'd taken my money and kept on. So I'm afraid I thought Travis would serve as the stick."

"You thought Angela was involved in *what* exactly?" said Jane.

"In the death of Irene March, of course," he said, his eyes looking especially shiny.

"That's for the police to decide," she said.

He laughed out loud. It was a rather attractive laugh, warm and hearty. "Haven't you heard?" he said. "They got who did it."

Jane tried not to let her jaw fall open.

He reached back into his briefcase. "Here. Last night's *Seattle Times*." He handed her a folded front section.

She took it and glanced at it. The headline read: "Arrest in Tiger Mountain Murder."

"Of course, there's no question of Angela's being involved in any hit-and-run in Electric City," he added. "The police already talked to her. She had an airtight alibi."

Jane tried not to look startled. She came back fairly quickly with another question. "Did you?" she said. "I imagine you had a key to that car too."

"Yes I did," he said. "Right on my key chain. But the State legislature was meeting in emergency session last year at this time. I was on the Senate floor in Olympia, voting late at night. A horrendous budget matter." Then he looked over Jane's shoulder and said, "Oh, here's Angela." Apparently Angela and her bruise had finished their cameo appearance at the royalty breakfast.

Jane took the paper and walked away with a quick nod. She was disgusted with both of them.

She went back to her car and read the article three times, vaguely aware of the Range Rover and its two occupants driving past her.

Maureen Louise Jenkins had been arrested by King County Police for the murder of Irene March. The police said that Mrs. Jenkins had arranged to meet Irene at a bus stop in a rural area of the county. She had prepared a backpack with a lunch. She had waited until Irene's back was turned, then struck her with a rock, pushed her over the side and flung the rock and the backpack after her in an attempt to make the crime look like a hiking accident.

"Police have still not disclosed a motive for the slaying," said the article, "though there is speculation that it involves a perceived threat to Jenkins's daughter, Amanda."

Jane suddenly realized that when she talked to Mrs. Jenkins, she'd missed something important. Amanda's mother never mentioned or asked if Irene had been found or was still missing. Why wouldn't she have been curious? Simply because she already knew the answer.

The police were also quoted as saying that physical evidence tied Jenkins to the crime. Her right thumbprint had been found on the plastic wrap around a sandwich, and a blue vinyl purse, identified as Irene's by co-workers, was found in the Jenkins home, a plaything for young Amanda.

The article said that Amanda Jenkins was now in the custody of her father and stepmother, who had flown up from California after the arrest. Amanda had been wrong. Her father wasn't dead at all.

The paper said she'd been wrong about something else too. "Despite a campaign to finance a heart transplant operation, the child was examined by doctors and found to be in good health."

The break in the case came, said the paper, when police discovered a Children's Protective Service report had been filed about Amanda Jenkins. Someone had seen Amanda sitting by herself in a car registered to her mother near Tiger Mountain on the Saturday morning after Irene was last seen, and they called police to say a child was left unattended in a car.

Police had traced the license number and handed the information over to CPS caseworkers. After a phone chat with Mrs. Jenkins, during which they learned Amanda was older than she looked, they dropped the matter but routinely filed the report in the state's computer where it would stay for a few years in case more reports on Amanda surfaced. And where the police found it when they filed their own report on her.

Detective Walters was quoted. "It was a lucky break that put the suspect near the scene of the crime at the right time," said Detective Walters. "Then, we built a case based on physical evidence. Eventually, Mrs. Jenkins confessed."

Jane put down the paper. In a way, she had helped solve the murder of Irene March, but would the board think she had? She'd given the police the Jenkins name. Maybe they'd let her have the money on that basis. She doubted it, though. The rules were pretty specific. It had to be something the police weren't doing.

Be realistic, said Jane to herself harshly. Who's to say the police wouldn't have found Mrs. Jenkins by themselves? The clipping in the safe-deposit box would have led them straight there.

Jane sat in her car at the curb, her hands on the wheel, feeling as if she had expended a huge amount of time and energy for absolutely no reason at all. She'd given the Raleighs back all their money. She'd planned now to tell the authorities that there was a good chance Angela was involved in a hit-and-run up in Electric City. Finding out who killed a helpless old lady. That would have been enough to soften the board's hearts.

And now Hank Raleigh tells her the police already talked to Angela about it. What was her alibi? Even if he was lying, there were a few fairly significant problems.

First, it would be hard to explain to the board the convoluted way she'd found that particular wrong to right. The old bastards wanted a written report, detailing her activities. But maybe she could come up with something creative. Her previous lies to the board had been lies of omission. For the scenario she had in mind now, she might have to commit a few whoppers.

Of course, the chief problem was that the whole thing would be useless if Angela wasn't convicted. Which brought up the whole question of why, if she was guilty, the police hadn't already caught her. A hot pink car that had appeared in a parade an hour away? Surely they'd be able to follow up on that. Maybe that alibi story was true.

Jane reached into her glove compartment for a state map. Who had jurisdiction up there in Electric City anyway, she wondered. The map revealed that five counties, each presumably with its own sheriff's department, met right around the dam: Okanogan and Ferry counties north of the Columbia; Douglas and Lincoln counties south of the Columbia; with between them a little panhandle belonging to Grant County, and including Electric City at its very tip.

Maybe that was the explanation. Too many jurisdictions. Five county sheriff's departments plus the tribal police all operating within the space of a few square miles. Jane didn't want to believe the authorities could have been so blasé about a little old lady being killed in a hit-and-run that they would have missed Angela and her hot pink car.

But what proof did she have now? The word of a probably drunken and certainly dead witness that a pink car had been seen there? The fact that Angela had painted the car and ditched it? These two facts were pretty flimsy.

What still remained unexplained, however, was the fact that Irene seemed to have been blackmailing Angela about it and she'd been paying. (Not much money, according to Angela, but money, nevertheless.) But Irene was dead too, so how could anyone prove anything about that aspect? Angela had already come up with at least three blackmail scenarios, none of which featured a hit-and-run in Electric City. She'd keep on lying and who could refute her? When it came right down to it, all of Jane's suspicions (and hopes for something to trot in front of the board) were based on two clippings.

Women were streaming out of the Elks Club now. Nice, small-town women who had time to run up cowgirl outfits for their daughters and give breakfasts and go to parades and tend old-fashioned gardens like the ones around the streets of Omak here, with baskets of fuchsias hanging from the eaves and pots of pansies and maybe some rhubarb for pies in the backyard.

Jane felt very sorry for herself and, for probably the first time in her life, she wished she'd grown up in a small town and married a nice steer wrestler, or maybe one of those smaller, more compact-looking bull riders who would have traveled the country and rodeoed with her, dancing the Texas two-step in honky-tonks on Saturday nights, then buying her a nice little house here so she could bake rhubarb pies and groom the pansies. A nice, uncomplicated cowboy without any neuroses or anything like that, just a sweet nature and great in bed. Maybe someone a lot like Jack Lawson.

Then she wouldn't have to be chasing around running into dead ends and getting terrorized by thugs like Travis (Jane's imaginary cowboy would have made short work of Travis for her) and having to deal with unpleasant people like the Raleighs. When the going got tough, Jane tended to fantasize about some nice man coming and taking care of her.

Because what did she think she was doing, anyway? Driving all around the state night and day, sleeping alone in crummy motels, messing into people's lives. And all the while, police quietly and efficiently did what the taxpayers paid them to do, and caught Irene's demented killer. Jane told herself she wouldn't dissolve into tears of frustration and drove slowly down Omak's main street and across a little bridge over to the Stampede grounds.

Crowds were streaming toward the area, past a carnival where girls screamed on the scary rides, and into a big parking area, where she parked next to a bunch of tough-looking grizzled bikers with black leather jackets that read "Riding Sober, Riding Free." Something told her that if you looked at them with even the hint of a snicker, they'd twist your head off, Caffeine Free Diet Pepsi surging through their bulging veins.

She picked her way through the sawdust parking lot to a sort of main drag where families and young couples cruised past booths selling cowboy hats, hot dogs, Indian jewelry, T-shirts, cotton candy, New Age music tapes, Western art and belt buckles. Not to mention the ubiquitous Northwest espresso stand complete with a sideline in Italian sodas.

Jane bought an iced latte and sipped it, walking slowly in the hot sun, watching people. She stopped thinking about her problems, and felt the poignant keenness that she often felt after a good cry or a failed love affair. It was not unlike the feeling she got when walking the streets of a new city— an intoxication of new sights and sounds and textures and colors.

There were a fair number of people in Western gear— Wrangler jeans, cowboy hats, boots—looking, Jane thought, elegant here, though she'd thought similarly dressed people looked eccentric when she'd seen them in airports and in cities. Maybe now she'd seen them on their own turf, they wouldn't look eccentric anymore.

There were also a few Indians in traditional clothing. A little girl was clearly delighted with a dress covered with bells that made a charming sound with each step she took. An adult man with long shiny braids covered in eagle feathers and buckskin walked with a little boy in similar dress but with the addition of a Chicago White Sox baseball hat. The man told the boy that if he had cotton candy it would ruin his supper.

Most of the people, however, seemed to be neither cowboys nor Indians. She realized since she had lived here last, a lot of Americans had taken to wearing a lot fewer clothes. Grown men and women seemed to be wearing shorts and tank tops, like children's playsuits, and their exposed arms and legs looked big and pale.

People seemed bigger here than in Seattle, and comfortable in their bigness. Maybe they were still eating the huge meals they'd needed to do hard work on ranches a couple of generations ago. Maybe they were the descendants of the big, tough people you needed to win the West.

After reluctantly sucking the last of the iced coffee from around the ice cubes, she ditched her plastic cup.

Every once in a while she would hear Spanish with a characteristically Mexican lilt and see smaller, darker families, strolling in an elegant Latin, paseo-like way. The women wore flattering dresses curving over their hips and stockings and high heels. The children were dressed as for church, the men wore neatly pressed long-sleeved shirts and long pants and leather shoes. Trust the Latins to make everyone else look scruffy. She smiled as a little black-eyed boy in a sailor suit picked up a feather from the ground and announced solemnly to his parents, "Una pluma de los indios."

She walked down further past the arena and sat in the grass under the shade of a tree for a while and listened to a woman who looked about fifty and sounded about eighteen playing the guitar from the back of a flatbed truck trimmed with blue plastic fringe.

She sang old-fashioned hymns that sounded like they came out of some Appalachian hollow in a lovely sweet, low voice. "I don't want to be a gold-plated Christian, with a heart as black as coal," she sang, and then one about a church in the wildwood all with a young boy playing the steel guitar behind her. Between the songs, she told how Jesus had cured her of leukemia when she was a young girl and how he was coming real soon, and how her ministry to cowboys took her all over the West. "Come and join us Sunday at the cowboy praise service," she said. "Even if you're not a cowboy."

After that, Jane made a pass by the other end of the Stampede grounds. Here was the Indian Encampment, an annual rendezvous of the Colville Confederated Tribe where teepees were set up and Indian families sat in webbed aluminum lawn chairs with their family names on the back in magic marker, visiting with each other and watching dancers with big numbers around their necks compete. The bells on their ankles shook in rhythm to the drums.

Then she walked over to the big chain link fence that ran along the top of the Okanogan River and looked across at Suicide Hill, where the horses would be racing later. It was a dusty dirt track down what looked like practically a sheer cliff. She couldn't imagine horses and riders clattering down there as Jack had described, and she realized that while she was only five hours away from Seattle, she was in a very different place where she was a foreigner. This was a feeling she relished. Her unhappiness at her failed case seemed suddenly less important.

33.

The spot Jack had picked out for her to watch the first running of the Suicide Race (there were four of them over the course of the weekend, one for each rodeo performance) was in the Okanogan River, with water almost up to her waist, her jeans clinging heavily to her, and Jack's arm around her. They stood there looking up at the sandy hill on the opposite bank where the riders were assembling.

A rope in the river marked off the course. In the water around them were enthusiastic locals who seemed to know a lot of the riders and were pointing them out from below.

She had left her shoes on shore—and the bottom of the river where she was standing felt silty and smooth on the soles of her feet. She got used to the cold current of the water fairly quickly.

Sprinklers were wetting down the steep course. At the top of the hill, silhouettes against the sky, were the horses and riders—and they were letting out war cries. On either side of the course, pressed against the chain link fencing that ran up the hill, were lots more people.

Further up the river, on the bank opposite the course, Jane saw a little boat from the sheriff's department and there were police with walkie-talkies on the grassy slopes.

Above, more chain link fencing held back more crowds. By the water's edge a man sat on a tall dappled gray horse. He wore full Western regalia, with elaborate leather chaps and vest incorporating the name of a beer company in its design. A black headset with microphone emerged from beneath his cowboy hat.

"Who's that?" said Jane.

"The rodeo announcer. The finish line is in the arena. He's telling the people back in the stands what's going on. We'll see the beginning of the race, but not the finish, and the people in the stands, depending on where they sit, will see them head off down the hill, and they'll catch the finish but they'll miss them crossing the river and see the end of the race."

"Seems like poor planning," said Jane.

"This is sort of a cross-cultural event here," said Jack. "These mountain races are a long-standing Indian thing. Traditionally they used to have them at another place—a town on the reservation further up the river called Keller—but it got flooded when they built Grand Coulee.

"Sixty years ago, when they started up the rodeo, they added the Suicide Race, and now it ends up in the arena. And the roots of the rodeo itself came from Spain via Mexico."

"Like the horses themselves," said Jane.

"The animal rights people are always all over us to close this thing down," he said. "People around here don't take to outsiders in Birkenstocks coming in and telling them what to do with their animals."

Or their own necks, thought Jane, as she saw some uniformed medics get into position at the bottom of the hill where the track met the river, and nonchalantly place a stretcher against the fence.

"The animal rights people say they'll close down the bullfights in Spain," she said. Jane felt slightly sick when the picador did his work, horror at the veil of blood over the animal and a woozy feeling when the life spilled out of the bull and it sank to the ground. But she could understand at the same time some of what the aficionado felt.

"A bullfight always seemed like a slow way to butcher an animal," said Jack.

"And a dangerous way to do the butchering," said Jane.

"But some young men like that danger," Jack said. "They don't feel complete without risk."

"I know," said Jane, unfairly annoyed that he was explaining this to her, of all people. But then how could he know? "My husband was a Formula One driver. He died on the track," she said.

"I'm sorry." He took his arm off her shoulder, as if he shouldn't touch her out of respect for the dead Bernardo. A lot of men felt that way about widows, she had learned. Even ones like Jack, who hadn't been particularly scrupulous about women with live husbands. "I didn't know. Are you sure you want to see this race?" He sounded genuinely concerned. He was probably just five years younger than she was, but he looked a lot younger now and sweet and untouched by life in a way that meant he could never really know her.

"Yes, I do," she said. "I don't get it personally, but I know that some people thrive on going as fast as they can, and taking physical risks." She put one arm around his waist and, reassured, he put his arm back around her and she put her free hand flat on his chest and spread out her fingers, as if trying to cover as much of the surface of him as possible. Compared to the water, he felt nice and warm.

The riders were lined up now, jostling for position at the top of the hill. Their war whoops floated down into the gorge, and around them the spectators responded with more of the same.

A gun went off and, amidst shouts from the hill and the riverbank, about twenty horses plowed over the edge down onto the track, kicking up a cloud of dust and mud, jostling for position, cutting each other off in a wild free-for-all.

The riders were all wearing orange life jackets over T-shirts and jeans and brandishing crops in their right hands with the reins in their left. They leaned far back in the saddles to accommodate the steep slope. A few hats flew off and one horse careened into the fence and twisted itself back onto the track.

It looked like the front-runners just managed to avoid a nasty pileup at the bottom of the hill, and then the horses plunged into the water, jerking the riders even further back at the impact. Dust turned to splashing water.

They had to cross the river at an angle, against the current, to get onto the path that led toward the arena. In contrast to their mad dash down the sandy slope, the field slowed down considerably as the horses swam, only their heads and necks visible above the waterline, pulling back and forth, a look that could almost be a look of concentration on their faces, but was probably, in fact, a look of effort.

The riders bobbed backward and forward, urging their horses on with their crops and with shouts. It was like a slow-motion segment in a fast-paced action film sequence. The tempo change, and the laborious feeling of the big animals swimming through water, heightened the suspense.

When the horses emerged dripping from the water, they seemed to fly up onto land, and the race went back into fast mode with the rhythmic sound of hooves on dirt. Three horses at least were now riderless but they kept up, reins flying, even, Jane saw, trying to muscle aside another horse or two while their riders, left behind in the river, swam ashore.

A second later the horses disappeared from view and headed toward the arena, but Jane could still hear a wave of shouting in their wake.

She caught her breath.

"What do you think?" Jack said.

"A hell of a lot more exciting than a day at the track," she said.

"Come on," he said. "Let's see who won. The tribal cop over there probably heard on his radio." He pulled her toward him and put his hands on her shoulders. "After that, I've got some time to kill before I play after tonight's rodeo," he said. "Let's go home and get out of these wet things. And then you know what I wish you would do for me?"

"What?" said Jane.

"I want to hear you sing," he said, brushing the hair away from her face.

It turned out he was a pretty good piano player, thwonking away by ear at chords while she sat next to him on the piano bench in his parents' living room. She sang "Scotch and Soda" and "Blue Moon" and "Begin the Beguine" and "A Room with a View."

And then she fed him the lines and they sang together—"Smoke Gets in Your Eyes" and "My Blue Heaven." He had a nice smooth baritone, but singing those old standards along with her, she had a feeling he was holding way back and that he also had a voice with a lot of ragged power.

"You're good," he said. "You're phrasing's great. You know how to sell a song."

"I love to sing," she said. "But I don't miss performing." She shrugged. "And my voice isn't anything very special. It's funny, I have a sort of sense of the voice I would have taken if I could have any voice—like mine with more color to it. And more power."

"I'm less and less interested in performing and more and more interested in songwriting," he said. "I want you to hear us tonight. We're doing a new song I wrote. It's something you could sing. A kind of smoky ballad."

"Play it for me now," she said.

He spread out his fingers over the keyboard and then they froze there for a second and he said, "No. I want you to hear it like everyone else does, so you can tell me what you think without having an idea in your mind from before."

"All right," she said, smiling at him. "I'm looking forward to it."

He put his arm on her shoulder. "You weren't heartbroken when you gave up singing, were you?"

She laughed. "Absolutely not. It was fun for a while. Then I started to feel silly."

"So you like what you're doing now?"

"Yes." She felt serious all of a sudden. "Now that I've finished what I was working on, I think I should tell you about it. I didn't mean to let any of that overlap—I mean, I don't want you to be upset with me, like you were before. I don't want you to think I haven't been honest."

He took both her hands. "I can't pretend I haven't been very curious. So tell me."

"I will," she said. "If you promise not to interrupt or make any judgments or ask any questions until I'm done."

He nodded and she began. She told him about Irene, and about Dave Twentyacres and the Jenkinses and the woman from Coulee City who'd seen Angela meeting with her and about Donna calling her and feeding her a phony story and grilling her. And then, taking a deep breath, she told him about her meetings with both Raleighs and about Electric City and the pink car there and Ella Mae Tinker.

She could tell he wanted to interrupt then, but she put a finger on his lips and went on, telling him about Coulee Dam and Travis.

This time he did interrupt. "He works for Hank Raleigh out at his place. I can't believe Hank Raleigh would unleash that psycho on you. Jesus!"

Then she told him about hiring Bob and scaring Travis, and he looked at her with a certain amazement and she thought to herself that he saw her now as a hard woman who didn't need anyone to take care of her.

And finally she told him that she was through with all of it, had returned the money and thought maybe she should tell the Grant County authorities that the Raleighs had been paying blackmail in connection with a hit-and-run and let them sort it out.

"My God," said Jack when she finished. "You've been pretty busy."

"That's right," she said. "I didn't mean to be running around trying to nail something on your ex-lover, but that's the way it turned out."

"Well I can tell you right now," he said, "that the Grant County Sheriff's Department knows all about her car. They asked her about it and she referred them to me and I told them the truth." He leaned very close to Jane. "She was with me that whole night. In the guest house on this ranch. And her car was parked in front of her place down by the river. They have a summer place here, you know."

"Where was her husband?" said Jane.

"He was in Olympia. Conducting the state's business." He got up and paced around the room a little. "Look, I know it sounds sleazy. It was, I guess."

Jane put up her hand. "Listen," she said. "I'm not asking for any explanations. It's none of my business." But of course, she couldn't help wondering what Jack, of whom she was becoming so fond, could have seen in Angela. Well, actually, she could see and that did upset her a little.

"But I feel like explaining," he said.

Jane laughed. "In that case, I won't stop you," she said.

"I know it sounds kind of dumb, but I felt sorry for Angela. I mean I kind of knew her all my life. She was a few years older, of course. I've always been a little intrigued by older women, to tell you the truth."

"One of your most endearing qualities," said Jane.

"Anyway, she was here by herself because her husband was back at the capitol, and my band performed and there was a big party afterward, and we got to talking and she was coming on to me and I wasn't sure what I was going to do about it. I mean I was attracted to her. She's a good-looking woman."

Jane nodded in a ladylike, good-sport way, even though she felt like adding: if you like that sort of cold, vulgar, hard-looking, overmade-up tart.

"And there was that princessy thing we talked about before. That feeling that she'd never been completely satisfied, and if you could do it, you'd be a real hero. And then," said Jack, "she kind of fell apart. Told me how miserable she was, even though everyone thought she was so rich and beautiful. She said her husband treated her like dirt, and she could never make him happy."

"If she couldn't make him happy, he loved being unhappy," said Jane, unable to restrain herself. "At least that's the impression I got."

He gave her a frown. "I'm just telling you how the evening progressed. Which is, I felt really sorry for her and thought she was kind of a tragic figure. He had children from another marriage and didn't want her to have any, which I thought was pretty low and selfish. Anyway, the upshot was I carted her away, and it was the beginning of an affair that didn't last too long, and was pretty tough anyway, seeing as she lived in Seattle and I was on the road. We managed to get together a half dozen times over about six months. She flew down to Las Vegas to see me one weekend—that's when she bought us those boots—and we planned to meet again, but we never did."

Jane wanted to know why, but she didn't ask. Instead, she said: "I'm sorry. The whole thing sounds painful."

"It was," he said. "For a very short time, and then the fog cleared. It was when I realized she'd never leave her husband, not unless it was for something equally secure."

Like the good-looking heir to a thriving apple business, young enough to be her husband's son, thought Jane. Angela wanted it all.

"And then," said Jack, "I realized I hoped she'd never leave her husband. I think I was almost relieved when she told me he'd found out and we'd better not see each other. I was ready to chalk it all up to experience. Recast the whole things as a sweet little fling. Wish her well and smile whenever I saw those boots in my closet."

"How did he find out?" she said.

He shrugged. "Beats me. To tell the truth, I didn't want to know the details. Cheating usually means lying. She had to lie. I didn't. But I tried not to know any of that part so the lies wouldn't contaminate me too somehow."

Jane wondered if Jack would have lied to protect Angela. If he had made up that alibi for the night Ella Mae Tinker died. Because if he wasn't lying, there was no reason for Angela to be paying off Irene March.

34.

She was glad it was going to take him a long time to set up. "Really," she said. "I don't mind being alone. I'm used to it. You don't want me hanging around. I'll drive down later. I'll be there in the front row, elbowing aside the other groupies."

"You want to go for a ride while I'm gone?" he said. "I'll saddle Hopscotch for you. You can unsaddle her and curry her like I showed you, can't you?"

"You trust me with your horse?"

"No. I trust the horse with you," he said. "And the ride'll do you both good."

"A ride, a bath, a nap," said Jane. "Then your concert. It sounds perfect."

And, she thought to herself, some time to think too. She found herself, not for the first time in her life, believing two things at once. She believed that Jack was telling the truth, and she believed that Angela's car had killed Ella Mae. But if it wasn't Angela behind the wheel, who could it have been?

While Angela was dallying with Jack, could Donna have gone for a spin up to Electric City? Donna hadn't flinched when she mentioned the car. Maybe she was a very good liar, her original Dracula saga notwithstanding. Could Jack himself have been driving? She rejected that idea. But who else, besides Angela's sister or Jack, would have been able to get their hands on the keys?

There was Hank, of course. He'd said he had a set of keys. But his alibi sounded rock solid.

While Jack saddled Hopscotch, Jane called Calvin in Seattle and left a message on his machine. She felt a little guilty because she hadn't reported in after her adventure at the dam. "Everything's fine," she said. "Can't wait to see you again and tell you everything that's happened. Hopeless case wise, things look hopeless, but at least I'm finishing up here. Can we find out when our old pal Hank Raleigh voted in Olympia on a special session last June tenth? And if anyone can account for him at two A.M. the next morning? I'll check back later."

She hung up feeling uneasy. Whenever she thought this was over, it wasn't. There was always some lingering doubt. And the central question, of course. Why was Angela giving money to Irene?

Jack brought the horse around to the front, and handed her the reins. "Here," he said, "I found an old pair of my sister's boots. See if they fit." He handed her the lace-up black boots with roundish toes, a fringed flap in front and a pair of plain steel spurs, well-worn examples of the shiny, old-fashioned little boots the young rodeo queens were wearing that season.

He took the reins back and Jane sat down on a big rock in the garden and smelled the sage and pulled on the boots. "They fit pretty well," she said. "Just a tiny bit big." She laced them up, then pulled her jeans down over them.

She waved goodbye to him from her horse, and was pleased to see that Betsy, the black and white dog, was joining her, scampering around sniffing eagerly as they made their way through the orchard. She felt confident on the horse and a cool green peacefulness in her surroundings.

It was about twenty minutes later that she reached the road and looked across to the packing plant. She hadn't planned to cross, but she saw something that surprised her.

There, not visible from the road, but clear from where her horse stood on a little rise, parked at an odd angle behind a huge pile of big apple bins, was what appeared to be the same Range Rover Hank Raleigh had been driving that morning.

She looked both ways and walked her horse across the blacktop. Hopscotch kept her head down and blinked, plodding along steadily, unaware of Jane's human curiosity. She was a little worried about Betsy, but the dog seemed streetwise and kept up with her.

She entered the gravel area next to the CA shed, and took in the scene in a glance. The little door in the center of the big door was slightly ajar. Next to it in the dust lay a tool with long handles covered in red vinyl—a bolt cutter she presumed—and a padlock, its hasp twisted.

The Range Rover was nearby. The passenger door was open and the engine was running.

She pulled back on the reins and Hopscotch stood there politely. A sudden movement to her left, by the river, caught her eye. A tree was shaking. It was shaking a little bit more than the trees around it.

She touched the horse's flanks lightly with her spurs and walked over there for a look. There, staring up at her, was Hank Raleigh standing next to a horse of his own. He was untying the reins from the tree she'd seen shaking.

"My God," she said. "What's happened? Your car is up here."

"I know," he said. "There's been an accident."

He got up on his horse and wheeled it around and up a

zigzagging little path until he was next to her. "I was going for help. It's—" He paused and looked at her with a face full of an emotion she imagined was shock. "It's Angela. She's killed herself."

"What?" Jane went back to the shed, clambered off her horse hastily and clumsily and went over to the shed, reins in hand, trying to remember to stay on the horse's left. She flipped open the door with the porthole. It was black in there except for a little circle of light from the thick window and a stripe from the open door. She saw a glimmer of gold lamé, a tumble of blonde hair.

"We've got to get her out of there," she said over her shoulder. What was he doing just sitting there?

"It's too late. You only last a few seconds in those places," he said. And then he said, "She took the car. I came after her on the horse by the river, but I was too late. It's pretty obvious that she twisted off that padlock and plunged right in."

"My God," said Jane, who was examining the door. The big door was sealed with what looked like a strip of caulking. Surely if that could be opened, fresh air would rush in.

"She killed that woman in Electric City," he said. "And that Lawson kid covered for her. I told her we'd get her the best lawyers in the world. But you scared her. What did you say to her this morning?"

"We can't just stand here," said Jane. "It's horrible."

It was all wrong. Why was he going to get help on his horse, leaving the car running there? Even if he knew it was too late, how could he leave the car there like that? Unless he wanted the little tableau to look like what he had just described, a suicide.

"Why aren't you taking the car? Why didn't you try to save her?" she shouted.

"Because I knew it was hopeless," he said. He walked his

horse over to her. "But you wouldn't know that. You might go in and try to save her."

A second later, he was off his horse and he had her around the waist.

She let out a scream and the reins jerked from her hand as he pushed her against the door to the shed. Betsy started barking furiously and came up and nipped at his boots. He tried to kick the dog away and, in the process, Jane managed to wriggle out of his grasp and off to the side where she promptly fell down on the gravel. She landed sitting down with her legs out in front of her next to the bolt cutters. She was horrified at being down while he was up, a shadow over her, his arms out ready to grab her again. She scrambled up as fast as she could and grabbed the bolt cutters on the way up.

It was useless, she decided. She wouldn't be strong enough or fast enough to use the thing as a weapon. In a second, he had her again, but he wasn't going for the tool. He was twisting her around so she faced away from him and toward the little door. If he wanted it to look as if she'd crawled in he'd have to get her in head first. She clung to the bolt cutters, which were about six inches longer than the little door he was trying to open with one hand while he controlled her with the other. She held it steady and while he tried to ram her headfirst in the opening he'd created, she managed to block the opening with the bolt cutters and keep herself out in the air.

He pushed her again and the tool caught her in the stomach and knocked the breath out of her, but he still couldn't get her through the opening while she held the tool horizontally.

He turned her around to face him and held her by the throat while he tore the tool away from her. She felt a cloud of dust as it landed with a metallic thunk, and then she felt his free hand join the other one on her body so he was holding her by both shoulders, facing him.

She braced her arms against the opening, leaned her back against the door and managed to get it shut. He seemed momentarily startled by the door closing, and loosened his grip.

She wrenched free, and fell to the side, ending up on her back with her feet in the air. He crouched down over her. She propped herself up on her elbows and kept kicking her feet, and he fluttered his arms indecisively, as if trying to decide how to subdue her.

Then she drew her right leg up and back and managed to drag one of her spurs across his face. She had summoned all the force she could. She felt the human flesh, so much softer than a horse's flank, yielding under the blade.

She'd made a diagonal slice across his face, and a trail of blood was appearing there. He let out a little cry, then she aimed her spur one more time straight for his eye and made contact. She dug it right in there and gave it a little twist with everything she had, using her thigh like a piston.

This time he fell back and rolled over into a crouch, clutching his face and screaming an unfamiliar masculine scream. She rolled away to the side.

Betsy was yapping at him while Jane scrabbled, keeping low, like a crab across the gravel, making her way to the Range Rover.

Hopscotch had moved further away, but Hank Raleigh's horse was cantering in a panic across the gravel and tossing its head. She barely escaped its hooves, but it ran between her and Hank as he pulled himself together and went after her. The horse slowed him down just enough for her to get to the car.

Panting, her heart pumping what seemed like gallons of

blood a second, her chest full of fear, she dragged herself into the seat of the car.

He was right there as she slammed the door shut, and so was Betsy. The seat was too far back from the pedals, adjusted for his own long legs. That would have given him away. He had driven here, not Angela.

He was scratching at the door handle now, his face against the window, his mouth agape. She could even see his gold fillings in that open mouth and she saw that the eye she'd spurred was covered with blood and twisted closed with pain, giving him a half-paralyzed look.

Sitting on the very front of the seat, her feet managed to find the clutch and the accelerator and she slammed the car into a gear she hoped was first. She didn't know where reverse was. That would have been better but it would have taken too long to find it.

The car bucked forward and she made a crazy arch and managed to find the hand brake and release it while he was clinging to the side of the car. She could see his hand wrapped around the side mirror. She heard Betsy's yapping further away. That was one thing fewer to think about. She'd been afraid she'd run over the dog.

She floored the pedal and drove as close to the huge pile of apple bins as she could, trying to knock him off.

She miscalculated by about a foot. Not only did she slam him off the side of the vehicle, she managed to strike several of the bins at just the right angle to topple a bunch of them over, like grabbing the bottom can of tuna from a grocer's pyramid.

By the time she wheeled away and got the vehicle over to the road and looked behind her, she saw his booted feet sticking out from beneath a huge wooden box.

On the other side of her she saw that Betsy had done her part too. She had herded both horses into a corner and was keeping them where they belonged with brusque and businesslike yaps.

35.

Some hours later, Jane sat on the sofa in the Lawsons' living room. It was a long room with a stone fireplace and a slab of wrought iron table and furniture in a rough tweed, all in a big Western scale that made her feel small. Betsy sat at her feet.

The house had been transformed from a sunny stillness to general headquarters for the sheriff. The air crackled with radios, the phone was ringing and there were people in various uniforms coming and going.

Jane had first spent what seemed like twenty minutes waiting for a patrol car on the road beside the packing plant. The whole while she'd been irrationally fearful that Hank Raleigh would stir himself and come after her again. After she saw a black and white sheriff's car and flagged it down, a lone deputy, a square-looking man with a small moustache, pulled over and took charge.

While she tried to tell him what had happened, he checked out the CA shed, asked her sharply how long Angela had been there and when he learned maybe half an hour, he just shook his head. Then he went over and tipped the apple bin off of Hank Raleigh and knelt down beside him, while simultaneously talking on his radio, asking for backup medical help, and a horse trailer for the two horses.

He turned to Jane. "He's alive," he said. "What the hell's been going on here?"

Jane was still there when they strapped him to a stretcher. He hadn't regained consciousness. She was there too when the refrigeration manager for the plant and the sheriff broke the seal and prepared to take out Angela's body.

At that point, a deputy was assigned to take Jane back to the house, where she promptly fell down on the sofa and felt her eyes fill with warm tears. She was crying, she decided, because she felt sorry for herself. Twice in one week—up at the dam and now, feeling her lungs panting for air for one horrible second—she'd been afraid she was going to die. Surely that wasn't what Uncle Harold had wanted for her. Or that board, not that they cared what happened to her. Not that anyone did, really. She was angry at them and at herself for buying into such a stupid scheme and being too desperate to have anything else going for her.

The deputy made coffee and brought her a cup. Stretched out on the sofa as she was, she probably looked like she'd been felled by the vapors, some Victorian woman weakened by tight corseting and hysteria, but then she decided that considering she'd been found next to one dead and one maimed body, maybe she'd better do her best to look like a victim and not a perpetrator, so she snuffled a little, which made her want to just go right ahead and succumb to tears.

The tears came at a more rapid rate, and she actually enjoyed the sensation of relief as they flowed down her cheeks. Now she was crying for all the pointless effort she'd put into this case, tears of frustration instead of self-pity. Then, as she gathered herself together a little and sipped the coffee, she cried tears of relief that it was all over.

The deputy, the same one she'd flagged down, was a saint. He said, "I know how you must feel," which was, of course, what a weeping woman wanted to hear—acknowledgment that tears were justified, and then he went to fetch a box of Kleenex from the bathroom.

After she'd had her refreshing cry, the sheriff came up to the house. He pulled over a dining room chair next to the sofa, and sat there with his chin in his hand. He was a patient-looking man with dark hair shot through with silver and soft brown eyes. He asked a few simple, open-ended questions and she told him everything.

She told him how friends of Irene were worried about her and how she'd run an ad asking about her in the *Times* and discovered Irene was blackmailing people using information from the clippings. She told how she met Donna and then found the clipping about Angela's car and been bribed by the Raleighs. She told them how she'd then found the second clipping—about the hit-and-run in Electric City, and how Donna had called her and learned she was in Coulee Dam, and how Travis had been sent to get the Raleighs' money back, and how she'd returned the money.

Then she told him all over again, for this was where she had begun, how she'd found the car, the bolt cutters, the padlock, Angela's body and Hank Raleigh unfastening his horse from a tree.

"I believe," said Jane, "that he had brought the horse there earlier, so he could ride back home and make it look like Angela had killed herself and left the car running. I know he drove the car there because the seat was so far back I could hardly reach the pedals."

The sheriff didn't seem interested in her theories. He just shook his head a little from side to side when she'd finished, as if overwhelmed by the Byzantine nature of her story. She was glad she'd left out some of the details: What she and

Bob had done to Travis. Where Jack Lawson fit into all of this, although the fact that she was his houseguest made their relationship pretty obvious. Most of all, she avoided explaining what she was doing messing in all this in the first place, and how Uncle Harold's peculiar testamentary trust worked.

The sheriff leaned to one of the two plainclothes detectives on the scene and said, "We better talk to Donna MacLaine. Can we get her up here? I'd like to get this all sorted out sooner rather than later."

Then the phone rang. Someone came into the living room and said it was for Jane. She went, slightly dazed, into the kitchen where there was an extension. It was Calvin. His voice seemed to belong to another lifetime entirely.

"So who answered the phone?" he said. "You got some cowboy friend over there?"

"It's a long story," said Jane.

"I called a client of mine in Olympia," he said. "A kind of lobbyist. I guess you'd call her that. She sets up after-hours events for legislators."

"Sounds like a procuress," said Jane.

"I got her off on that charge in Thurston County," he said with a tinge of professional pride.

"What does she know about Hank Raleigh?"

"Just that on the date in question, the emergency session budget finally went to a vote at ten-thirty at night. His vote's on record. Then there was a general celebration afterward in a nearby cocktail lounge. Hank Raleigh was there when my friend left, around midnight. She remembers because he was waiting to use the phone and she was on it and he was kind of crabby."

Jane sighed. "Thanks," she said. He could have made it maybe to Ellensburg by two, but certainly not to Electric

City. "Listen," she said, "I better go and leave this line open."

"What *is* going on over there?" said Calvin.

"Hank Raleigh tried to kill me and he did kill his wife," said Jane.

"My God," said Calvin.

"The police are questioning me now," said Jane. "I managed to inflict great bodily harm on him during the struggle."

"Struggle? Jane, what have you been up to? Say, you don't think you'd better have some representation, do you? Is that friendly questioning, or what?"

"I think it's all okay," she said.

"You *think?* Was Bob Manalatu involved in some of this mayhem? Remember, I didn't know why I was sending him over there."

"Just relax," said Jane. "The villain of the piece is clearly Hank Raleigh. God, Calvin, even though he was trying to kill me, what happened to him was pretty awful. He ended up underneath one of those huge apple bins they have here. As big as a shed. With just his feet sticking out. Like the Wicked Witch of the West under Dorothy's house."

"That was actually the Wicked Witch of the East, her sister," said Calvin. "She was the one who got crushed by the house."

"That fits," said Jane. "Hank Raleigh was from the East. Vermont or Maine or something judging by his accent."

"I knew he was from back east, but I didn't know it was New England." Calvin's voice took on a rare tinge of excitement. "You'll never guess what Wendy Webber overheard on Irene's personal phone call the last day she was at work."

"What?" said Jane, looking around to see the sheriff was standing next to her. Her "what" had a certain shrill tone to it that caused him to raise one eyebrow.

"Some guy called her and said he wanted his fifty grand back and he was going to get it too, now that he knew who she was and where she lived. Wendy thought it was maybe an escrow matter."

"What does that have to do with Hank Raleigh?" said Jane, who only managed a flicker of concern that Calvin was so chummy with the unspeakable Wendy Webber.

"She said the guy never identified himself," said Calvin. "But that he had a very distinct New England accent."

Jane said goodbye, hung up the phone and turned to the sheriff. "I just learned something else," she said. While she was explaining what Calvin had told her, all the while wondering why Irene had fifty thousand dollars of Hank Raleigh's money in the first place, she heard Donna's voice in the living room.

Without thinking, Jane brushed aside the sheriff and went to her.

"Oh my God, Donna," she said. "I'm so sorry."

"I never liked Hank Raleigh," Donna said, her eyes redrimmed. "I never liked him. I've been afraid for her for a long time, and I never knew why, but I must have known it was him that could hurt her."

Jane led Donna to the sofa and sat her down. The sheriff moved toward them. Jane sat next to Donna and took her hand. "I'm so sorry," she said. "I know you did what you could to help her."

The sheriff cleared his throat and started to say something, but Donna snapped at him. "Just a minute," she said. "I want Jane to tell me what happened."

The sheriff opened his mouth as if to get back control of the situation, then he appeared to think better of it and shut his mouth and sat back and listened.

Jane and Donna faced each other and Jane told her how she'd ridden into the area, and seen Hank untying his horse, how he told her the suicide story and that it was too late to save her and how then he'd tried to make it look like Jane had tried to save her.

Donna twisted her hands in the hair at her temples and pulled her hair back from her forehead and closed her eyes. "I talked to her today. After that breakfast. She and Hank went home and she called me and she said he had something you gave him that made him angry."

"What?" said Jane.

Donna shook her head. "Then she said 'I gotta go' like she could handle him. She always thought she could handle him. Then she hung up." Donna began to shake.

The sheriff leaned forward a half inch and said very softly, "Did you give him something of hers, Mrs. da Silva?"

"A check," said Jane. "A check on an account she had on a bank in Omak. Now that I think about it, I bet he didn't know about that account. I think you'll find fifty thousand dollars in it."

36.

Jane turned to Donna. "She had a prenuptial agreement with Hank Raleigh, didn't she? She more or less told me she did when we met in Bellevue."

Donna nodded. "That's right. I think she would have left him but she hated to turn her back on all that community property. It's not very nice, but I think it's the truth."

Jane turned to the sheriff. "I think Angela found a way to siphon off a lot of the estate and hide it before she left him. She told him she was delivering blackmail money. But Irene March never asked for fifty thousand dollars. She asked for a thousand, according to Angela."

"What did Irene March have on my sister?" said Donna.

"Nothing," said Jane. "Hank wouldn't pay fifty thousand to hush up an affair. Or even a shoplifting charge. That's what Angela told me he thought he was paying for. And he wasn't paying blackmail for Angela hitting and running in Electric City, either. She had an alibi."

Donna looked confused, and the sheriff looked enigmatic. Jane wasn't sure he was following, but she kept on, because she was thinking as she was talking, and the facts all fell into place and tumbled out.

Donna looked very pale. "This hit-and-run. It was the same time as the Stampede? Last year?"

"That's right," said Jane, leaning forward. "The night you and Angela partied with Jack Lawson and his band. The night Hank was in a special session at the legislature. The night a pink car killed an old lady in Electric City."

Donna leaned back on the sofa cushions and tried to take a deep breath but it came out in a kind of palsy. "Hank called me that night. Around midnight. From Olympia." Right after Calvin's friend monopolized the phone, thought Jane.

Donna put a hand to her forehead. "I was kind of pissed off because I had to go home and take care of my kids and Angela was still having a good time. And I guess I was jealous of her too, with a rich husband worrying about her and calling me looking for her.

"It was pretty clear she had the hots for Jack. In fact, they were falling into each other's eyes at the bar like a couple of teenagers."

She took another deep breath. Steadier this time. "And besides, I'd had a few beers. Otherwise I probably wouldn't have said what I said."

"What," said the sheriff, "did you say?"

"I said I didn't know where Angela was. Then I said it was too bad he was down in Olympia, because it looked like his wife had a pretty good chance of getting laid. And then I made a stupid little pun, you know. 'A trip to Electric City,' I said. Because that's the name of the band.

"He got really mad. I never heard him like that before. So I backed off and laughed. I didn't want to give Angela away. So I just laughed and said, 'Yeah, up in Electric City.' Then I said I was just kidding."

"I see," said Jane. And what would Hank Raleigh do then? He'd figure out the fastest way to get east of the mountains. Which might well be the way she got Bob Manalatu over here. In a plane. She hadn't thought of that before, because she hadn't pictured Hank Raleigh being in a hurry.

But it made sense. The skies over Washington State were full of people hopping over the Cascades and avoiding a long trip through one of the few mountain passes.

And when he got here, he'd go to their house by the river. Hoping his wife would be home waiting for him. He'd find the car there and no one home, get behind the wheel (he'd already acknowledged that he had a key to it on his key ring) and tear up to Electric City. With maybe a few drinks in him.

"He must have flown from Olympia," said Jane.

The sheriff turned to his deputy. "You know, our very own legislator commutes to Olympia in a little Piper Cub. Give him a call, will you, and see if he gave Hank Raleigh a lift over here after that special session last year? If that doesn't work, check with the Omak airport. I think Mrs. da Silva might just be on to something."

37.

"I'm so sorry, my dear," said Bishop Barton—the one member of the board for whom Jane actually felt a flicker of affection. "But I know you're very plucky and you'll get on with it and try again." She managed a wan smile.

The others had chickened out and sent him to break it to her. When she had heard he'd be coming by himself, she had braced herself for rejection, but it was still humiliating. He sat in her living room, white-haired, hunched in his boxy black suit with the gleam of purple beneath the jacket. He smiled back at her, his round, florid face like some jolly toper from an old Dutch painting, and delicately sipped the second of the two large martinis she had carefully prepared for him.

He explained gently between sips that some of the other board members had said the police had solved the murder of Irene March. That Jane's stumbling onto the crime scene after Hank Raleigh had murdered his wife was accidental. That Hank Raleigh, who had been convicted of killing his wife, was not expected to stand trial for the hit-and-run killing of Ella Mae Tinker.

Jane protested that the Grant County Sheriff's Department had unofficially closed the Tinker case, convinced that

Hank Raleigh had been responsible. She'd been through it all before, when she'd made her presentation to the full board, but she wanted to make sure he understood.

The state legislator from Omak had been willing to testify that Hank Raleigh seemed very anxious to find his wife that night they flew back together from the special session in Olympia. And Donna was willing to say she'd steered her brother-in-law to Electric City. There was the police report mentioning the pink car. There was the fact Hank was willing to pay fifty thousand dollars to a mousy little woman who waved a clipping about the incident at his wife.

But, with tight budgets, a dead witness, a guilty verdict in the murder of Angela, and Raleigh's long sentence, they'd decided to pass on trying to make the case.

The bishop listened to her rehash the case along these lines (she knew it was pointless now, but she couldn't stop), his gnarled hand clutching the martini glass, a gentle expression on his face. Whether his saintly demeanor was an example of Christian fortitude in the face of her monologue, or whether it was simply that the gin and vermouth had kicked in, she wasn't sure. He tottered off with a few more kind words and the assurance that she could stay in the house while she tried once more.

She closed the door behind him, fell on it and had a nice cry, after which she slammed things around the kitchen and cursed all the geezers on the board, with the possible exception of the bishop, who had managed to give her the impression he would have granted her the money but was outvoted by his sterner colleagues.

After a period of grief, Jane managed to appreciate the good news when Calvin said his struggle to make sure Donna inherited all the money in Angela's Omak bank looked good. Hank Raleigh couldn't inherit from someone he'd killed.

And things seemed calm at the Columbia Clipping Service. Mrs. Webber had a new boyfriend, a realtor, and spent a lot of time away from the office and seemed less intense.

Monica had given notice. She was going to use the money she'd inherited from Irene to go to graduate school and become a librarian.

The clipping service employees had decided to give Mrs. Thibadeau the remaining dishes with orange poppies on them. It came out at Hank Raleigh's trial that the caretaker at his country property, Travis Slocum, had broken them when clumsily searching for materials relating to a hit-and-run in Electric City. His fingerprints, on file for several previous arrests for assault, had been found on the broken shards.

Still pending was Maureen Louise Jenkins's trial. Her lawyer said she would plead guilty by reason of insanity, and that she still believed her daughter was dying. Her trial, in Kind County, was scheduled for next month. (Justice was more swift in Okanogan County.)

Her daughter, Amanda, was now in the permanent custody of her father.

One day, Jane went to the mailbox and discovered a letter from Jack Lawson. It was wrapped around a cassette.

"Dear Jane," it read.

"I wrote a song that is getting a lot of airplay in selected markets and is slowly making its way up the country charts. Should it keep going, and should you hear it someday, I'd like to think you heard it from me first.

"It's a song about Angela, and I found myself worrying you'd think I had somehow trivialized her death or exploited it.

"The song had to be simple. All good songs are, as you know. It started out more complex and more specifically about Angela; it changed to become something else.

"It's about a greedy woman who lost her small-town ways and can never be happy. The guy who's singing the song is torn because he loves her for the glitz as well as for what she used to be, and he knows she's two women and he can't have either.

"It's a kind of stomping, honky-tonk song, not really sad at all, just kind of wistful and ironic.

"My dad wants me to fly with him to Taipei on some apple business later this month. Unless this song keeps doing what it's doing, I'll be coming through Seattle. I'll call you. I hope you still want to sing and dance with me. I'll apologize once more for losing it when you didn't show up at my concert. If I'd known what you'd been through I never would have yelled like that. It's taken me a while to get it all sorted out in my mind.

"Love, Jack."

Jane put the cassette in the machine. From the first notes, starting out with just a lonely little fiddle line, then coming in with a driving bass, and the opening lines: *Rodeo queen in a pink corvette, rhinestones on her hat, she's out for all that she can get,* delivered in an anguished, growly baritone, Jane figured he had a hit. It was corny and sentimental and pretty damn good. Jack Lawson wouldn't be coming through town on any apple sales trip anytime soon.

Which was all right, she supposed. She was preparing herself to scrounge for another case, even though she might have to finance it with Visa. She needed something the board would eat up, and she was sure there was something out there that would be just perfect.